"I don't want t
said

But did she? From ~~~~~~
on Jordan, she had found ~~~~~~
one hand on me, I'll—"

"I won't touch you, Emily." He straightened his spine. In spite of the lingering trail dust and the prison-issue denims, Jordan exuded the dignity of an honorable man. "You have my word as a gentleman."

"Who do think you are? Rhett Butler?"

The right corner of his mouth quirked in a grin. "At your service, Miss Scarlett. Get in," Jordan said.

Emily crawled inside, and the warmth of the light-weight sleeping bag snuggled around her. When Jordan joined her inside the bag, there was barely room to move. She couldn't escape without waking him. And she wasn't altogether sure she wanted to leave him.

It had been years since she'd been intimate with a man, and she'd forgotten how pleasant it was to lie close to a large masculine body. Tempting fate, she wriggled against him. His breath whispered deep and slow, echoing the rhythm of his heart. His natural male fragrance mingled with the fragrance of her soap. "Jordan?"

He was silent, already sound asleep. True to his word as a gentleman. *Damn it.*

Dear Harlequin Intrigue Reader,

Welcome to a brand-new year of exciting romance and edge-of-your-seat suspense. We at Harlequin Intrigue are thrilled to renew our commitment to you, our loyal readers, to provide variety and outstanding romantic suspense—each and every month.

To get things started right, veteran Harlequin Intrigue author Cassie Miles kicks off a two-book miniseries with *State of Emergency*. The COLORADO SEARCH AND RESCUE group features tough emergency personnel reared in the shadows of the rugged Rocky Mountains. Who wouldn't want to be stranded with a western-born hunk trained to protect and serve?

Speaking of hunks, Debra Webb serves up a giant of a man in *Solitary Soldier*, the next installment in her COLBY AGENCY series. And you know what they say about the bigger they come the harder they fall....Well, it goes double for this wounded hero.

Ann Voss Peterson takes us to the darkest part of a serial killer's world in *Accessory to Marriage*. The second time around could prove to be the last—permanently— for both the hero and heroine in this gripping thriller.

Finally, please welcome Delores Fossen to the line. She joins us with a moving story of forced artificial insemination, which unites two strangers who unwittingly become parents...and eventually a family. Do not miss *His Child* for an emotional read.

Be sure to let us know how we're doing; we love to hear from our readers! And Happy New Year from all of us at Harlequin Intrigue.

Sincerely,

Denise O'Sullivan
Associate Senior Editor
Harlequin Intrigue

STATE OF
EMERGENCY
CASSIE MILES

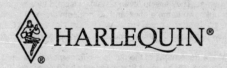

HARLEQUIN®

TORONTO · NEW YORK · LONDON
AMSTERDAM · PARIS · SYDNEY · HAMBURG
STOCKHOLM · ATHENS · TOKYO · MILAN · MADRID
PRAGUE · WARSAW · BUDAPEST · AUCKLAND

ISBN 0-373-22645-4

STATE OF EMERGENCY

ABOUT THE AUTHOR

Cassie Miles lives in Denver, one of the fastest-growing cities in the country, with the traffic jams to prove it. She belongs to the film society and enjoys artsy subtitled cinema almost as much as movies where stuff blows up. Her favorite entertainment is urban, ranging from sports to museum exhibits to coffeehouse espresso. Yet she never loses sight of the Rocky Mountains through the kitchen window.

Books by Cassie Miles

HARLEQUIN INTRIGUE

122—HIDE AND SEEK
150—HANDLE WITH CARE
237—HEARTBREAK HOTEL
269—ARE YOU LONESOME
      TONIGHT?
285—DON'T BE CRUEL
320—MYSTERIOUS VOWS*
332—THE SUSPECT GROOM*
363—THE IMPOSTER
381—RULE BREAKER

391—GUARDED MOMENTS
402—A NEW YEAR'S
      CONVICTION
443—A REAL ANGEL
449—FORGET ME NOT
521—FATHER, LOVER,
      BODYGUARD**
529—THE SAFE HOSTAGE**
584—UNDERCOVER PROTECTOR
645—STATE OF EMERGENCY†

*Mail Order Brides
**Captive Hearts
†Colorado Search and Rescue

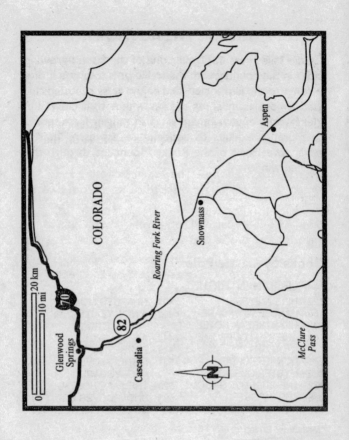

CAST OF CHARACTERS

Emily Foster—The former emergency-room nurse seeks solitude and peace in the Colorado mountains where she works for Search and Rescue.

Jordan Shane—The Florida-based computer chip manufacturer, arrested and accused of murdering his estranged wife, makes a daring escape and is on the run.

Lynette Afton-Shane—The Aspen jet-setter and owner of two ski lodges is shot before she can divorce Jordan.

Brian Afton—Lynette's brother inherits the bulk of her estate when she dies.

Sean Madigan—The professional skier who lives in the guest house on Lynette's estate had an intense relationship with the deceased.

Deputy Ed Cooper—Sloppy police work leads to his downfall when he slides off a cliff.

Deputy Frank Kreiger—The overzealous law enforcement officer secretly loved Lynette and wants her murderer punished.

Dr. Spence Cannon—The local doctor, a good friend for Emily, also works for Search and Rescue.

Pookie—The golden retriever puppy is neither a watchdog nor a detective, but he helps solve the crime.

To Rosie. Hi, Mom!

Prologue

Jordan Shane woke with a shudder. The guest bedroom in his wife's house was cold as a morgue. The bedsheets and comforter weighed on his legs like a blanket of snow. He always felt half-frozen in the mountains, even now in the middle of summer.

A white sliver of light cut through the midnight dark. The bedroom door stood slightly ajar.

"Lynette?" He whispered his wife's name. There was no reason for her to come to him in the night. They hadn't been intimate for eleven months. They didn't live in the same house. Most of the time, they weren't even in the same latitude.

Jordan's home and his business were in sun-baked Florida on the Gulf coast where semitropical breezes played in the lush green palm fronds. Most of the time, Lynette stayed here in Aspen, Colorado, where she owned two ski lodges and lived in the biggest damn house he'd ever seen. She called it a château. He called it a hotel because of the constant stream of friends and relatives who were usually taking up space in the sixteen extra bedrooms, not to mention Sean Madigan, a professional skier who lived in the guest house, or the housekeeper who had a good-size apartment behind the downstairs kitchen. Lynette didn't like to be alone...not even with her husband.

She had, however, made an effort at privacy for Jordan's midsummer visit. There were no business associates, no guests, no cousins, no friends. The granite château-hotel was eerily vacant.

Jordan had come to discuss the dissolution of their estranged marriage. This afternoon, when he proposed divorce, she agreed, asking only that he postpone legal action for a month to give her time to clean up a few business details. The end of their marriage would be amicable. No hard feelings. Their relationship just hadn't worked out.

From the very start, they shared zero common interests. But Jordan had been blinded by Lynette's astonishing physical beauty—her long, shining black hair, sapphire eyes and perfect creamy skin. Even now—with the marriage basically over—he fondly remembered her lush curves and full breasts. The thought of her naked body warmed him, and he reached across the king-size bed, hoping against the impossible that she might have joined him. For old times' sake.

Groping at the pillow, he touched metal. His fingers closed around the grip of a handgun. His memory of Lynette's perfume vanished as he caught the whiff of cordite and powder. This lightweight Glock automatic had recently been fired.

Jordan bolted from the bed, turned on the lamp and scanned the guest bedroom. Lynette's antique furniture contrasted his laptop, printer and global cell phone. Nothing seemed to be out of place.

But somebody had been here. Somebody had left the gun.

He checked the clip, making sure the pistol was still loaded. He grabbed the cell phone before he opened the bedroom door and peered into the second-floor landing. One side of the hallway was open with a cherrywood railing that overlooked an atrium foyer. On the other side were the closed doors to guest bedrooms, all vacant.

His wife's master bedroom suite was fifty yards away, at the south end of the house. Her double doors were wide open.

"Lynette!"

His voice echoed against the dark wainscoting and white walls, hung with original artwork. He didn't call her name again. He was dead certain she wouldn't answer.

Wearing only his boxer shorts, Jordan raced toward her suite. He burst through the sitting area into her white bedroom, stark as a glacial landscape. Track lighting blazed reflections against a wall of mirrors. At the foot of the four-poster bed, Lynette sprawled on the plush white carpet, stained crimson with her blood. Her lacy white nightgown hiked up to her thighs. She'd been shot in the chest.

Dropping the gun, Jordan fell to his knees beside her. At the base of her throat, he felt for a pulse. Nothing.

"Help!" Jordan yelled. The housekeeper ought to be downstairs. "Rita, help."

Lynette's blue eyes stared, blank and gelid. Her skin felt cool. She couldn't be dead! There was color in her cheeks.

Jordan punched 9-1-1 into his cell phone. "Ambulance! Send an ambulance!" He gave the address. "How do I do CPR? Tell me!"

"Sir, if you will just stay on the line, I can—"

He threw down the phone. If there was life in Lynette's body, he had to act fast. He straightened her legs. Her bare arms were slippery with blood. When he lifted her upper body, her head tilted back and her glossy black hair tumbled over his arm. For a moment, he cradled her against him. He'd wanted to end it. "But not like this. My God, not like this."

Rita Ramirez, the housekeeper, appeared in the doorway, wearing a yellow chenille robe.

"Rita," he said, "you've got to help her."

The housekeeper took a backward step. Her hands flew to cover her mouth. "*Mios Dio,* Jordan. What have you done?"

Chapter One

"This is the wound." With a red marker pen, Emily Foster drew two parallel dots, representing the fang marks of a rattlesnake, on the arm of a seven-year-old Brownie. The other eight girls and the troop leader stood in a tight circle around the Formica-topped table in the Cascadia Search and Rescue headquarters. "Can anybody tell me what to do next?"

"I know," said an angelic little redhead. "You gotta shoot the dang rattler."

"The snake will be gone." Emily preferred *not* to discuss snakebite treatment in her first aid lectures. Given her druthers, she'd never talk about reptiles at all—those slimy, sneaky, altogether terrifying creatures. But kids always asked about worst-case scenarios. Potential encounters with rattlesnakes, cougars and grizzly bears were a lot more dramatic than learning how to identify poison ivy. "Anybody know what we do next?"

"Suck out the poison," said Libby Hanson, the daughter of the troop leader. "Then spit it out."

The red-haired cherub gave a naughty smirk. "What if somebody gets bit on the butt?"

"Gross," said a tall, feminine girl with a long braid that hung to her waist. "I wouldn't *ever* suck *anybody's* rear end."

"Except for Johnny Jamison," the naughty angel said.

"Settle down, girls." Yvonne, the troop leader and mother of four, spoke with the voice of authority, but the Brownies weren't listening. They'd caught an extreme case of the giggles.

"Settle down," Yvonne repeated. She held up her hand in the sign for quiet.

Those who weren't making sucking noises on their arms were wiggling their skinny little bottoms at each other.

"Quiet!" Yvonne threatened, "Or no snacks."

Immediate silence descended, and Emily nodded an appreciative thank-you. She'd never been comfortable with children, especially not in a group. Controlling them was like juggling spaghetti. "Actually, we don't recommend the suck-and-spit method, anymore. First, we clean and disinfect the wound." She pantomimed that action. "Then wrap an Ace bandage above the wound. Not too tightly. Most of all, you want the victim to remain calm."

The supposedly snakebit Brownie eased into a prone position on the tabletop, and Emily completed the treatment by taping a folded gauze pad over the bite. "This is to apply direct pressure to the wound. Now, what's next?"

"Get help," said Yvonne's daughter.

"That's right." Emily gave a thumbs-up. "Any other questions?"

Tall and Feminine raised her hand. "Is that your real hair color?"

Emily touched her curly blond ponytail. "Yes."

"I wondered 'cause your eyes are kind of a weird green and not blue like most blondes."

"Let's get back to first aid, shall we?" Emily loosened the Ace bandage on her volunteer victim's arm.

The irrepressible angel asked, "Did you have anybody die from getting bit by a rattler?"

"Never."

"But you've seen people die 'cause you're a nurse."

Before she moved to Cascadia three years ago, Emily had experienced more than her share of senseless, violent death when she worked in a Denver hospital emergency room. God, yes, she'd seen people die. The helplessness and horror branded deep into her soul. Real-life death wasn't an appropriate topic for seven-year-old Brownies. "The important thing," she said, "is to avoid danger. Can you tell me the first rule of mountain safety?"

"Think ahead and be careful," they recited back to her.

"Second rule?" Emily asked.

"Be prepared."

"And if an accident happens?" she prompted.

"Keep calm. Call 9-1-1. Use first aid."

"I don't get it," said Tall and Feminine. "9-1-1 is Sheriff Litvak's phone number. Why is it the same for Search and Rescue?"

"The 9-1-1 dispatcher contacts S.A.R.," Emily explained.

"Does he call you at home? Like, what if you're busy?"

"Drop everything and come running," Emily said. "We usually meet right here, behind Dr. Spence's office."

The headquarters for the mostly volunteer S.A.R. unit

based in Cascadia, Colorado, was the size of a two-car garage and almost as glamorous. The furnishings included secondhand tables, chairs, desks and an ancient refrigerator. Their rescue equipment, however, illustrated state-of-the-art preparedness with skis, snow shoes, carry litters, pitons and miles of nylon rope. Sophisticated aerial-photograph maps covered every wall. There were walkie-talkies, a satellite phone and two computers—electronics that were beyond Emily's comprehension.

Concluding her demonstration, she passed out miniature first aid kits with the address and phone number for Cascadia S.A.R. attached with a sticky label. From past experience, she knew that most of these kits would be used as toys, but at least the girls would be thinking about safety.

Dr. Spence Cannon, a young and much-loved general practitioner, poked his head through the door that connected with the offices for his regular practice. "I thought I heard some mice down here."

Excited, the Brownies flocked around him. "We're not mice!"

"Then how do you explain those big ears?" Spence tugged at a couple of their braids. "And these long tails?"

"I'm an eagle," said the redhead. She spread her arms and began to soar.

"Yeah? Well, I'm a wolf." Libby Hanson bared her fangs and snarled.

Tall and Feminine struck a pose. "I'm a supermodel."

Emily stepped back beside Yvonne, and they watched as Spence and the Brownies settled around a table for Kool-Aid and snacks. "He's great with kids," Emily said.

"You bet," Yvonne agreed. "We're so lucky he settled here. With that streaked blond hair and those baby blue eyes, Spence could've made big bucks with a practice in Aspen."

Though Cascadia lay only an hour's drive from the fabled ski area, this small working-class community was a million miles distant in terms of economics. Cascadia couldn't be described as a resort. It wasn't a picturesque mountain town with châteaus, chalets and cutsey shops. Most of the people who lived here worked in Aspen. Their homes were humble cabins off the beaten path or trailers or rented rooms in the barracks-like motels.

"Spence fits in here," Emily said. "He's a nice guy."

Coming from her, "nice" represented a genuine compliment when applied to an M.D. In her years as an emergency room nurse, she'd developed a potent hostility toward the usually egotistical doctors.

"Thanks for talking to the kids," Yvonne said. "Those first aid kits are nifty. How did our underfinanced S.A.R. afford them?"

"We received a contribution that was specifically earmarked for mountain safety training and first aid. Ten thousand dollars."

"Wow!" Yvonne's eyes popped wide. In addition to motherhood duties, she raised and trained rescue dogs—an endeavor that could always use extra financial aid. "Who is this benefactor? Somebody from Aspen?"

"Somebody who's dead. Lynette Afton-Shane."

"Oh my! You know I hate to brag, but I've been to that house. The Afton Château. Big stone monstrosity. Gorgeous antiques."

"How did you manage that?"

"It was a kid thing." Yvonne clucked her tongue and lowered her voice, not wanting the Brownies to overhear.

"That poor woman. Being killed in cold blood by her own husband."

"I don't think Jordan Shane did it," Emily said.

"Do you know him?"

"Not really. I've met him twice."

The first time had been over a year ago when he attended one of her mountain safety lectures in Aspen. The second time, he came personally to her cabin to deliver the contribution. He insisted the ten thousand dollars be credited to his wife's name even though the check had been written on his personal account.

"Come on, Emily. I want details. What's he look like?"

"Dark brown hair. He wears it kind of long." When she'd met Jordan, he was another woman's husband. It would have been improper for Emily to notice his cleft chin, high cheekbones and smouldering dark eyes. She had absolutely no right to admire the breadth of his shoulders and the way his snug Levi's outlined his muscular thighs. "He has a southern accent. I think he's from Florida or something."

Yvonne's dark eyebrows lowered in one of those reproachful mother looks. "Please don't tell me you have a thing for him."

"How could I? He's married."

"*Was* married," she said darkly. "Now, he's a murderer."

"He's *accused* of murder," Emily corrected. She'd been following the much-reported case in the newspaper. "The trial hasn't even started."

"Correct me if I'm wrong, but wasn't he found standing over the body with a smoking gun in his hand? And there was nobody else in the house? No sign of forced entry?"

"That's right," Emily conceded.

"He had motive, too," Yvonne said. "I heard the couple was talking divorce, and Jordan would lose out on her inheritance."

Nearly everybody in the surrounding mountain communities had already decided that Jordan Shane, the outsider, was guilty of murdering his popular, wealthy spouse. On the strength of negative local opinion, Jordan's attorney had obtained a change of venue for the trial.

"I don't know," Emily said, "but Jordan Shane just doesn't act like a murderer."

"As if you'd know." Yvonne gestured toward the giggling girls and Spence. "Why not hook up with somebody like him?"

"Spence? No way. There's one thing I learned as a nurse—don't fall in love with a doctor."

"Why not?"

"It never works." She'd found out the hard way. "Besides, I've already selected my favorite beau. His name is Pookie."

Yvonne gave a disbelieving snort. "Pookie is a golden retriever puppy and not very bright."

"But he keeps me warm at night," Emily said. "Which reminds me, I've left him home alone too long. I should be going."

Before Yvonne could launch into a birds-and-bees explanation on the difference between sharing your bed with a dog and sleeping with a man, Emily bid her hasty goodbyes and left the Cascadia S.A.R. headquarters.

Though community service played an integral part in her life and the demonstration with the Brownies justified her minimal monthly stipend from Search and Rescue, she was glad to have this task over. With her Saturday morning errands already accomplished, she was free to spend the rest of the weekend curled up with a good book or hiking with Pookie or starting on the million and one maintenance chores she needed to do before the first snowfall.

Emily slipped behind the wheel of her old Land Rover, a vehicle too ancient to be considered an SUV, and drove through town. In less than twenty minutes, she was bouncing along the seldom-traveled graded road that led to her even more desolate turn-off. Emily's log cabin—which had been in her family for as long as she could recall—bordered on National Forest land and she had no neighbors, except for the chipmunks, the elk and the hummingbirds. Sometimes, she went for days without hearing another human voice.

Though she occasionally worried about turning into an eccentric tangle-haired hermit, Emily loved her secluded mountain lifestyle. Tucked safely in her cabin, she no longer needed daily doses of antidepressants. Her anxiety attacks seldom occurred anymore. She'd made the right decision when she left behind the frenzy of activity and constant tension of the big city E.R. where life-and-death situations were daily, if not hourly, occurrences. The pressure had been too great. Now, at age thirty-two, solitude was preferable, even necessary.

She parked at her cabin, surrounded by conifers on a ridge warmed by the western sun. Outside the vehicle, she stood for a moment. On this crisp September afternoon the skies stretched above her in deep, endless blue. God, it was beautiful! A brisk wind brushed against her cheeks and tangled in the curly blond wisps that escaped her ponytail. Autumn was her favorite time of year. The changing aspen leaves colored the slopes with shimmering gold. Fresh snow glistened on the distant high peaks near the continental divide.

A flash of caramel-colored fur loped toward her. She'd been trying to train Pookie, following the program that Yvonne outlined, but Emily secretly enjoyed the way her puppy wiggled all over with crazed joy every time he saw her. And she adored his muffled woofs.

"Moof, moof." Pookie launched himself at her. His overlarge paws groped at her thigh, and his tongue lolled out of his mouth.

"How did you get out?" she asked as she scratched behind his ears. "I know I left you inside."

"Burf moof." He sat back and cocked his head to one side, giving her the doggy equivalent of a shrug.

"Raccoons," she muttered. Those masked vermin could break into anything. They must have pushed open a cabin window.

With Pookie following, she climbed the front steps onto the porch. Her front door was unlocked. Had she left it that way? As soon as Emily stepped inside, she was grabbed from behind. The cold bore of a pistol dug into the small of her back. A harsh voice whispered, "Don't scream."

Though she'd taken self-defense classes in the city, her mind went blank. The sudden assault stunned her, and she froze. Her breath caught in her chest. Her heart paused midbeat.

"I won't hurt you," he said. There was the hint of a southern accent in his voice. "I need your help, Ms. Foster."

He knew her name. "Who are you?"

He said nothing. His muscular forearm clamped across her throat, exerting slight pressure on her windpipe. Her body pressed against his, and she could tell that he was very tall. The top of her head barely cleared his shoulder. Struggle was futile. Even without the gun, he could easily overpower her.

What did he want? She trembled, unable to accept this harsh reality. She was supposed to be safe here. Her breath returned in a frantic gasp.

Her impending panic had no effect whatsoever on Pookie. The puppy bounced around them, stumbling over his own paws and seeming to enjoy this new game. "Murf, bork, bork."

"Please," Emily said, "let me go."

"I'm thinking about it."

He was toying with her, reveling in his superiority. An edge of anger cut through her terror. She had to act, to escape from him. Her arms tensed as she prepared to thrust her elbows backward into his midsection. Caution tempered her actions. *Remember the gun.* The worst thing she could do was to anger this person and cause him to lash out. In a controlled voice she said, "You wanted my help, and I'll do what I can. Just don't hurt me or my dog."

"Fair enough." He released his grip.

Free from his grasp, she pivoted and faced him. He wore prison-issue denim pants and a blue workshirt with a black number stenciled above the pocket. His dark brown hair hung shaggy and unkempt. His upper left arm was bloody. More blood smeared his face below the cheekbone. Returning her gaze, his expression hardened in dark, silent desperation.

"Jordan Shane," she whispered. "You escaped."

She'd been wrong about him. Until this moment, Emily had believed in his innocence. But innocent men don't run. Jordan Shane was a cold-blooded murderer. In his right hand, he held a .22 caliber automatic, trained toward her midsection. "That's my gun," she said grimly.

"Hope you don't mind if I borrow this peashooter."

She kept the unloaded pistol in a wooden box on the top shelf in her closet. And the ammunition was stashed in her underwear drawer. He must have searched her house. The thought of a murderer going through her personal belongings disgusted her.

And yet, Pookie snuggled congenially against him. Weren't animals supposed to have a sixth sense about danger? Emily warned herself not to take Pookie's judgment too seriously. Coldly, she said, "I didn't notice a car outside. How did you get here?"

"I parked in that shed behind your house and latched the door. Hope you don't mind."

Of course, she minded! She was not in the habit of harboring escaped criminals. His phony politeness didn't fool her for one minute. Jordan Shane had not dropped by for a spot of tea. "What do you want from me?"

"I'm in need of medical attention. I've been shot."

Even if she hadn't seen the blood, Emily would have suspected serious injuries from the occasional tremors that shook his shoulders. His breathing was shallow. His complexion blanched white.

This was a far different Jordan Shane than the handsome benefactor who had visited her cabin a year ago. When he'd been here before, he had a deep Florida tan. Six weeks in the Pitkin County jail erased that healthy glow. He looked thinner but not at all frail. His features were sharpened, as if his ordeal had sliced close to the bone.

As she stared at him, her instinctive empathy emerged. It was an emotion more deeply ingrained than her fear or rage. For as long as she could remember, Emily had been driven to reach out to those who needed help and nurturing. She was a natural-born nurse. She truly believed in the motto of S.A.R.: "...That Others May Live." In this case, however, her instincts were dead wrong. Jordan Shane was a dangerous man. "I can't help you," she said. "If I did, I'd be aiding and abetting a criminal."

"Not if I force you," he said, casually displaying the gun. "I didn't come here to get you in trouble, Ms. Foster."

"Then why? Of all the places in the world you could have run to, why did you come to me?"

"It was logical." Jordan took a step away from her and leaned against the arm of the plaid sofa. He was light-headed, but he didn't think his condition came from loss of blood. More than likely, he was disoriented by his own audacity. He'd never been the sort of man who acted without thinking, and now he was on the lam from the Pitkin County sheriff. At this very moment, a massive search effort would be getting underway.

"Logical? You came here because it was logical?"

"That's right."

His mental process was a little fuzzy, almost as if today's events had happened to someone else. He clearly remembered being left in a windowed room at Sardy Field in Aspen. He was being transported to Denver where his trial was slated to start on Monday. Another prisoner waited with him. With no explanation, Deputy Frank Kreiger had entered the room, removed their shackles and cuffs and left them alone again.

The other guy went to one of the windows, unfastened the latch and pushed it open. Fresh air washed inside, and Jordan was drawn toward the scent of freedom.

"I don't understand your definition of logical." He

heard Emily speaking. Her voice echoed as if she were talking from the bottom of a deep well. "Would you explain?"

He truly didn't know. Jordan hadn't consciously decided to escape, but he was suddenly outside, ducked down and running alongside the hangar toward the tarmac.

Gunshots exploded. A stinging heat penetrated his left arm. He turned halfway around and heard a bullet whiz past his cheek. The other prisoner lay flat on the ground, awaiting recapture.

Jordan ran. He dodged and backtracked through the airport where he'd been dozens of times before. He found the employee parking area. After he hot-wired a late model Dodge, he drove away from Aspen. He had no clear escape route in mind but found himself on the road leading toward Cascadia. He remembered the directions to Emily's cabin from when he came here to drop off the contribution. He also recalled that this location was remote with no troublesome neighbors.

He offered her a summary explanation. "I remembered that you were a former emergency room nurse, and I figured that you'd know how to deal with a gunshot wound."

"I do." Her green eyes narrowed. She was guarded, suspicious and wary. Perfectly normal reactions. She probably believed, like everyone else in Pitkin County, that he had murdered Lynette.

"Patch me up, Ms. Foster, and I'll be on my way."

"Please call me Emily," she said with an admirable show of bravado. "After your armed assault, I think we should be on a first-name basis."

The corner of his mouth twitched. It had been weeks since he'd smiled. "You have a sense of humor, Emily."

"A sense of survival," she corrected. "And I'd feel a whole lot more comfortable if you'd get rid of the gun."

She held out her hand as if he'd be stupid enough to surrender his weapon. "I think not."

"Don't you trust me, Jordan?"

"Hell, no." She was a law-abiding citizen who would turn him over to the cops in two blinks of an eyelash. "Let's get this over with."

Though he suspected the gunshot had resulted in nothing more serious than a painful flesh wound, he wanted her professional opinion. The bullet slice across his cheek was more worrisome—partly because it wouldn't stop bleeding and partly because the wound was inches away from a fatal shot to his skull.

He pointed toward the kitchen where he had assembled her medical supplies. During the half hour he'd been alone in her house, he'd made friends with the dog and conducted a fairly thorough search of this cosy two-bedroom cabin. She had no television, no VCR and no computer. Her bookshelves were crammed with hardback reference works and an eclectic selection of paperback fiction, including a lot of science fiction and medical thrillers. She had a decent sound system and an extensive collection of blues and classical CDs.

Though most of her furniture was worn around the edges, nothing looked shabby. She decorated with warm, bright colors—a patchwork quilt on her bed, dozens of framed prints on the walls and flowers. Emily had captured the outdoor sunlight with glass vases of wildflowers and a golden arrangement of aspen branches on the kitchen table.

When they entered the kitchen, she assumed the brisk attitude of a nurse. "Take off your shirt."

His left arm was stiff, but he managed the buttons

while still keeping a grip on the gun. Underneath he wore a white cotton T-shirt.

"Take off both shirts." She stood at the sink with her arms folded beneath her breasts. "I see that you gathered up a lot of bandages and brought them to the table. You shouldn't have rifled through my things, Jordan."

"You should've kept your front door locked."

"I hardly ever lock up when I leave." She shrugged. "There are too many other ways to break into the cabin. If someone intends to rob me, I might as well save myself the trouble of fixing a broken window."

"Generous," he said.

"Besides, I've been hoping that my ferocious watchdog would be a deterrent to crime."

"He's a good little fella. What's his name?"

"Pookie."

"Well, there's your problem," Jordan said. "If you want him to be a watchdog, you've got to name him Spike or Killer."

"For your information, Pookie comes from *pukka* which is a term of nobility and respect in India."

"Why not name him Ghandi? Here, Ghandi."

"Moof, snoofle, moof." The dog jumped up, ignoring the gun, and licked Jordan's bare forearm.

"Weird bark," he said.

"No worse than his bite."

As he looked down at the loose-limbed golden retriever puppy, Jordan felt the corners of his mouth curving upward. Another smile.

Slowly, it was beginning to dawn on him that he was free. After six weeks of jail time, he was out in the world again, unshackled, unfettered. Freedom meant he had options, choices, the opportunity to do more than to declare his innocence over and over until the words sounded hollow and empty.

"Your T-shirt," Emily said. "Take it off and come over here to the sink."

He did as instructed. Though he wasn't sure how far he could trust Emily, Jordan believed she'd do a good job of nursing. From the first time he saw her, giving a lecture on mountain safety, he'd been impressed by her professionalism. He remembered sitting at the Aspen Ski Patrol meeting with Lynette at his side. Their marriage had already begun to fall apart, but Jordan had been making an effort to share in her interests. Still, midway through the meeting, he'd become fascinated by Emily Foster. Her curly, maize-colored hair and the vivacious color in her cheeks contrasted his wife's cool beauty. As a married man, Jordan would never do anything but look, but he certainly had taken in an eyeful. Being in Emily's presence made him feel like springtime after the winter chill of his ice princess wife. Poor Lynette! She hadn't deserved a bloody death. It wasn't right that her killer would go unpunished.

"Ouch!" He reacted as Emily washed his wound with stinging antiseptic.

"Betadine antiseptic to prevent infection," she said. "It's a neat exit wound. The bullet burned right through without hitting the bone. You're lucky."

"I guess." Although getting shot in the first place didn't seem much like a stroke of good fortune, he had reason to hope. His improbable escape gave him a second chance, and he needed to make use of this opportunity.

She sat him down beside the kitchen table. Before she dressed the wound, she went to the refrigerator, took out a carton of orange juice and filled a tall glass. "Drink this. And you should probably eat something."

"Thanks." He hadn't eaten since breakfast, and it was already past two o'clock in the afternoon.

When she went to work on his arm, Jordan barely felt the pain. He was too busy thinking, considering the options. His first priority was to evade capture. "With your S.A.R. work, you're in contact with the sheriff's office."

"That's right," she said as she skillfully applied gauze and wrapped the bandages.

"What happens when they go after an escapee?"

"I'm not involved in that kind of search," Emily said, "but I imagine the deputies will fan out in the most likely areas for searching. They'll probably bring in blood-hounds."

"How can they track the scent if I'm in a car?"

"You'd be surprised," she said. "Not all dogs are like Pookie, you know. There was one legendary bloodhound from Denver who found a body days after the murder and miles away from the supposed scene of the crime."

It sounded pretty far-fetched to him. "What else?"

"Probably helicopters. And roadblocks, of course."

He'd been thinking about the roadblocks. By now, the sheriff must have determined the make, model and license plate number on his stolen vehicle.

"There," she said as she finished the bandaging. "The cut on your face is more of a problem. Facial wounds tend to bleed a lot, and you're going to need stitches."

She strode toward the kitchen door.

"Hold it!" Jordan raised the pistol. He couldn't allow himself to be lulled into a false sense of security, no matter how charming Emily seemed to be. She could make a quick call to 9-1-1 and pinpoint his location. She could make a break for her car. "Where are you going?"

"In your search of my house, you apparently missed the closet in the second bedroom. That's where I keep a lot of my equipment, including a backpack of medical supplies. I have the stuff I'll need for stitching in there."

"If you don't mind, I'll accompany you."

"I mind," she muttered. "I don't like being a hostage."

He wasn't exactly thrilled about his role as hostage-taker. But he didn't have an option.

The closet in the second bedroom was surprisingly large, and she'd neatly stored much of her S.A.R. equipment inside. Jordan's gaze lit upon a heavy-duty walkie-talkie combined with a battery operated cell phone. With his uninjured right arm, he picked up the communication device. "Can you use this to pick up the police radio?"

"I have no idea," she said as she grabbed a red backpack. "I hardly know how to turn it on. Electronics aren't my thing."

Fortunately, Jordan was an expert in all things mechanical. His company in Florida manufactured high-tech computer chips. As they returned to the kitchen, he activated the walkie-talkie. Within minutes, he was picking up the police band radio.

"I'm impressed," Emily commented. "When it comes to mountain survival and emergency medical aid, I do a good job. But that thing baffles me. I hate carrying it on searches."

As she disinfected the wound on his cheek, Jordan focused on the static reports from the walkie-talkie. The sheriff had already set up roadblocks on the main highway and some of the major roads leading away from Aspen. Had they come this far? Had they thought of Cascadia?

"The stitching is going to hurt," Emily said. "I don't have anesthetic. Maybe I should just use a couple of butterfly bandages."

But he might be on the run for days and wouldn't have a chance for further medical attention. He needed a more permanent solution than a couple of bandages. "Stitch it up."

He could manage the pain. What he couldn't stand was being recaptured again. There was no way in hell he'd go back to jail.

She handed him a bottle of ibuprofen. "Take three."

He washed down four tablets with another swig of orange juice. "I'm ready."

As she prepared to stitch, he stared at the curved needle. If she wanted, Emily could inflict serious damage on his face. He nudged the nose of the gun against her rib cage as a reminder. "Don't try anything cute."

"I'm a nurse, Jordan. And I take pride in my work. I won't hurt you any more than I have to. Try not to move around."

He closed his eyes and retreated deep into his head, seeking a meditative core of stillness. Instead of tensing his body, he willed himself to relax. In an almost objective state, he felt the needle pierce his flesh. He acknowledged the stab and, just as quickly, dismissed the resulting pain.

He inhaled a deep breath before she stitched again. Behind his eyelids, he saw cool blue Gulf waters lapping against the Florida sands. He imagined gentle breakers washing over him, soothing his mind and his spirit, lifting him above the throbbing agony.

He didn't flinch. The stitching was necessary. The hurt was nothing compared to the thought of spending a lifetime in prison for a crime he did not commit.

"Done," she said.

When he opened his eyes, he glimpsed a fleeting gentleness in her eyes. For an instant, Emily almost looked like she might hug him. He wanted her touch, yearned for her attention, her affection. If he had only one person to believe in his innocence...

"That's all I can do," she said. "You promised to leave."

Stiffly, he nodded.

Jordan's attention returned to the police radio. They were setting up roadblocks near Cascadia. He couldn't use the car for his escape.

Logically, a plan fell into place. He would escape on foot across the mountains where it would be harder to find him. He was, however, ill-equipped to handle mountain survival by himself. He needed an expert. He needed Emily.

"Get your backpack," he said. "You're coming with me."

Chapter Two

From the start, Emily knew they would have a problem: What would Jordan do with her when he went on the run again? He couldn't simply wave goodbye and stroll out the door. He couldn't leave her behind as a witness.

She thought he might tie her up or disable her car. She feared he might knock her unconscious. But she never dreamed his solution would be to take her with him.

"Why, Jordan? Why do you want me to go with you?"

"Makes sense," he said.

"No, it doesn't."

"Think about it."

"You want to use me as a hostage." A helpless pawn, he'd use her as a bargaining chip to gain his freedom. The idea disgusted her. Emily had never been a docile woman. She was descended from warriors. Her father had been in Vietnam, and she liked to think she was like him. "I warn you, Jordan. If you take me with you, I'll do everything in my power to make sure you're recaptured."

"Then I'll have to keep an eye on you."

Shirtless, he sprawled in the ladder-back kitchen chair with his long legs splayed, gathering his strength after her emergency medical care. His stoic endurance when she stitched his facial wound had astounded her. He hadn't cried out, hadn't even twitched a muscle. His intense self-control and determination worried her. This man wouldn't give up without a fight.

She watched his bare chest rise and fall with each heavy breath. Despite six weeks of jail time, he was in decent physical condition. The span of his shoulders and chest narrowed to a lean torso. She guessed his age to be mid-thirties, a few years older than she was.

He was damned attractive, she ruefully acknowledged. When she'd been dressing the wound on his arm, his flesh warmed beneath her hands. When she'd inadvertently brushed against the black, springy hair on his chest, the texture enticed her. For a moment, her fingers yearned to stroke that hair, to glide across his muscled body. With a jolt, she'd returned to her senses.

Emily couldn't allow herself to entertain fond thoughts about Jordan Shane. He was an escaped convict, a criminal. Her duty was to return him to police custody.

She snapped, "You can put on your shirt now."

He did as she ordered though his injured left arm was somewhat inflexible. He left the bloodstained, prison-issue workshirt unbuttoned.

Her gaze lifted to his face. She had covered his stitches with a white antiseptic dressing, but she could still see the angry red swelling on the left side of his face.

"I need you to come with me," he said, "because of the roadblocks. I can't use the car. I'll have to escape on foot."

"Are you crazy? It's mid-September. The temperatures at night are below freezing. It might even snow."

Casually, he reached down to pat Pookie who had taken up a position on the floor beside Jordan. "That's why I need you. I don't know how to survive in the mountains. I'm just a computer nerd from Florida."

He certainly didn't look like a nerd with those broad shoulders and darkly handsome features. But he didn't look like a murderer, either. Appearances, she reminded herself, could be deceptive.

He rose to his feet, towering over her. "Pack your gear. Plan to be gone for a week."

"A week?" Her voice rose to a squeak. "But who'll take care of Pookie?"

At the sound of his name, the puppy bounded to his feet. His head whipped back and forth, glancing between Emily and Jordan. "Murfle, moof."

"We'll bring the dog along," Jordan said. "Let's move."

Because she was always ready for an emergency call from S.A.R., Emily was quickly able to assemble two backpacks with sleeping bags, climbing equipment, medical supplies and freeze-dried food for herself and Jordan as well as puppy chow for Pookie.

"Do you have maps?" he asked.

"In the top left drawer of my desk."

"I don't suppose you have a G.P.S. unit."

"What's that?"

"G.P.S. stands for Global Positioning Satellite. A signal bounces off satellites and triangulates on your position. It gives longitude and latitude, accurate within ten meters, then references area maps."

He'd lost her after the word "triangulate," but Emily nodded as she always did when someone explained technology. "I don't have one of those."

While she completed her packing, Emily plotted an escape of her own which didn't involve satellites or triangulation. Simple was better. If she could break away from Jordan, she'd make a run for her car which was parked less than thirty yards from the front door. One fast sprint and she'd be behind the wheel. She'd drive away and not look back until she'd contacted the sheriff's department.

She had to go now. Once they got out on the trails, escape would be far more difficult. A dash to the car was the best solution, quick and decisive. Yet, she heard a whisper of remorse, echoing quietly in her conscience. Jordan had begun to trust her. He'd tucked the .22 automatic into the waistband of his Levi's. Somehow, it seemed wrong to betray him.

"I'm finished." Fastening the last straps on her pack, she sat back on her heels. Escape plans loomed foremost in her mind, and she didn't dare look directly at Jordan. He might guess what she was planning. "I should go to the bathroom before we leave."

"Emily?"

Her gaze darted nervously to his face. Did he know what she was planning? "What?"

"Are you okay?"

"Peachy keen." She masked her tension with sarcasm. "This is my favorite way to spend a Saturday, being held hostage and kidnapped into a forced mountain trek."

"I didn't intend for this to happen."

The ring of sincerity in his softly accented voice irritated her. "Oh, please! What were you planning to do when you left here? You couldn't just leave me here. You knew I'd call the sheriff."

"Believe this, Emily. I don't want to hurt you."

"You have a strange way of proving that." She stood and confronted him. "You grabbed me around the throat when I walked through the door."

"I needed to get your attention."

"What if I'd struggled? How would you have subdued me?"

"I was pretty sure you wouldn't make a fuss," he said. "You're not that kind of woman."

"Not like your wife?"

He recoiled as if she'd slapped him. Though his expression remained unchanged, his eyes flared with suppressed anger. "I'm only going to say this once. I didn't kill Lynette."

"Then why are you afraid to stand trial?"

"Innocent men and women are convicted every day." His shoulders straightened. He stood over six feet tall, and he seemed to grow stronger by the minute. "I won't go back to jail. I'd rather die."

"You can't live outside the law, Jordan."

"Let's go."

This was it. Her best chance to make a run for the car. "I'll be with you in a minute."

She left the back bedroom and hurried toward the bathroom. She shoved the door closed with a loud slam, hoping he'd think she was inside, and palmed her car keys from her jeans pocket. Quietly, she eased toward the front door. In her heavy-soled hiking boots, total stealth was impossible, but she only had a few steps before she was outdoors. Was it enough of a headstart?

As she stepped onto the porch, Pookie bashed open the screen door. The dog bounded down the three stairs. "Moof, moof."

From the back bedroom, Jordan called out, "Emily, what's going on?"

Now or never! She leapt down the porch steps and raced toward the stand of Ponderosa pines where she'd parked her ancient Land Rover. *Please, God, let it start on the first try!*

She heard Jordan behind her but didn't look back.

Would he shoot her? The muscles between her shoulder blades tensed, expecting a bullet.

Her boots skidded on the loose gravel, costing her valuable seconds. She had to make it. The Land Rover was only ten feet away.

Her arms stretched out, reaching for the driver's side door.

Before she touched the handle, she was tackled from behind. Jordan fell on top of her. She hit the ground hard.

With the wind knocked out of her, she couldn't breathe. She was stunned. A tingling darkness danced in her peripheral vision. Jordan's weight pressed down, heavy as the tons of snow in an avalanche. She was suffocating. Air. She needed air.

In an instant, he was off her. He rolled her onto her back, and she gasped. The first breath burned her lungs. She exhaled, then gulped down another breath. Her blurred vision cleared. She looked up at his face, silhouetted against overhanging pine boughs and blue sky.

He leaned over her. Closer and closer, he came. His mouth was almost touching hers. Instinctively, she wanted to close her eyes and welcome the taste of his lips joining with hers. Instead, she shoved at his chest. "What are you doing?"

"Mouth-to-mouth," he said.

"Don't need it."

She gasped again, then her breathing settled. No serious damage had been done.

"I'm sorry," he said. "This shouldn't have happened."

None of this should be happening. Emily squeezed her eyes closed then open again, as if she could change reality with a blink. She shouldn't be lying on the ground with an escaped convict kneeling beside her. She shouldn't be excited about the possibility of a kiss.

This was all his fault. Why did he have to be such a sympathetic person? She would've felt better if he slapped her. Instead, he was gentle and apologetic.

Ignoring his own injury and pain, he helped her to her feet. She leaned against him, intensely aware of his warmth and strength. Her hand slipped inside his unbuttoned shirt as she braced herself. When she touched him, he shivered. And she knew his reaction wasn't due to a sudden chill. It was the opposite. He was hot for her. And she felt the same way about him. A terrible magnetism drew them together. "This couldn't be any worse."

"That's where you're wrong," he said. "Do you hear that?"

A distant whir signalled the approach of a helicopter. Emily should have guessed that the chopper pilot, Harrison Perry, would fly by and check on her. They'd worked together on several S.A.R. missions. Last winter, they'd gone out on a couple of dates.

Jordan hustled her back inside the house. He turned her toward him and held her arms, forcing her to look directly at him. "Quick. Tell me about the chopper."

"A police helicopter. The pilot is a friend of mine. He checks up on me."

"What do you usually do when he flies over?"

"I step outside and wave."

The noise of the rotary blades racheted loudly. He was hovering over her cabin. Outside, Pookie danced an enthusiastic but clumsy puppy welcome.

Jordan peered deeply into her face. His dark eyes glowed hot as charcoal embers. "I'm not a killer."

"But the evidence—"

"If I'm recaptured, a great injustice will be done. Please, Emily, give me this chance."

"I want to believe you." The noise from the chopper was deafening.

"Go outside and let the pilot see you're all right."

She nodded.

"Emily." His voice was low and intense as he stepped away from her and took the gun from his waistband. He didn't need to state his threats. The presence of the weapon was reminder enough. "You hold my life in your hands."

Emily went onto the porch. Now was her chance to turn him in. She could easily signal Harrison Perry, letting him know she was in trouble. She could scream. She could make a thumbs-down gesture. He'd find a place to land and radio to the sheriff. Deputies would surround them. This ordeal would be over.

But what if Jordan truly was innocent? What if he'd been framed for a murder he did not commit? His escape attempt might be the last nail in his coffin. The death penalty was seldom used in Colorado, but life in prison was worse. She imagined Jordan being locked away forever with shackles on his wrists and ankles. How could she do that to him? She was a nurse. Her life was dedicated to nurturing.

She stood outside her cabin with Pookie at her side. The dog's liquid brown eyes seemed to accuse her. *Don't do this to him.* She looked up at the chopper and felt her lips pull back in a false smile. The downdraft from the rotary blades swirled around her. Her arm lifted and she waved. For good measure, she made an *O* with her thumb and forefinger to let Harrison know she was okay.

He waved back. Then, like a giant dragonfly, the police helicopter moved away. He hovered low, searching the wooded landscape for an escaped convict, searching for Jordan. The noise faded to stillness as she stood, unmoving. Possibly, she'd just made the biggest mistake of her life.

She heard Jordan approach. He said, "You did the right thing."

That remained to be seen. "Harrison will report that everything is okay in this area. It'll give you a little more time for your escape."

"It'll give *us* more time."

When she turned, Emily saw that Jordan was already wearing his backpack. In his hand, he held a length of nylon rope which he looped over her head like a lasso and cinched around her waist.

"What's this?" she demanded.

"Insurance," he said. "In case your conscience needs a little reminder."

Furious, she yanked at the rope. "A leash! You've got me on a leash!"

"It's no use in tugging, Emily. This is a fisherman's knot. On a double rope like this, you won't be able to untie it because the other ends are attached to my belt."

"I hate this!"

"Too bad," he said. "I need both hands free for climbing, so I can't carry the gun. But I need some way to control you."

After everything she'd done for him—treating his wounds and chasing away the chopper—he repaid her with a rope. To control her. She wanted to tell him off, but Emily was utterly incoherent with rage.

Since she had no alternative, she stomped back toward the house and maneuvered into her backpack. She'd been a fool not to signal the chopper. She wouldn't make that mistake again. On the trail, she'd take her revenge. This wouldn't be an easy hike in the mountains and she would definitely leave a trail.

With adrenaline pumping, she left the house and set out toward the open field at an aggressive pace. The rope pulled her up short and she whirled around. "Now what?"

"We should stay under the cover of the trees until nightfall. Your friend with the chopper might be back."

"Fine," she snarled.

"I suggest we head in a roughly northeastern direction," Jordan said. "Back toward Aspen."

"That's about the dumbest thing I've ever heard. Everybody's going to be looking for you in Aspen. Why would you want to take that risk?"

"Investigation," he said.

"Of what?" She'd just about had it with his cryptic responses. Even if he didn't think she'd understand his logic, she deserved to know what was going on inside his head. "Tell me, Jordan. Just what do you think you're going to investigate in Aspen?"

"I'm going to find out who murdered my wife."

AFTER TWO HOURS and twenty minutes of hiking, Jordan ached in every cell of his body. The gunshot wound in his arm was nothing compared to the screaming muscles in his thighs and lower back. The tight throb of the stitches in his face penetrated his cheekbones and spread across his skull. Though he'd been in the high country for a couple of months and had acclimated to the altitude, his lungs couldn't suck enough oxygen from the thin mountain air.

It didn't help that Emily chose consistently uphill routes or that she purposely pushed back tree branches and allowed them to snap back at him. Though she claimed to hate the rope that tied them together, she yanked at the cord every five minutes, sending a jolt through his midsection.

Still, Jordan hadn't complained. Neither he nor Emily had spoken for over half an hour.

The only one who seemed happy about their cross-country trek was Pookie. The dog bounded ahead of them, scrambling over rocks and darting through the firs. The dog suddenly froze, alert and watching. Had he seen something? Were the searchers approaching?

"Hold it," Jordan said.

"Why?" Emily halted and turned toward him. An evil grin spread across her lovely face. "Are you tired?"

Damn right! But he'd never admit weakness to her. "Pookie sees something."

The hairs on Pookie's back stood up, then he charged through the trees. His bark was different, deeper. "Whooo-whoo-woof."

"What's that mean?" Jordan whispered. "Why's he making that kind of noise?"

"I don't speak dog," she said archly.

He directed her toward the cover of a prickly shrub and ducked down. Clumsily, he retrieved the gun from his backpack. Truly, this pistol was a peashooter. With a .22 caliber automatic, he couldn't trust his aim at any distance. But it was better than nothing.

"Moof." Pookie bounded back toward them, almost strutting. The pup looked real proud of himself.

"What was it, boy?" Emily grinned at the dog. "A vicious chipmunk? An evil deer?"

Pookie gave a full-body wiggle.

"Nothing to worry about," she said. "Unless you're afraid of being recaptured by an army of rabid tree squirrels."

Easy for her to say. Emily wanted to be found.

Jordan thanked his lucky stars for her momentary lapse into kindness when she'd waved the helicopter away. His escape could have been over at that moment, but she'd saved him. He didn't expect that sympathy again.

"Ready?" she challenged.

"Let's make tracks."

She set out at a fast pace, and he was hard-pressed to match her speed. Her energy amazed him. Surefooted as a bighorn sheep in Kletter boots, she hiked higher and higher on slender, almost nonexistent forest trails. Uphill, dammit, always uphill.

He wished he had a pair of hiking boots like hers. Jordan's shoes were cheap, canvas, prison-issue sneakers that offered little traction and no protection against the rocks he constantly tripped over. But there was another lack in his mountain climbing gear that worried him more. He didn't have a jacket.

Though Emily owned a warehouse of camping supplies, including two sleeping bags, she wasn't prepared with a parka in his size. Come nightfall, Jordan was going to be mighty chilly. By God, he hated these mountains. The climate was cold and arid, inhospitable to human life. Rugged terrain gave him no pleasure. The jagged spires of rock were teeth waiting to tear into his flesh.

Stumbling again, he stared down at the dry bed of pine needles below his feet. In the fall, there wasn't much green in these forests, and it wasn't the brilliant tropical green he was accustomed to seeing in Florida. Colorado's palette ranged from khaki to the army drab of pine and spruce.

A tug on the rope told him they were headed uphill. Again. He glanced up toward Emily. Since she was leading the way, he should've had ample time to admire the fit of her snug Levi's, but Jordan was denied even that small diversion. From the rear, she looked like a big red backpack with legs.

Finally, they reached a pinnacle on a high ridge. There was no more up. Finally, they'd be hiking downhill.

The first few steps felt good. The change in muscle groups refreshed him. After they'd covered a couple hundred yards and entered an aspen grove, his legs turned to rubber. He couldn't control his momentum. The space between them shortened. He was only an arm's length away from her backpack.

Then, inexplicably, Emily stopped short.

"No!" He barely dodged around her. But he couldn't stop. His equilibrium was off. Flailing, he crashed through the slender white tree trunks. The rope pulled taut, and Jordan went down flat on his back.

Emily followed, almost tumbling. In an amazing display of agility, she stayed on her feet.

Half-stunned and totally exhausted, Jordan looked up through the aspen boughs. His wounds throbbed, but he willed the pain away. In the fading light of dusk, the air took on a golden hue. The leaves trembled delicately like a shower of golden coins, nature's wealth. Numbly, he said, "It's beautiful."

She squatted beside him. "Don't tell me you've never seen an aspen before."

"Only from a distance, and I never understood why you people get so excited about a couple of yellow trees."

"You don't really appreciate Colorado, do you?"

"'Fraid not." Jordan was a southern boy, born in Atlanta where the lush hardwood forests were far more forgiving than the stern, rugged Rockies. Even then, Georgia's hilly terrain had been too much for him. All those trees felt claustrophobic. On the Gulf coast of Florida, he found wide vistas and open space, palm trees and sultry, ocean-scented air.

He inhaled a deep breath. The cool breeze smelled fresh and earthy. And the gold shimmered all around him.

When he looked up at Emily, hovering over him like an angel, her face seemed to glow. Her curly blond ponytail glistened like warm honey. She wasn't strikingly beautiful, not like Lynette. Emily was the sort of woman who might be overlooked in a crowd, but when you noticed her, you knew you'd discovered a hidden treasure.

She clambored to her feet and dusted off her jeans. Disdainfully, she said, "If you think you can make it that far, there's a stream up ahead."

"Okay." He forced his legs to move.

Beside the trickling stream which was only a few feet wide, they shed their backpacks and sat side by side on a wide weathered rock. Though Jordan was still enjoying the golden leaves, he felt a warning chill in the air. The sun was about to dip behind the mountains. He started to pull off his shoes, thinking how good the cold, clear stream water would feel on his ten stubbed toes.

"Don't," she said.

"Why not? My feet are killing me."

"On a hike, it's always better to keep your feet dry. Besides, putting your shoes back on again will be sheer agony." She groaned. "I don't know why I bothered to tell you. You deserve the pain."

Her job was healing. He didn't think she'd willingly allow suffering. "What's that motto for S.A.R.?"

"...That Others May Live." She glared at him. "But I don't think it applies to escaped convicts."

He called on her wisdom again. "I know you're carrying a little water purifier in your pack. Is it safe to drink from the stream?''

She shrugged. "You take your chances."

But Jordan followed her example, taking a swig of lukewarm liquid from the canteen in his backpack. Not as satisfying as scotch and soda, but it was liquid. With all this exertion, keeping hydrated was important.

Pookie, on the other hand, seemed to think the Rocky Mountain spring water was just fine. The pup splashed through the glistening ripples.

"Pookie!" Emily reprimanded. "Get out of there."

"Moof, woof." He slipped on a rock and got completely drenched.

"How am I ever going to train him?" Emily asked.

"Leave him be. He's just a pup."

"But he needs to start learning now or he'll never be any use as a rescue dog."

"I understand about working dogs," Jordan said. This was the closest they'd come to a conversation, and he wanted to prolong the moment, to win her trust. "When I was a kid, I had a bluetick hound that I trained for weeks to be a good hunting dog."

"Do you hunt?"

"Not anymore," he said. "Do you?"

"No, but I have two older brothers who used to go hunting all the time. I'd go with them." But Emily had never taken pleasure in stalking and shooting. "I'd patch them up when they sprained their ankles or cut themselves with their hunting knives."

"You liked nursing even when you were a kid."

"It comes naturally." In spite of her warrior heritage, she didn't need to kill anything. She carried on the family tradition by being a healer, just as her father had taken on the job of medic before he was killed in Vietnam.

She watched as Jordan dug into his backpack, pulled out the walkie-talkie and tuned to the police band radio. Listening to the static dispatches, he stretched out on the rock and stared up into the quaking aspen leaves. Though she considered his hatred for the mountains to be a damning quality, she couldn't quite believe he was a murderer.

Still, she removed the package of tissues from her pocket and tore off a small piece which she dropped to the ground. All along their route, she'd been leaving markers which Jordan was too preoccupied to notice.

"I have a question for you," she said. "If you despise the mountains so much, how did you end up married to a woman from Aspen?"

"We met while she was on vacation in the Florida Keys, had a whirlwind courtship and got married before we figured out that we didn't have a single thing in common."

"Opposites attract," Emily said.

"But they don't stay together for long. We were married for two years and probably lived in the same house for only two months of that time."

"The newspapers said you were going to ask her for a divorce."

"That was why I came to Aspen," he said.

His lack of apparent emotion seemed odd. The newspaper reports had hinted that Jordan's motive for killing his wife was passion. "Did you still love her?"

"Not love. Not hate." He stretched the muscles in his back. "There weren't any strong emotions left."

"And you asked for the divorce?"

"That's right."

"What did she say?"

"She agreed. It was all real civilized and calm. But

she asked me to wait a month so she could clear up some kind of financial problem with her estate.''

If Emily eliminated passion as a motive, it had to be the money. Lynette Afton-Shane was a multi-millionaire who owned two ski lodges and prime real estate. Even by Aspen standards, her wealth would be considered impressive. ''How much do you inherit?''

''We had a prenuptial agreement that gave each of us ten percent of the other's estate.''

''In Lynette's case, that might be a million dollars,'' Emily said.

''I really don't know,'' Jordan said. ''I wasn't in her class financially, but I do okay. I have my own computer hardware manufacturing company in Florida with twenty-seven employees.'' And Emily remembered that he'd written the ten-thousand-dollar contribution to S.A.R. on his own account. Jordan certainly didn't project the image of someone who needed to kill for the inheritance.

He bolted to a sitting posture on the rock, concentrating hard on the reports from the police band radio. ''They're coming closer to Cascadia. Do you have those maps, Emily?''

She reached into a zippered pocket on her backpack and pulled out three different maps.

He unfolded the worn paper and studied the detailed terrain which included topography and landmarks as well as roads. Though Emily wasn't good at map-reading, she had an innate sense of direction in the mountains that seldom led her astray.

''Does this stream have a name?'' he asked.

''I don't think so. It's too small.''

''But you've been here before,'' he said. ''You knew there was a stream at the bottom of the hill.''

''I knew because I heard the rushing water,'' Emily

explained. "Plus, we're at the base of a slope, and the presence of aspens generally indicates that the water table lies close to the surface."

He pinpointed their location on the map. "I'd say we're about here."

Pookie bounced up to them, paused and shook himself, sending out a spray of ice-cold stream water.

"Not on the map," Jordan said. "Geez, Pookie. Get a grip."

"You were the one who didn't think he needed training," Emily reminded him as she corralled the wet dog in her arms, then pushed his butt to the ground. "Sit, boy."

"Moof," Pookie said.

Jordan's attention returned to the map. "Pretty soon, it's going to be too dark for the helicopters to search. We need to stay far away from the roads." He pointed to a small black rectangle that didn't seem too far from their location. "What does this represent?"

"A warming hut for hikers and cross-country skiers."

"Warming hut?"

She explained, "It's a small cabin that people can use if they get stuck in bad weather. It may be a good place for us to spend the night."

His eyes narrowed. "It also might be the first place for searchers to look. The sheriff's department has maps like this, don't they?"

She nodded but didn't offer any advice. When it came to the bottom line, Emily didn't want to aid in his escape. Jordan's guilt or innocence was for the courts to decide.

To ensure somebody figured out that he'd taken her and Pookie with him, she'd left a trail from her cabin that a blind man could follow. At every opportunity, she'd broken branches off trees and trampled shrubs as well as dropping shreds of tissue and all the change from her pockets.

"It's going to get cold tonight," Jordan said, watching her for a reaction. "And I don't have a jacket."

Her recommendation would be to risk staying in the shelter of the warming hut and avoid the potential danger of hypothermia. But she said nothing.

"I need a good night's sleep," he said. "And time to recover from my injuries."

Again, he assumed correctly.

Jordan asked, "How far to the warming hut?"

"A few hours if we stay under the trees. Less time if we step out in the open."

"With your bright red backpack marking our location like a signal flare," he said bitterly. "It's a chance I'll have to take. We'll go by the most direct route."

He tucked away the maps, rose to his feet and shouldered his backpack, flinching slightly as the strap brushed his wounded arm. His ability to endure painful injuries without a single complaint was impressive, but Emily refused to acknowledge any positive attribute in Jordan Shane. She didn't want to like him and certainly wouldn't help him.

He led the way from the aspen grove into a wide-open field of dried buffalo grass and weeds. With virtually no cover, they'd be visible from half a mile away. If there were search parties in the area, they'd be spotted.

Apparently, Jordan had realized the same probability because he came to a halt. He threw an arm in front of her. "Don't move."

Emily looked down. Three feet away, a snake slithered off a sun-warmed rock at the edge of the path. A snake! Adrenaline shot through her veins. God, she hated snakes! Oh God!

Chapter Three

Seconds after Jordan noticed the snake—which was only three feet long and probably a docile, nonpoisonous variety—three things happened simultaneously. The reptile vanished in the high grass. Emily let out a shriek louder than an air-raid siren. And she leapt in a gravity-defying vertical jump, about three feet in the air.

Then she started running across the open field. Fastened to her by the nylon rope, Jordan had no choice but to follow at top speed. His feet beat the ground. His heart pounded. He hadn't intended to set a new record for the four-hundred-meter dash across the world's most rugged terrain.

His plan was to baby his aching muscles until they got to the warming hut where he could collapse into bed and recuperate. Dammit, he'd been gunshot today. Twice. But he couldn't stop running. Emily sprinted with such arm-churning force that if he held back she'd yank him off his feet and drag him on his belly across the mountain meadow.

Any chance at a quiet, subtle sneak across the wide-open land vanished. If there were any searchers in the vicinity, they must have been alerted by Emily's eardrum-piercing scream. Jordan tried to watch in all directions as he ran. Were they closing in? Were they converging? The reports on the police radio had named the Cascadia area. Would the next bullet strike his heart?

On the far side of the open meadow, Emily screeched to a halt on a hillside below a stand of conifers. Her frantic gaze darted. Her head swiveled. Her arms clenched across her breasts, and her fingers curled into tight little fists. Unnecessarily, she said, "I hate snakes."

Pookie echoed, "Brrr-oof."

"No lie." Jordan bent double, trying to catch his breath. Though his chest heaved with the effort of consuming enough oxygen, the run seemed to have loosened him up. His muscles were tingling instead of throbbing.

"I can't believe this." She spoke in breathy half-sentences. "A few hours ago. I lectured. To Brownies. About snakes. Were you...scared?"

"No." In Florida, there were lots of snakes. They'd never bothered Jordan. "I don't think that one was poisonous."

"Don't care. I hate them all."

From their vantage point on the hillside, he turned to scan the open meadow behind them. He looked for the glint of fading sunlight on a long-range rifle. He listened for the sound of manhunters calling to each other, for barking bloodhounds, for the whir of helicopter blades.

Only the soft whisper of mountain breezes disturbed the perfect silence. He saw no movement, no evidence of searchers. However, if and when the sheriff's deputies came this way, their direction was obvious. The wild race across the dried grasses trampled a path straight as an arrow pointing the way toward Jordan.

He was well-aware that seeking shelter in the warming hut—a clearly mapped landmark—was risky. But he needed warmth and comfort for a good night's sleep and recovery. His escape efforts might last for days, even weeks, and he couldn't take a chance on falling ill.

He turned to Emily. "Nothing like that is going to happen again."

"I didn't plan to see a snake," she said.

"I thought you were an expert outdoorswoman, certified in mountain survival."

"Unless there's a snake," she said in a small voice.

After her consistent display of mountaineering skill and wisdom, he detected a subtle shift in their relationship. Her unreasonable fear of snakes had given him an edge and elevated him from the status of mountaineering idiot to potential survivor. He felt gratified to finally be the one with the answers. "I'm pretty sure snakes in these parts are headed toward hibernation. At nightfall, they hide away. It's too cold out here for reptiles. We won't see another one."

"Do you promise?" With the back of her hand, she wiped sweat from her forehead. A convulsive tremble shook her slender body.

Though he wanted to take her into his arms and offer reassurance, Jordan still wasn't sure whether she'd hug him back or slap him upside the head. He suspected the latter. "Do you want to sit and rest for a few minutes?"

"No! I want to put as much distance between us and that reptile as possible."

"Suits me." He took the topographical map from the pocket of his Levi's. "First, let me get my bearings."

Staring in a northeastern direction, he spotted a high, jagged outcropping of granite. "Are those the chimney rocks marked on the map?"

"Yes," Emily said. "Let's get going. I can find my way to the warming hut."

Not only did he mistrust her willingness to help him, but dusk was rapidly turning to night. The local landmarks would be invisible in the dark, and he'd have to rely on the compass.

Almost due north, he spied a hogback that was marked on the map. In his head, Jordan calculated the triangulation and set their course for twelve degrees northeast on the compass. "When we approach this hut, there's probably a road. Right?"

"A path," she said. "It should be maintained by the Forestry Service."

He balanced her compass in the palm of his hand. The setting sun was behind them. He could already feel the chill in the air. "Let's go."

Keeping a steady pace, they climbed hills and crossed other meadows. As night surrounded them, Jordan took the lead, keeping them on track with the compass.

Behind him, Emily stumbled. "Ow! Jordan, I have flashlights in the backpacks. We should use them."

"Here's a better idea," he said. "Why don't we just hang a neon sign that says Escapee Here."

"Searchers won't be out this late," she grumbled. "If they are, we'll see them coming. Because they'll be smart enough to use flashlights."

A valid point. He concentrated on watching for glimmers of light in the surrounding forest. Though he was less likely to be tracked in the dark, shadows made him wary of an ambush. Every sound magnified. The snap of twigs beneath his feet. The rustle of wind. Occasional screams from predator birds. And Jordan was the prey. Well-armed deputies with guns and shackles were after him. Searchers led by bloodhounds. They could be waiting at the warming hut, setting a trap.

"How do you know where we're going?" she demanded.

"I'm using the compass."

"We should've already reached the hut," she said. "It's late. We need to stop soon."

"We'll find it."

"You know," she said, "people get lost in the mountains all the time. These are miles and miles of open country."

"I said, we'll find the damn hut."

He'd learned the principles of coastal navigation while sailing on his fifteen foot sloop in the Gulf of Mexico, and the same logic applied on dry land. Though he could also take his bearings from the constellations, the Colorado sky was unfamiliar to him. Brilliant stars, unobscured by moisture or fog, shone too dazzling bright to be anything more than a distraction. Therefore, Jordan didn't take the time to look upward. He concentrated on placing one foot in front of the other, aiming in the right direction, finding shelter from the cold that froze his sweat against his body.

Stepping through a wall of forest, they entered a small clearing with a trail leading due north.

"This must be the path," Emily said. "I'm surprised you were able to find it."

Frankly, so was he. "I had to find the way. Quitting isn't an option."

She stepped around him to take the lead again, but he tugged gently on the rope, halting her forward progress. If a trap had been laid at the warming hut, he wouldn't give Emily first chance to signal.

"I'll go first. There might be an ambush." Once again,

he removed the gun from his pack. "Don't make any noise."

"What's your plan?"

"Pookie." Though the pup had lost much of his earlier vigor, Jordan expected a lot of barking if they encountered other people. "He'll warn us if anybody else is around."

They followed the path for less than a mile when he saw the dark square shape lurking amid the trees. Unlit, the warming hut appeared to be deserted, but Jordan held back, waiting for Pookie to make the first approach.

The dog didn't disappoint him. In a flash of golden fur, Pookie bounded up to the cabin door, sniffed and came back to them without a single moof.

"Okay," Jordan said. Sheer relief warmed his blood, fighting the cold that penetrated his flesh and chilled his bones. Only a few more steps. He could make it. "Now we can use the flashlights."

The inside of the one-room warming hut was primitive, but it looked like a Hilton hotel to Jordan. The only window was tightly shuttered, but the beam of his flashlight shone on a sink and a wood-burning stove. Several futon-like mattresses were stacked in a corner. There was a grimy table and two wooden chairs. He shed his backpack and lowered himself onto the seat. The hard wood felt more comfortable than plush velour.

Emily demanded. "Unfasten my leash."

Though he couldn't imagine how she'd find the strength to take off running, he couldn't give her the chance. "Not yet."

"But I'm starving, and Pookie needs to be fed. How am I going to prepare food while I'm tethered by this stupid cord?"

He sure as hell didn't want to shadow her movements

around the cabin. Summoning his last reserve of strength, Jordan moved his chair against the door which was the only way in or out. He sat before untying the nylon rope from his belt. "Knock yourself out, Emily."

She stretched and flexed her muscles as if she'd been bound, hand and foot. Then she got busy. Her first task was finding a hurricane lamp on a high, grimy shelf. Taking a votive candle from her pack, she struck a match and filled the glass lamp with flickering illumination.

Jordan watched through half-closed eyelids as she hustled and bustled, digging through the backpacks, assembling all her equipment. She reminded him of an exotic golden bird feathering her nest, creating a home.

Jordan exhaled slowly, using his willpower to dismiss the aches and pains of his wounded, battered body. This time, however, he didn't retreat to memories of sultry, green Florida. He was content to be here. Emily's presence was strangely comforting.

"Water," she muttered. "We need water."

A rusty hand pump stood beside the sink. Gamely, she grasped the handle and pushed down, again and again, until she was rewarded with a spurt of gritty, reddish-brown liquid. Pumping more vigorously, Emily finally achieved relative clarity. Still, she warned, "This isn't for drinking, only washing."

After feeding Pookie and giving him water, she assembled several unappetizing packets of freeze-dried food. "I need hot water for this."

"No fire," he said. Much as he'd like the heat, they couldn't risk sending up smoke signals.

"Don't need fire," she said.

Her emergency supplies included a small Sterno-powered hotplate. While their dinner warmed, she scrubbed the sink and wiped down the table. She also dug into her pack and produced a lightweight space blanket. "Wrap yourself in this."

Though it hurt his masculine pride to be huddled by the door with a blanket around his shoulders, Jordan was too chilly and tired to object. He took the bottle of ibuprofen from his pocket and swallowed three. To avoid thinking about the pain, he watched Emily.

With a strange lack of typical feminine vanity, she rolled up her sleeves and scrubbed her arms. Her eyes squinted shut as she splashed water on her face. Stepping away from the sink, she unfastened her ponytail. Her curly hair billowed past her shoulders in a golden cloud. It looked soft.

Jordan rubbed his thumb and index finger together, imagining the silky texture. He wished he could take the brush from her hands and stroke through that mass of thick wonderful hair.

Without consulting a mirror, she pulled it back into a ponytail. He'd never known a woman like her—completely honest, straightforward, without artifice. She wouldn't engage in the manipulative games most women played, and Jordan found those character traits very appealing. Maybe it wasn't an accident that his escape route led toward Cascadia. Maybe fate had directed him to Emily.

She dished the food onto small plastic plates and added two bottles of water. "Come and get it."

He shouldn't leave the door, shouldn't offer her an unguarded exit. "Take off your boots," he said.

"What?"

"You can't make a getaway if you're barefoot."

She rolled her eyes. "I'll take off my shoes if you'll come to the table. This isn't gourmet dining, but the taste is better when it's warm."

He dragged his chair across the rough wood plank floor and joined her. After six weeks of eating alone in jail, Jordan wasn't sure he could manage civilized conversation. "Well," he said. "We made it."

"*You* made it. This is *your* trip," she reminded him. "I'm just the hostage, dragged along for the ride."

He'd never use her as a shield, would never do anything to put her in danger. But that fact needed to remain his secret. If she had nothing to fear, she'd run from him. He took a bite of something with brown, orange and greenish lumps that vaguely resembled stew. "Not bad."

"Be sure to drink all the water. Keeping hydrated is important." She frowned. "I probably shouldn't be giving you survival tips."

"Probably not," he said sardonically. "If you're nice to me, I might grow on you."

"Like a fungus."

Undeterred, he said, "You might even start to like me."

"I try not to get too friendly with escaped convicts," Emily said. In spite of her hostility toward Jordan, she felt a grin begin to spread. "There's not much future in the fugitive-hostage relationship."

"Not true in my case," he assured her as he scarfed down another spoonful of freeze-dried stew. "I'm innocent, and I'm going to prove it."

His statement was so utterly artless that she couldn't help wondering if he spoke the truth. Earlier, when he talked about his deceased wife and the lack of passion in their marriage and proposed divorce, he'd been very believable. "Earlier, you mentioned investigating in Aspen, finding the real killer."

"That's right."

"What could you possibly hope to uncover?" She'd

kept track of the evidence through the newspaper reports. "Sheriff Litvak himself supervised the investigation."

"Don't get me wrong," Jordan said. "I don't think Litvak was out to frame me. But once he decided I was guilty, he stopped gathering data. There's got to be something he overlooked."

"Like what?" She enumerated the facts on her fingers. "He has the murder weapon, a gun that was registered to your wife and has only your fingerprints. There was no evidence of a break-in at the house. And an eyewitness, the housekeeper, saw you standing over the body."

"Kneeling," he said. "I'd found Lynette's body and called 9-1-1. I was kneeling beside her, trying to figure out how to do CPR or stop the bleeding."

"You don't know CPR?"

"I'm not an EMT like you. There was nothing I could do to save her."

His gaze met hers, and she saw a deep sadness in his dark brown eyes. Emily had almost forgotten that Lynette Afton-Shane had been a living, breathing woman. She was more than an anonymous victim. She'd been Jordan's wife.

He said, "From the coroner's report, I learned that CPR wouldn't have done any good. Lynette was shot through the heart. Her death was almost instantaneous."

"Accurate marksmanship," she said. "That might be a clue. Are you good with a gun?"

"Powder burns showed that she was shot at point-blank range. Not much skill required."

From what Emily recalled of the newspaper articles, Jordan claimed to have been sleeping down the hall when his wife was murdered. "Why didn't you hear the gunshot?"

"There was a silencer on the weapon. Plus, Lynette's

house is huge. I used to call it Hotel Afton-Shane because she generally had the sixteen bedrooms packed full with friends and family.''

"But no one else was staying there on the night she was killed."

"Just me."

"Why?" she asked.

"I wanted privacy to discuss our divorce. Crowds make me jumpy as a flea on a dog." As he relaxed, the southern lilt to his voice became more pronounced. "Most of the time, I'm real content to be alone with my computers and software."

"Me, too," she said. "Not with a computer, of course. But I've always been able to entertain myself."

"And that's why Lynette and I were alone at the house."

Emily understood why the sheriff had settled on Jordan as the most likely suspect. His request for a solitary weekend made it sound like he had something nefarious in mind.

Yet, he wasn't a fool. Why would he kill his wife when no other suspects inhabited the guest rooms in the house? "No sign of a break-in," she mused. "But surely other people had keys."

"Unfortunately, no. Lynette kept a lot of valuable artwork so her security was tight as a bear trap. There were no extra keys."

"Somebody might have dropped by," Emily suggested. "Your wife would've opened the door to let them in."

"That's what I told the sheriff," Jordan said. "A late-night guest. When I found her body, Lynette was dressed in a mighty fancy nightgown for somebody who was planning to sleep alone. But the doorbell rings through to the housekeeper, Rita Ramirez, in her first-floor apartment behind the kitchen. And Rita didn't hear anything.''

''Maybe your wife met them before they rang the bell.''

''How would she know when they arrived? There were no phone calls made to or from the house. Plus, this late-night visitor wouldn't have been able to leave after Lynette was shot. She had the kind of security system where you have to key a number into a computer to open or close any of the doors or windows without setting off an alarm.''

His sadness faded, and a grim determination took its place. His mouth set in a straight stubborn line, and his eyes seemed even darker, smouldering with a carefully banked fire. She sensed the strength of his character and the fierce willpower that drove him beyond the limits of exhaustion and pain. If anyone could find the murderer, Jordan could. Unless…he was guilty himself.

Purposefully, Emily mentally separated herself from the magnetism that flowed from him, enveloping her and making her see things his way. She wasn't ready to take his side. Not yet, anyway.

In a more clinical frame of mind, she noticed the sterile bandage covering his stitches was dirty after the day's exertions. ''I should check your wounds,'' she said, ''before we go to sleep.''

''Let's do it now. I'm about ready for sleep.''

''Take off your shirt and wash up.''

He went to the sink and peeled off his shirt. ''I want you to show me how to treat these wounds myself. When you're gone, I'll need to know what to do.''

''As long as there's no infection, you shouldn't have a problem. Keep the wounds clean and use lots of antiseptic.''

While he worked the pump at the sink, the lateral muscles in his back rippled. The candlelight cast a leaping shadow behind him on the plain log wall as he used her soap to scrub his bare arms and chest. He shivered. "Cold," he said. "I'm always cold in the mountains."

"You should dress in layers." She sounded as prim and prissy as a mountain safety handbook. Her lips sealed. If she honestly spoke her mind, she'd babble about his muscular upper body and how the proportion of his shoulders to his narrow waist took her breath away.

Shirtless, he returned to the chair. "Ready."

After she'd stripped off the gauze bandages and inspected the wounds, she had to admire her own handiwork. "I did a good job with those stitches. You'll have a scar, but it won't be too bad."

"One scar more or less doesn't matter," he said. When she stepped away, he slipped back into his shirt. "Here's something else I've been thinking about regarding the circumstances of Lynette's murder. She asked me for a month to clean up her financial affairs before I filed the paperwork for the divorce. Why?"

"It doesn't seem odd to me." Emily's finances were so simple that all the documentation for her savings, checking and ever-dwindling mutual funds could be stored in a shoebox. Still, every year at tax time, she spent a few weeks straightening receipts and sorting documents. "Maybe she was just disorganized."

"Not Lynette. This was a woman who made a daily list and crossed off every item with a neat, straight line."

Emily's eyebrows raised. "I've heard of people like that. Efficient people."

"Not your thing?"

"I manage with what really needs to be done, but I tend to get sidetracked. I'll start out the door, planning to put up the storm windows for winter, but I'll notice the color in the wildflowers and end up playing Frisbee with Pookie.''

She glanced over at the golden retriever puppy who was sleeping near the door. Pookie must have been dreaming of a rabbit chase because his paws twitched and he mumbled his trademark ''moofing'' noise.

Jordan said, ''What about when you were an E.R. nurse? You had to be efficient.''

''I had to be fast. In a triage situation, there isn't time for distractions.'' But nursing was so much more than technical delivery of necessary medical procedure. Emily naturally leaned toward whole patient care. Whether it was holding a hand or soothing a fevered brow, she tried to comfort. She talked to people. And she listened. She heard their dying words.

Sharp memories prickled like nettles, and she forced herself back to the present. Now was definitely not the time to slide into painful remembrance and allow her self-control to lapse. She must be more tired than she realized.

From across the table, Jordan watched her intently. He asked, ''Where did you go, Emily?''

''Nowhere.'' She'd never told anyone about her panic attacks brought on by E.R. stress, and she didn't intend to start with him. Mentally, she closed the door on her past. ''We were talking about you, about your wife's finances. Do you think the motive for her murder was monetary gain?''

''Yes,'' he said simply.

Emily asked the next obvious question, ''Who inherits?''

''A tenth goes to me. I think there are a couple of other cash stipends to cousins, but her brother, Brian, gets the house and the businesses. Sean Madigan, the professional skier, lives in the guest house near Lynette's château and he receives the deed to that cabin, free and clear.''

"Did the sheriff investigate all these people? Do they have alibis?"

"Brian claimed to be surrounded by witnesses at a party. Everybody else claimed to be home asleep."

"Which no one can prove or disprove."

"I'll find proof," he said. "The killer won't go unpunished."

Determination was well and good, but he'd set himself an impossible task. The sheriff—with all his law enforcement resources—couldn't discover evidence that implicated anyone but Jordan. How could he, as a fugitive, hope to do better?

"I'm sorry, Jordan, but your investigation doesn't sound too promising," Emily said. "I don't know how you hope to nab this murderer unless he suddenly develops Tourette's syndrome and blurts out a confession."

His intensity relaxed as he chuckled. "I like your sense of humor."

"You sound surprised."

"It's unexpected," he admitted. "Your occupation in emergency medicine isn't something I generally associate with comedy."

"That's what you nonmedical people don't understand," she said. "My work puts me in life-and-death situations. I need to be able to laugh. Otherwise, I'll start crying and never be able to stop."

She heard the bitterness in her own voice. And the pain. Her emotions were far too close to the surface, threatening to break though. Before she could blurt out anything else, Emily rose from the table and busied herself at the sink, washing dishes. What was it about Jordan that compelled her to reveal personal memories? Was it his desperation? He was in a fight for his life, his freedom, his peace of mind. Certainly, it wasn't because she trusted him.

Padding across the wood plank floor in her socks reminded her that Jordan had taken her shoes. He'd put her on a leash and forced her to break the law. She had absolutely no reason to sympathize with him.

Stiffly, she said, "If you don't mind, I need to go to the bathroom."

"Leave your boots here," he said. "Don't get lost in the dark."

When she opened the cabin door, Pookie woke. "Moof, moof."

She ruffled the fur on his head. "You should probably come with me, dog."

"Good thinking," Jordan said. "If anybody is outside watching, Pookie will find them."

"Great," she muttered as she stepped into the darkness. "He's turning my dog into a lookout. If I don't watch out, Pookie will be driving the getaway car."

It was too cold to consider an escape, especially without shoes. Even if Emily had the physical capability to run, she wasn't sure that she would leave Jordan. *Of course, she would. At the first opportunity.* Even if he was innocent, he shouldn't have escaped police custody.

Back inside the cabin with Pookie, she saw that Jordan had managed to drag one of the double-size mattresses off the stack.

"Only one?" she asked.

"We're going to zip the sleeping bags together and sleep on one mattress," he said. "Otherwise, I'd have to tie you up, and I wouldn't want to do that."

"Wouldn't you?" Emily tried to raise enough anger

to protest, but today's exertions had taken their toll—physically and emotionally. She could only manage a weak gesture. "You grabbed me at my house, tackled me in the front yard and tethered me with a leash. You enjoy tormenting me."

"I'm too tired to argue. Just help me zip the bags together."

"I don't want to sleep with you," she said. But did she? From the first moment she laid eyes on Jordan, she found him attractive. "If you lay one hand on me, I'll—"

"I won't touch you, Emily." He straightened his spine. In spite of the lingering trail dust and the prison-issue denims, Jordan exuded the dignity of an honorable man. His accent deepened in an echo of the Old South. "You have my word as a gentleman."

"Who do you think you are? Rhett Butler?"

The right corner of his mouth quirked in a grin. "At your service, Miss Scarlett."

Muttering to herself about overbearing southern gentlemen, Emily fastened the bags together.

"Get in," Jordan said.

She crawled inside, and the warmth of lightweight thermafill snuggled around her. When Jordan joined her inside the bag, there was barely room to move. She couldn't escape without waking him. And she wasn't altogether sure she wanted to leave him.

It had been years since she'd been intimate with a man, and she'd forgotten how pleasant it was to lie close to a large, masculine body. Tempting fate, she wriggled against him. His breath whispered deep and slow, echoing the rhythm of his heart. "Jordan?"

He was silent, already sound asleep. True to his word as a gentleman. *Damn it.*

Chapter Four

The candle had burned out. Darkness filled the small cabin, and Jordan blessed the absence of light when he woke. In the Pitkin County Jail, there had always been a glare from the guard station or from outside the windows. Here, the silent ebony night surrounded him, refreshed his senses and gave him peace. Here, in a warming hut on a mountainside, he was a free man.

Not only was he free but he shared the dark with a remarkable, beautiful woman. An unwilling woman, he reminded himself. She didn't want him to touch her.

However, while they'd slept inside the double thermal bag, he and Emily had inadvertently arranged themselves like nesting spoons. His wounded left arm gently rested upon her from shoulder to hip. Her back snuggled against his chest. Her wildly curling hair tickled his chin.

He couldn't be blamed for finding himself in this altogether pleasing position. It wasn't his fault they'd drawn together in slumber. Emily couldn't be angry about an unconscious embrace.

Unmoving, he reveled in her femininity, her softness. In the dark, unable to see her, he remembered the rainbow of gold in her hair, her rose petal lips and delicate throat. Her body remained a mystery to him because she'd spent the day hidden under a backpack, jeans, shirts and hiking boots. Even so, he could imagine her well-toned muscles and slender curves. Her body, he assumed, would be perfect.

The fingers of his left hand flexed ever so slightly, and he felt the swell of her hips. He glided his hand lower and cupped her buttocks. Her sleeping body enticed him, and he grew hard with longing. He wanted her, wanted to rub against her. At the thought, his erection strained at the zipper of his jeans. If Emily woke right now, he was pretty damned sure she'd be outraged.

Careful not to disturb her, he eased his left wrist toward his face so he could read his wristwatch. As the muscles in his upper arm contracted, the gunshot wound ached with a hard throbbing pain. Emily had said the wound would heal, and he believed her. He had to hope for the best. An infection would slow his escape and make him vulnerable.

With the wristwatch next to his nose, he read the glow-in-the-dark numerals. Four-thirty, predawn. If he wanted to stay a free man, Jordan needed to get moving. He also needed a plan. Yesterday, he'd instinctively headed back toward Aspen and hoped he wouldn't be caught. Today, he had to be smarter.

First of all, he needed to obtain the proper clothing for mountain survival. A jacket with a hood. Maybe a sweatshirt. Decent boots and warm socks. Unfortunately, he couldn't stroll into the nearest backpacking store and buy his supplies.

If he had a computer and modem, his problem would be solved. He could go online and order whatever he needed. Jordan was not only familiar with software and the Internet, he'd invented some parts of it. With his years of expertise, he knew how to hack around the system, set up dummy addresses and bounce a signal through so many filters it couldn't be traced.

But where could he find a computer? As far as he knew, his laptop was still at Lynette's house in Aspen. To get it, he'd have to break in, breaching the security system. Too risky. There had to be another way.

Emily wiggled against him, unintentionally teasing, driving rational plans from his head and sending his brain directly into his crotch. A groan rumbled in his throat. He leaned inches closer to her ear, caught the lobe between his teeth and lightly tugged. She made a tiny sound. Was she encouraging him? Maybe if she rolled over in her sleep and kissed him before she was fully conscious, she would forget who he was and why they were here. Maybe she'd—

He heard a loud panting from across the room. The thud of puppy paws crossed the wood plank floor. Pookie's tongue slapped against Jordan's forehead. "Moof, woof."

"Not now, dog."

Apparently, those words were the command for playtime because Pookie bounded on top of the sleeping bag. Instead of waking with a seduction, Jordan and Emily tangled together inside the bag.

"Roof, ruff." The puppy attacked whichever body part was moving.

Emily's sweet pliance turned into flailing elbows.

Protecting his injured body, Jordan shoved her away and hauled himself out of the bag. Blindly, he stumbled toward the door and opened it. Moonlight and cold mountain air spilled inside. Pookie scampered out.

Growling, Emily demanded, "Is it morning?"

"Close enough," he said, retrieving his flashlight from beside his pack and hoping that his arousal would subside before she noticed. He shone the flashlight beam in her eyes. "Do you have another candle in your pack?"

"Turn that thing away from me." She threw a hand in front of her face. "I'll get the candle. You'll never find it."

He spotlighted her movements as she went to her pack, found another votive candle and placed it inside the hurricane lamp. A soft glow filled the one-room hut as she turned toward him. "Now what?"

Pookie the Demon Dog scampered back inside, waggled himself at Jordan and went to his mistress, Emily, for a good-morning hug. "Moofle, ruff."

Though fond of the puppy, Jordan momentarily considered shaving off that golden fur and wearing it as a coat. He closed the door with a slam. "I'd like to get moving before the sun comes up. I need warmer clothes. Do you have anything?"

She delved into the depths of her backpack and pulled out a knit woolen cap and one-size-fits-all mittens. "Wrap yourself in the space blanket. It's lightweight and designed to conserve your body heat."

The silvery blanket would also reflect like a mirror when the sun came up. "This thing would be a beacon to searchers. You don't want me to get caught, do you?"

"Don't I?"

He couldn't tell what she was thinking. Last night, Emily had seemed ready to believe in him. But now? She avoided his gaze as she donned her own jacket and a red knit cap with a tassel.

"You know I'm innocent," he said.

"All I know for sure is that you're on the run from the law and you're forcing me to go with you."

He struggled to tie the blanket around him. As his body wakened, he recognized aches and pains in places he never knew he had muscles. Jamming the plain black cap on his head, Jordan suspected he looked like a total ass. But when it came to a choice between vanity and hypothermia, he'd choose warmth.

He found the plastic bottle of ibuprofen and tapped out four tablets. When he reached for his canteen, he was surprised to find it filled to the brim. He turned toward Emily who was putting together a breakfast of granola bars. "Where'd you get the water?"

"Last night I ran some from the pump through the purifier. It's not Perrier, but it won't make you sick."

"Planning ahead. That's good." She knew how to do these things. Her work for S.A.R. made mountain survival second nature to her. That was why he'd brought her with him.

Before they left the hut, Jordan listened to the police band radio. Searchers were already mobilizing. It sounded like a legion of armed men with helicopters and bloodhounds were taking the field, all of them intent upon finding him.

Terse orders and responses came through the dispatcher. The area immediately surrounding Aspen seemed to be the epicenter of the manhunt. Though they hadn't yet discovered that Emily was missing, Jordan heard the words he dreaded through the static, "Cascadia. Northeast quadrant. We've got a trail."

Jordan remembered their frantic sprint across the open field, the trampled grasses. "Damn it."

Using the topographical maps, he set their course toward the Roaring Fork River.

Emily looked over his shoulder as she munched a granola bar. She shook her head. "You're walking into trouble."

"I have to go to Aspen. There's something I need."

"What?"

"My laptop computer. It's at Lynette's house."

"A computer? Oh, sure. That's a real essential survival tool. A computer is worth risking your life."

"I wouldn't expect you to understand. You're too busy communing with nature to bother with the Internet."

"Internet, my eye." She pointed to the chair. "Before we head out, let me take one more look at those stitches on your cheek."

The wound on his face felt tight, but it wasn't nearly as painful as the rest of his body. Still, he sank onto the chair.

Gently removing the sterile bandage, she assured him, "I'm not doing this because I care about what happens to you. It's just that I feel professionally responsible for your medical care."

"Give it up, Emily. You're not a good liar."

"What do you mean?"

"I think you're beginning to care about me."

"Not a chance," she said.

"Last night, you asked enough questions about the murder to convince yourself that I'm innocent. You know the truth. I was framed. I had no reason to kill Lynette."

"That's for the courts to decide," she said.

His gaze lifted to her face, noticing the light sprinkle of freckles across her nose. Her lashes were thick, a dark brown like her eyebrows. Her cool green eyes concentrated intently as she used a Betadine swab to clean his wounds. Her attitude was clinical. She didn't see him as a man. To her, he was only a patient, and he hated that.

Jordan could accept her anger, even her disgust. But he wouldn't stand for indifference. "Look at me, Emily."

Her lashes fluttered as she focused upon him.

He entered the windows of her soul and deep inside,

he recognized a spark—an intimacy that belied any nurse-patient intentions.

Before she could object, he held her nape below the curly blond ponytail. He pulled her toward him and kissed her moist, sweet lips. Her surprised gasp faded to a womanly moan as she kissed him back. Her mouth moved against his. Her lips parted. She welcomed his tongue into her mouth, and he tasted her hunger, nearly as strong as his own. Before their journey ended, he knew they would make love.

When he released her, she stepped back. Dazed, she trembled. For a moment, she seemed to forget that she was a hostage and he was a fugitive. Her dark hostility lifted, and she shone beautiful as a sunrise.

Then, she blazed. "How could you! Jordan, you promised not to touch me."

"That promise was only good for last night." In spite of a sharp twinge of pain from the newly dressed stitches in his cheek, he grinned. "It's a new day, Emily."

"There will never be enough days for me to forgive what you've done to me." She lifted her hand and touched her tingling lips, unable to believe that he'd kissed her. Worse yet, she'd kissed back. Anger surged inside her. "Damn you, Jordan."

Still, he grinned. He was arrogant and proud of himself for stealing a kiss. An involuntary shiver crept through her. What a kiss! It felt like she'd been waiting all her life for him. Last night, she'd wanted him. Her resolve had weakened. But she was stronger now.

Above all, Emily knew the difference between right and wrong. "I won't let you turn me into an accomplice. I work with the sheriff's department. I'm not a criminal."

"Neither am I," he said simply. "Let's go."

She readied her pack and eased the straps onto her

shoulders. Last night, she found reasons to believe he'd been framed for his wife's murder. Last night, she wanted to help him, even if it meant breaking the law.

But she'd been wrong. How could the truth come through an illegal escape? Whether or not he'd committed murder, it wasn't her place to decide. A verdict resulted from the opinions of a judge and jury. Jordan had to face trial.

Last night, he'd said that innocent people were convicted all the time, and she suspected that was true. The court system never claimed to be infallible, but the system offered room for appeal, for mistrial, for evidentiary hearings. Even with flaws, the justice system worked. Emily believed in the American way of life. Her family legacy. She remembered, as a little girl, saluting the flag. Her father had died a patriot in Vietnam, defending their way of life. Helping an escaped criminal meant disregarding her father's memory. How could she do that? She'd dedicated herself toward being someone her father would have been proud of. As an E.R. nurse, she fought life-and-death battles.

She steeled herself against Jordan. "You can't take the law into your own hands."

"Ready?" He held the door open.

"You could turn yourself in. We can use the walkie-talkie to contact the searchers. They'll go easy on you if you show you're willing to—"

"I won't go back to jail."

His determined tone offered no room for compromise. And she was equally convinced. She crumpled the granola bar wrapper in her hand to use as a marker after they set out.

When he took out the coil of rope, she said, "Not the

leash. Not in the dark, Jordan. We're clumsy enough in full daylight.''

"Fair enough," he said. "I trust you not to make an escape attempt."

"And if I did?"

His dark eyes were hard as anthracite as he reminded, "I still have the gun."

She followed him outside into the bracing chill. Through the spired treetops, the half moon hung low in the western sky. "You wouldn't shoot me."

"Don't test me," he said grimly. "I'll do whatever it takes to escape."

As they left the maintained trail, she surreptitiously dropped a piece of the granola wrapper. For good measure, she snapped a low-hanging branch on a tree.

Pookie stood beside her, looking up. His trustful puppy eyes seemed to accuse her. Emily fought a rising sense of guilt, telling herself over and over that turning Jordan over to the authorities was the right thing.

By ten o'clock in the morning, after five hours of hiking, Jordan had packed away the reflective blanket. They had taken care to stay under the cover of the forests. On a small rise at the edge of a clearing, he paused. "There's something wrong," he said.

Emily clenched the tissue in her hand. All along their route she'd been dropping tiny shreds. "What could be wrong?"

He took the high-powered binoculars from her pack and scanned the landscape. "I don't see anyone, but it feels like they're getting closer."

As if on cue, she heard the distant ratcheting whir of helicopter blades.

"Get back," Jordan ordered. "Take off your pack and stash it under the shrub."

She shoved her bright red pack under a chokecherry bush, ripe with berries.

"The red jacket," he said. "Hide it."

She did as he ordered. There was only one reason for a chopper to patrol in this desolate area. The scope of the manhunt had tightened. The trackers had picked up the clues she'd been leaving.

Emily should've felt glad that her ruse had worked. He was going to be caught. Instead, a dark foreboding settled upon her. What if she'd been wrong? What if he truly couldn't obtain justice? If he was caught and convicted, her actions on the trail would have condemned him.

He grabbed Pookie by the collar. Then his strong arms closed around Emily and he pulled her down behind the bushes. "I'm not making a pass," he said. "I just don't want you or Pookie getting some crazy idea that you should run into the open and signal your buddies in the helicopter."

The chopper came into sight. Flying low, the runners nearly skimmed the tops of the trees as they navigated in a loose grid pattern.

Though circled within Jordan's arms, Emily doubted that he could hold both her and the dog. If she struggled, she might break free. Her gaze focused on the clearing, only twenty feet beyond their hiding place. Unemcumbered by her pack, she could race into the clearing and signal the chopper.

But she didn't move.

His voice was a tense whisper in her ear. "I haven't told you what it was like to be in jail for six weeks. Waiting for the legal system to come up with an answer for my trial, I had no power, no recourse. Day after day in a square gray cell."

Too easily, she imagined what it was like. Her own

father had been in jail. Weeks before he died, he was a POW in Vietnam, locked in a cage. No recourse. Helpless.

"Always cold," Jordan said. "In jail, it was never dark enough to get a good night's sleep. At first, there was a rage inside me. It burned like wildfire."

The helicopter was directly overhead. She felt the downdraft. Every muscle in her body tensed, waiting for them to be sighted.

But the chopper did not pause in its overhead swoop. Not hovering for even a second, the searchers moved on.

Jordan continued, "After four weeks, the fire in my soul went out. I lost hope. No matter how many times I proclaimed my innocence, nobody believed me. It seemed like nobody ever would."

The memory of a father she'd never known tortured her conscience. He must have felt the same way Jordan did.

"I'd rather die," he said, "than go back to jail."

As the noise of the helicopter faded, Jordan released her. He took out the police band radio and listened intently, picking out the pieces of intelligence through the static transmission. Searchers had found evidence of their stay at the warming hut.

With dread, Emily heard the report. "…heading northeast. Looks like somebody's leaving a trail. Scraps of tissue."

Startled, Jordan looked up. She saw the pain and fury in his eyes. He knew he'd been betrayed.

He grasped her wrist, uncurled her tightly closed fingers. The crumbled tissue fell from her hand.

"You've been helping them," he said.

She could only nod as fear spread through her body.

What would he do to her? How would he take his revenge?

"Why?"

A sob caught in her throat, but she didn't cry. She was a soldier's daughter, the child of a hero. "I thought I was doing the right thing."

Disgusted, he dropped her hand. From his backpack, he retrieved the gun. His voice was harsh. "I needed your skill to survive. Instead, you've left a trail so clear that Pookie could follow it."

Staring at the barrel of her own .22 automatic, she tried to defend her actions. "I had to help the searchers. You're an escaped—"

"I'm an innocent man." He stared hard into her eyes. "Somewhere in your heart, you believe me. I know you do."

"That's not the point, Jordan." Her words sounded hollow. "You have to let the justice system do its job."

"The system turned against me. The press is howling for my blood. The good people of your mountain community hate me, like they hate all outsiders. They're a goddamned lynch mob." He held her chin, forcing her to look into his eyes. "I thought you were different, Emily. I thought you were independent enough to make your own decisions."

"Are you going to shoot me?"

He winced, as if her suspicion caused him physical pain. Then he placed the pistol in her hand. "Check the clip, Emily. It's not loaded."

With trembling fingers, she verified his statement. Not loaded! But why? "I guess when you searched my house, you couldn't find the ammunition."

"The bullets were in your underwear drawer," he said.

"I didn't load the gun because I didn't intend to use it. I'm not a killer."

She'd made a mistake, a terrible misjudgment.

Believing that she helped the cause of justice, she'd betrayed an innocent man who had been falsely imprisoned. The parallel with her father stung her conscience. She would never forgive herself if Jordan was caught before he had a chance to prove his innocence. "I was wrong."

"Yeah." He took the blue nylon rope from his pack. "I'll leave you here, tied to a tree with enough water and food to last until you're found. Shouldn't take long. I imagine you've left enough signposts to this very spot."

"I have," she admitted. "Not that it made much difference. I've worked with these guys, Jordan. Professional trackers are capable of picking a trail from thin air. Plus they have bloodhounds. You'll never make it."

"I have to try." He slipped a loop around Pookie's neck and tied it so the dog wouldn't accidentally strangle himself. Then he turned to her. "Hold out your hands, Emily."

But she could help him, truly help. She knew enough tricks to throw searchers off the trail. At least, she could slow them down. "You need me," she said.

"Like a surfer needs a shark."

"Before now, I didn't understand." She wanted to tell him about her father, his imprisonment. But she'd never spoken of his death. Never shared that pain with another human being. "Give me a chance to make this right."

He hesitated, rope in hand. "I'm listening."

"My father," she said, "died for unjust reasons that no one ever truly explained to me. He wasn't a criminal, but he was in prison. In Vietnam."

Jordan watched her steadily, unblinking.

"My mother told me he was a hero, but I never really knew him. He died before I was two years old. I've always tried to live in a way that would make him proud of me. Jordan, I think he'd want me to help you."

"It was hard for you to say that."

"Real hard," she said. "I got you into this mess, and I can get you out. I'll help you for the rest of today. After that, you're on your own."

"You betrayed me, Emily. How do I know I can trust you?"

"Because I know where you can get a computer," she said. "At the S.A.R. headquarters in Cascadia, we have two computers that are almost never used."

"A laptop?"

"I think so. It's a fold-up thing with a battery so it can be used on the trail."

Her gaze traveled beyond his shoulder. At the peak of the hillside behind them, she glimpsed a reflection of something metallic. A gun? She pointed. "They're closing in."

He whirled and grabbed the binoculars. "Where? I don't see them."

"By that flat granite stone at the top of the hill. It's less than a mile away."

He focused. "Two men. One of them has a rifle."

"You need me," she repeated. "You won't make it to nightfall by yourself."

He lowered the binoculars. "You've got a deal. What do we do next?"

With renewed vigor, Emily tore through their backpacks. "We travel light, eliminate all but the bare necessities."

"If we leave this stuff here, they'll know you're with me."

"Might be useful," she said. "If they know you have a hostage, they won't be so quick to use their guns."

All that was left when she finished were the sleeping bags, the medical supplies, rope, matches, granola bars and canteens of water. She picked up the tissue he'd discarded on the ground.

"We'll go uphill," she said. "Moving across the flat rocks, we won't accidentally break any branches."

"But we'll be out in the open," Jordan said. "Even if the chopper doesn't come back, those guys behind us must have binoculars."

"We'll only be exposed for a little while. Then, we're going to lay a false trail."

He caught hold of her arm and turned her toward him. "Are you sure this will work?"

Emily looked him straight in the eye. "I won't betray you again, Jordan."

"I believe you." He didn't have much choice. Jordan knew he couldn't outsmart the trackers on his own. He had to trust Emily and hope her change of heart was true.

Falling into step behind her, he hiked straight up, climbing over rocks. The ache in his muscles became unnoticeable as adreneline drove him forward. He imagined the searchers closing in, lifting rifles to their shoulders, sighting on his back. In his mind, he felt the bullets tearing through his flesh, disabling him, making him vulnerable to capture.

At the edge of a high cliffside, they ran on uneven terrain, covering ground. His breathing sounded as loud as a turbo engine to his ears, alerting everyone within twenty miles to his presence. They rounded the corner of the rocks, and Emily leaned against the granite wall, gasping.

"So far, so good," Jordan said. If anyone had been

monitoring their progress, they'd lose sight of them at this point. "Now what?"

Scanning the flat outcropping of granite, she motioned him forward until they came to a vertical crevasse between two towering boulders. Emily stepped inside the rock chimney. From side to side, the crevasse was only a few feet wide. Jordan had seen rock climbers inch their way up similar formations with their feet braced against one wall and their back against the other. He stared up. From the ground to the top of the boulders was probably thirty-five to forty feet. He wasn't thrilled about the prospect of scaling this height. "Don't tell me we need to go up this thing."

"We're going to make the searchers think we did," she said. "If they think we made this climb, they won't be able to pass up the challenge of following. Lift me up."

Bending, he grasped her around the knees and elevated her to a height of about ten feet. She carefully placed a scrap of tissue on a stubborn shrub that clung to the granite surface. "Okay. Put me down."

"Clever," he said. Since the searchers were following her marked trail, they'd probably waste a lot of time climbing the rock chimney. "Now we go downhill."

"Not quite yet, but soon. Then we'll double back toward Cascadia."

They went deep into the forests, headed in a southwestern direction—sometimes forward, sometimes backtracking. They forded a stream in a zig-zag pattern.

Jordan pressed for speed. In the shadows of trees, rocks and shrubs, he felt encroaching danger. Had their ruse at the rock crevasse been successful? He didn't dare to stop and look. Not yet. Not until they'd put distance between themselves and the trackers.

At the base of another jagged cliff, they approached a trail that wound below the rocks. Emily held up her hand, signalling a halt.

"We've got a decision to make." She pointed across the narrow wooded canyon to a flat promontory on the opposite side. "That's Mammoth Rock. It's easily reachable on a dirt road, and it's the best look-out point for miles around."

He took the binoculars from the pack and peered through them, adjusting the focus. Lowering the glasses, he scanned with his naked eyes. "I don't see anyone."

"Two options," she said, taking a long sip of water from her canteen. "We can move along this path under the cliff where we'll be easily visible. Or we can stay under the trees in the canyon. The route through the trees will take longer."

He glanced at his wristwatch. It was almost two o'clock in the afternoon. Not that time mattered. The ticking clock was irrelevant. They needed distance to escape.

"It's a risk," he said.

Jordan squatted down, thinking. He prided himself on being a rational man, capable of making measured intelligent decisions. But he wasn't in the boardroom now. Absently, his fingers tangled in Pookie's fur. The puppy had behaved well, sticking close to them as they moved swiftly. It was almost as if Pookie sensed the danger.

Jordan's brain adjusted to his new situation. He was a fugitive, on the run. He needed speed. "We'll take the faster route and hope there's no lookout on Mammoth Rock."

Cautiously, they stepped onto the path. Emily went first, moving fast, and Jordan followed. He felt the sun on his face. In the open, they were as obvious as ducks in a shooting gallery.

Loose gravel crunched loudly beneath his feet.

He kept pace with her. Uphill again. They moved quickly on the narrow path below the cliff.

A gunshot echoed through the canyon.

Chapter Five

The rifle blast echoed in Jordan's ears. Magnified by his vigilant caution, it sounded louder than a thunderclap. They'd found him! He was caught!

He leapt forward on the trail, driven by an urge he couldn't explain. In spite of his need for self-preservation and escape, his first instinct was to protect Emily. She'd frozen midstride, stiff as the jagged rock spires that rose above them.

He grabbed her arm and she whirled toward him, stark confusion in her eyes. But there was no time to explain. He lifted her off her feet and pulled her with him behind a rock at the edge of the path. Her tense arms and legs compressed into a tight ball. "Emily, are you okay?"

"I don't know."

"You're not wounded, are you?"

"Of course not." Her eyelids blinked rapidly. She appeared to be shocked rather than frightened. "I can't believe they're shooting at us. Aren't the police supposed to yell something first? Like freeze?"

"I'm not sure of proper criminal etiquette." He tried to reassure her with a smile. "It's okay. They're not after you. If you stay down, you ought to be safe."

"You want me to hide?"

"I want you to be sensible."

"I'm not a coward." Color flooded back into her cheeks. "I won't let somebody hunt you down like an animal. There are procedures to be followed. It's not right."

He wondered how she'd come up with all these stringent rules about right and wrong, but now was not the time for a philosophical discussion. Danger had caught up to him. He had to act quickly.

Though Jordan hadn't seen their assailant, he guessed that the rifleman was on Mammoth Rock which placed his trajectory above them, the perfect vantage point for a marksman. The rock they hid behind offered very little protection, even less when Pookie joined them and flattened himself against Emily's thigh.

The dog moaned. "Rrrrr. Mrrrr."

Jordan glanced at both of them. His gang. A curly-haired blonde and a Pookie. Oh yeah, he was a fearsome fugitive, a real threat to society. He rested his forehead against the rough granite surface of the rock, tempted to bang his skull until he knocked himself unconscious.

Though it might be pleasant to stop thinking and give up, he didn't want to wake up in jail. Once again, he needed a plan.

Jordan peeked out from cover. A steep ravine separated them from Mammoth Rock. At the base of the gravel path was forest land, trees. If he could make it down the hill...

"I'll signal them," Emily said. "They won't shoot me."

"Don't be so sure." When he'd escaped from the airport, there had been no offer of safe surrender. Only bullets.

Another shot rang out. The stone beside Jordan's

shoulder shattered. Before he ducked down, he saw the glint of sunlight off a rifle on Mammoth Rock.

He huddled down beside Emily. "The bad news is that we're pinned down."

"And the good news?"

"I think he's a lone gunman," Jordan said. That wouldn't last for long. Even if the lookout hadn't already radioed his position, his gunfire would draw other searchers. Each moment that passed added to the danger. "I'm going to make a run for it. You stay here, Emily."

Her green eyes shimmered with unshed tears. Her lower lip trembled. "I'm sorry, Jordan. This is my fault."

He wanted to ease her guilt, to tell her that he probably wouldn't have survived the previous night if she hadn't explained about the warming hut. If there had been time, he would've told her how much he admired her skill and her spirit. But there were only moments between Jordan and capture.

He leaned forward and brushed her lips with a kiss. "Goodbye, Emily."

"Don't leave me," she whispered.

"Honey, I'd like nothing more than to stay." He'd like to hold her, to kiss her until her tears melted into sweet desire. But he wasn't free. "Goodbye."

"What are you going to do?"

"I'm going to dive down this cliff and hope he can't get a clear shot in the trees. Hold onto Pookie's collar so he won't come after me."

"Jordan, no. You'll be killed."

"I'll make it," he said grimly.

From a crouch, Jordan sprang into the open. He plunged over the edge of the high path onto a gravel slope. It couldn't have been more than ten yards before he'd be hidden by tall forest. The soles of his sneakers skidded.

Repeated gunfire cracked around him.

Stumbling, falling, he reached the pines.

EMILY'S HEARTBEAT pounded louder than shots from the repeating rifle. She feared for Jordan's safety, prayed for his escape.

She peered around the edge of her hiding place. On the opposite cliff, the rifleman stepped out from behind a tall boulder. He wore a deputy's uniform. Swiftly, he moved to the rounded edge of Mammoth Rock which was shaped like a prehistoric wooly mammoth. The deputy stood above the place where the mammoth's eye would have been. He was looking down into the trees below, trying to get an angle for his next shot.

She couldn't allow this to happen, couldn't allow Jordan to be hunted like prey.

Despite Jordan's warnings, Emily surged to her feet. At the very least, she could provide a distraction. With arms raised above her head, she waved at the deputy. "Help," she shouted. "You! You've got to help me!"

Beside her, Pookie chimed in, "Roof. Woof. Woof."

The deputy looked toward her. Sunlight reflected off his dark glasses. For a terrifying instant, his rifle aimed toward the center of her chest.

"Don't shoot!" Emily yelled.

The long pewter-colored bore of his rifle lowered again. Intent upon sighting Jordan, he took another step forward. And his foot slipped.

She watched as the uniformed man lost his balance. He went down hard. The rifle fell from his hands and plummeted off the edge and into the trees. Unable to stop his fall, the deputy slid on the rounded side of Mammoth Rock. His fingers clawed, frantically seeking a handhold.

"Use your boots," she shouted. With traction from his hiking boots, he might be able to cling like a fly on the surface of the rock. If not, it was a dangerous drop, over thirty feet.

Helpless, she could only stand and watch as the deputy lost his grip and tumbled down the face of the rock.

"Are you all right?" Emily yelled.

No answer.

"Hey, deputy!" she tried again. "Are you conscious? I can help you."

Still silence.

Her priorities shifted into rescue mode. With the medical supplies in her pack she could handle emergency care for the deputy, but there was no way she could lift him to the top of Mammoth Rock for evacuation. Managing a litter was a two-person job, and she didn't have the proper equipment.

With help from another person, she might be able to rig something with ropes. But Jordan was already on the path to escape, and she didn't expect him to look back. He'd already said goodbye. *Goodbye.* His words dropped into her mind like pebbles into a smooth pond. The concentric ripples spread until she was consumed with regret.

Though she should have been glad that her hostage ordeal was over, she never really knew this complicated man. He was brave and stoic when confronted with physical pain. His terse verbal responses belied a remarkable depth of intelligence, yet he had a wicked sense of humor. And honor, she thought. Above all, Jordan had behaved like a gentleman. Except for that one stolen kiss. With a sigh, she lightly touched her lips, remembering

the moist pressure of his mouth against hers and the pleasure of their forbidden embrace.

Now, he was gone. How would he survive in the
mountains without her help? He hadn't taken the medical
supplies. What if his wounds became infected?

Her gaze lifted toward the distant horizon. He was out
there, somewhere, running for his life. All she could do
was to wish him well. *Godspeed, Jordan Shane.*

"Come on, Pookie."

With her furry companion—the only male she could
ever really trust to stay by her side for better or worse—
Emily climbed down from the path and hurried into the
forested area, headed toward the spot where she'd seen
the deputy fall.

The moment she saw the body, she feared the worst.
Sprawled against the rocks, his right leg was twisted at
an unnatural angle. At the very least, his knee was badly
sprained. But she was more concerned about the bloody
laceration on his forehead, a probable concussion. He appeared to be unconscious.

Stripping off her pack, she knelt beside the injured
man. Without his sunglasses, she recognized the deputy.
His name was Ed Collins. He had taken part in previous
S.A.R. operations, but she'd never socialized with him.

Beneath his leather jacket, his chest rose and fell with
every breath. A good sign.

Leaning over his face, she spoke loudly, hoping for a
response. "Wake up, Ed. Ed Collins, I want you to wake
up right now. Come on, Ed."

His eyelids snapped open. His narrow, weathered face
twisted in a grimace of pain. Then he gasped. "You're
that nurse from Cascadia. Emily?"

"That's right." She offered a professional smile. Moments ago, the deputy had aimed a rifle at her chest, but

she couldn't hold that against him. He was doing his job.
"You need to lie still while I check you out."

"Like hell I will."

When he started to sit up, she firmly restrained him by
holding his shoulders. "In a fall," she explained,
"there's always a danger of spinal cord injury. Or you
might have a busted rib that could puncture your lung if
you move around."

Hopefully, the worst-case scenario would scare him
into submission. Emily didn't have the patience to deal
with a difficult patient. "Do what I say, Ed. And you just
might be all right."

"Moof, moof," Pookie echoed. The dog kept his distance from Ed, pacing nervously about eight feet away.

"Lie still," Emily repeated.

"That's a load of crap," he muttered. "I'm okay."

"I want you to look at my face," she said, still worried
about concussion. "Try to focus. How many fingers am
I holding up?"

"I see three skinny twigs waving at me. God, you're
a mess. What the hell were you doing with that fugitive?"

"I was a hostage," she said coldly. When Pookie
started growling, she had to agree. Ed Collins was a most
unpleasant person. "How many fingers now?"

"Go play nurse with somebody else. I'm giving the
orders here."

He shoved her aside and bolted to a sitting position.
Apparently, his back was not seriously injured. However,
when he tried to stand, his right knee collapsed beneath
him and he went down with a yelp of pain. "My leg!"

"Could be broken," she said with a distinct lack of
sympathy.

Groaning, he dragged himself into a sitting position,

leaning against a rock. His macho attitude faded in a string of curses that ended in a whimper. He wiggled uncomfortably against the rock and unfastened his belt buckle.

"What are you doing?" Emily asked.

"Taking off this damned utility belt. There's about twenty things poking into my back."

"Do you have a walkie-talkie? We can radio a chopper for emergency evacuation."

"In my car. Parked on top of Mammoth Rock."

He tore off the belt, placing his sidearm holster, handcuffs, pepper spray and sundry bits of other police equipment beside him, within easy reach. Then he whined, "Give me something for the pain. I need it."

Digging into her pack, she found a plastic bottle of ibuprofen. She handed it to him along with her canteen.

"Is this all you've got?"

"Yes," she said.

"I'm better equipped than you are, nursey." He dug into his trouser pocket and pulled out an amber prescription vial. Gruffly, he explained, "Chronic headaches."

"What's the dosage?"

"One a day," he said.

"Ed, I really don't think you should—"

"Too bad." Before she could stop him, he downed four pills and tossed the canteen aside, allowing her precious water to spill onto the gravel soil.

Angrily, Emily snatched the water container and screwed on the lid. It always seemed that the worst patients were people with training who ought to know better. In the case of Ed Collins, that stereotype held true. Hoping that his pills would relax him, possibly even put him to sleep, she inspected his head wound before dealing with the more painful leg injury.

"It's a superficial laceration on your forehead," she said as she swabbed with disinfectant. "But you're going to have a bump."

"Tell me something I don't know." His eyes glared angrily, fully conscious and aware. If he had a concussion, it was minor. "Damn it, I should've nailed that son-of-a-gun. I had a clear shot."

"Shoot first and ask questions later?"

"Those were my orders." He winced as she placed a sterile bandage on his forehead. "I was aiming for his legs. That's why I missed. I should've shot him in the chest."

Thank goodness for Ed Collins's lousy aim. "You know, Ed, I never thought that was standard operating procedure for the police. Aren't you supposed to offer the fugitive a chance to surrender first? Especially when there's a hostage involved?"

"How the hell was I supposed to know you were a hostage? You could've been helping him escape."

Emily felt a slight twinge of guilt. She had no room to make accusations about Ed's professional behavior. Her alliance with Jordan should have silenced her criticism. Still, she said, "An ambush doesn't seem right."

"The guy is a cold-blooded murderer. I should've shot him in the head." He exhaled slowly. His pills were beginning to do their work. "Besides, I could use the money."

"What money is that, Ed?"

"The bounty. Ten thousand bucks."

Even in the wild west of Colorado, the sheriff's department didn't offer dead-or-alive bounties. This was a clue, a big one. Emily had wondered how Jordan, a high security prisoner, managed to escape from police custody. Had his escape been arranged, even encouraged by the authorities? Was the plan to shoot him down as an escapee?

That would mean he'd been framed. And, if framed, he was innocent. Trying to hide her excitement, Emily asked, "Who's offering this reward?"

"Ten thousand dollars." His eyelids drooped. His jaw slackened. "I'm just doing my job."

"It sounds like a setup, Ed. Was Jordan supposed to be shot and killed while he was escaping?"

"I dunno." He was fading fast.

"Concentrate, Ed. I need to know."

"About what?"

"The ten thousand dollars. Who was offering the bounty?"

He waggled his finger at her. "I got my eye on a dirt bike. Are you going to fix my leg or not?"

"Maybe you can give me some answers first."

"Nope." His eyelids fluttered and slammed shut.

Emily wouldn't get any more information from Deputy Collins. But he'd given her something to chew on. It seemed that someone didn't want Jordan to come to trial. They wanted him dead. Was it a cover-up? A frame? More than ever, she was convinced of Jordan's innocence.

She readied the SAM splint, a flexible aluminum frame covered by a layer of malleable foam which could be adjusted to fit almost any sprain or break. When properly shaped, the splint would be stiff enough to immobilize Ed's leg until he could receive in-hospital medical attention.

When she straightened his leg to splint the knee, he shuddered violently but didn't wake up.

This time, Emily didn't try to rouse him. She checked his vital signs, made sure his breathing was unobstructed and went to work on his leg. After she was done here, she'd climb around the edge of Mammoth Rock and use the deputy's car radio to call for help in evacuation. Collins seemed to be resting comfortably. He'd be okay for a few minutes on his own.

"Moofle, woof. Whoo-woo." It was Pookie's happy bark.

Emily glanced over her shoulder and saw Jordan hiking toward them through the trees. In the shadows of the forest, he paused before stepping into the open. He stood so very still, that she thought he might not be real. His return might be a mirage.

But Pookie galloped toward him with all the lopsided grace of an unstrung marionette. "Whoo-woof. Yip, yip, yip."

Jordan fended off the wild doggy embrace. "Down, dog."

To her surprise, Emily's heart soared at the sight of him. He'd come back to her. Jordan hadn't really said goodbye after all.

Her excitement was so great that she couldn't properly wrap the tape on Deputy Collins's splint. She abandoned the EMT effort and stood. Though she never considered herself to be particularly romantic, she envisioned running toward Jordan in slow motion with dappled sunlight all around them. She would leap into his arms, and he would twirl her in a wide circle.

Despite the danger, he'd come back. He needed her.

He stopped a few feet from her. His face was streaked with trail dust and sweat, smearing the bandage over the stitches on his left cheek. His denim jeans were filthy. His shirt, bloodstained at the left shoulder. Yet, she thought him handsome and unbelievably sexy.

Their gazes spanned the short but uncomfortable distance. So much had happened between them in such a short time. She'd resented and betrayed him. She'd protected him, kissed him. In her mind, Emily was in his arms, passionately embracing him and devouring his lips with kisses. In reality, she felt hesitant, unsure of what came next in this bizarre relationship.

She swallowed her tension and said, "I thought you'd be long gone by now."

He shrugged, favoring his uninjured right shoulder. "Not yet."

"You keep turning up."

"Like a bad penny."

She wished he'd tell her how much he missed her though they were only apart for minutes. Or that he'd admit that he couldn't go on without her, that he was drawn to her. But Jordan wasn't the talkative sort.

He nodded toward the deputy. "Is he okay?"

"I think so." Emily returned to the task at hand, kneeling beside the deputy and wrapping the SAM splint with tape. "You should be safe for a little while. The deputy's walkie-talkie is in his car, parked at the top of Mammoth Rock. He never had the chance to radio his position to the others."

"I overheard some of your conversation," Jordan said as he peered over her shoulder. His nearness delighted her. The cadence of his southern accent pleased her ears.

"Did you hear what he said about the bounty?" she asked.

"No."

"Apparently, somebody is offering ten thousand dollars for your return, dead or alive. I had the distinct impression that dead was preferable." Pleased with her own deductive ability, she continued, "I think your escape was a setup. Somebody wanted you to make a run for it. Then, you'd be shot dead as an escapee.''

"Who?''

"That means you're innocent, Jordan. You were framed.''

"I'm aware of that,'' he said drily. "Have you got a name for me, Emily. Who's offering the bounty?''

"I don't know.'' She frowned at Collins. "He passed out before he could tell me.''

"Why is he unconscious?''

"He had some kind of prescription pills for headache. I advised against taking them, but he thought he knew better.''

"How about his upper body?'' Jordan asked. "Any injury to his arms?''

An odd question. She finished the splint and turned toward Jordan. "Why do you care?''

A broad smile stretched below the bandage on his cheek. "Because that's a mighty fine leather jacket the deputy is wearing. Nice boots, too.''

"Is that why you came back?'' Disappointment shot down her romantic fantasies. Jordan hadn't returned for her. He had other things in mind. Practical things. Logical things. The man didn't have a single romantic bone in his entire body. "You hung around because you wanted to steal the deputy's jacket and hiking boots?''

"And his vehicle.''

Jordan spoke without a shred of remorse. He'd heard enough of the deputy's comments to Emily that he was ready to charge over here and slap this jerk's rude mouth. "The deputy isn't going to need his jacket. We'll cover him with the reflective space blanket and use his radio to let the searchers know where to find him. This guy is going to a nice, warm hospital bed.''

"You could show a little respect," Emily said. "Deputy Collins risked his life in the line of duty."

Not the way Jordan figured. This cop had hidden behind a rock and fired on an unarmed woman and a dog. Collins hadn't shouted a warning, hadn't offered a chance to surrender peacefully. Deputy Collins was nothing more than a bushwhacker, a back-shooter. Jordan wouldn't waste time feeling sorry about the accidental fall of a coward.

"If I ever see Deputy Collins again," Jordan said, "I'll be sure to thank him for the clothes."

Careful not to wake the sleeping lawman, Jordan removed the leather jacket. Taking off the boots was a bit more difficult, especially since he didn't want to make a mess of Emily's splint, but he managed to untie the laces.

In minutes, Jordan was dressed in Deputy Collins's clothes and shoes. The jacket pulled tight across the shoulders, but the Kletter boots were close to perfect. He did a little shuffle and stomp, much to Pookie's delight.

"Happy feet," Jordan said. "What do you think, Pookie?" The dog mirrored his clumsy dance, adding a couple of loose-limbed puppy pirouettes.

Jordan grinned at Emily. "Maybe I'll be able to keep up with you now. Let's go before the other searchers figure out where to look."

"Aren't you forgetting something?" Her lips pursed in a tight angry circle. "His sidearm. And you could probably find the rifle."

"Don't want them," he said. "I'm not a marksman, and I don't want anybody else to get hurt. Come on, Em. Get into your pack."

"Excuse me? Am I to understand that you want me to come with you?"

"Yes." What was the matter with her? The way she'd

been looking at him when he came out of the woods had been steamy, sexy and welcoming. Now, her eyes were a matched set of green ice cubes. "Are you teed off because I'm stealing the boots and jacket?"

"Not really." She frowned. "I mean, of course I am. Dammit, just leave, Jordan. I'll stay here and keep an eye on Collins."

"I thought he was okay. He didn't need any more medical attention."

"Probably not." Avoiding Jordan's gaze, she made a shooing motion with her hand. "Go on. Get out of here."

They didn't have time for her to throw a hissy fit. Determining the cause of a woman's unreasonable anger could be an all-day affair. When he'd been married to Lynette, Jordan sometimes spent hours getting the silent treatment, trying to guess how he'd offended. But he frankly didn't expect such manipulative behavior from Emily. "You're coming with me."

"Why should I?"

He sensed that she was fishing for something, but he didn't have a clue about the right thing to say, so he blurted out the first logical argument that occurred to him. "You made a deal. You promised to stick with me until the end of today."

"Moof, moof," Pookie emphasized.

"I gave my word," Emily said slowly. "And I'm not a liar."

"Let's go."

Jordan went first, climbing the steep, winding path to the top of the flat cliff that lead to the Mammoth Rock formation. In his new boots, the hike felt less strenuous. His toes weren't slammed with every misstep. Though they'd been running since before dawn, his aches and pains had faded and his brain was starting to work. Ironically, his thoughts focused not on escape but on Emily. Somewhere between stepping out of the forest and tying his new boots, he'd said or done the wrong thing. Somehow, he'd ticked off this green-eyed, blond-haired bomb.

He wanted to know why, but didn't have time to figure it out. Not now.

At the summit of Mammoth Rock, he sighted the deputy's Jeep with a sheriff's logo on the doors. Emily made a beeline for the driver's side.

"Hold it," he said. The only mountain skill Jordan had acquired while living in Aspen was an ability to drive on the hairpin turns and two-lane byways. He wasn't great in snow, but these roads were dry. "I'm driving."

"Whatever." She backtracked to the passenger side. "Are you planning to hot-wire the deputy's Jeep?"

"Not necessary." He reached into the jacket pocket and pulled out a set of keys. "Even though he didn't know it, Deputy Collins was very, very good to me."

Behind the steering wheel, Jordan wiggled into the padded bucket seat. The upholstery wasn't luxurious Corinthian leather but, after sitting on rocks, the Jeep felt like a Rolls Royce. It would be a relief to drive rather than hike. Unfortunately, they couldn't go far. As soon as they called in the location of the injured man, he expected an immediate APB on the Jeep, and they'd have to ditch it.

From his backpack, he produced Emily's walkie-talkie. "I'll set this to communicate with the searchers. Give them your name, tell them you're a hostage and describe the location for Collins."

"I should also advise that they'll need a helicopter for emergency evacuation."

"Don't get chatty," he warned. "It's easy to accidentally give away too much information."

"I understand," she said tersely.

"And you might want to fasten your seat belt, Emily."

He cranked the key in the ignition and backed off Mammoth Rock. The four-wheel drive responded easily to his touch as they jostled over the narrow, rutted path. When he turned onto a two-lane graded road, he said, "Make the call."

"So soon?" she asked.

"I'd rather wait until tomorrow," he said, "but I don't want to leave poor old Collins lying out there unprotected."

While she reported in, he punched the accelerator, taking the sharp curves at a fast pace. Within minutes, the searchers would respond, and Jordan wanted to put some distance between himself and the helicopters. He checked the odometer. They'd gone four miles on the road. It wasn't far enough.

The Jeep swiveled down a hairpin descent. On a relatively straight stretch beside a creek, he burned the gravel. Nine miles.

Jordan careened off the two lane onto a turnoff. At a deserted cabin, he snuggled the Jeep close to the wall under the eaves. Two tall spruce trees provided cover on the other side. Jordan cranked down the window and listened for the ratcheting sound of helicopter blades.

Beside him in the passenger seat, Emily sputtered. "I can't believe how fast you were going. You drive like—"

"Like a good old boy from Hazzard County," he said. "I had a lot of backwoods practice when I was growing up."

In a flat monotone, she said, "Yee-haw."

"Help me listen. Do you hear a helicopter?"

When she leaned out the passenger-side window, he

couldn't help but admire the delicate curve of her throat. No doubt about it, she was a pretty woman. Strong, too.

He didn't want her to leave him at the end of the day. They needed to have a talk, to clear the air. Though he'd almost rather be pinned down by gunfire, Jordan had to attempt one of those relationship discussions with Emily.

"There it is," she said. "The chopper."

He heard the distant whir. Though he couldn't see the helicopter, the noise grew louder. Then, gradually, it faded.

"He passed us," Jordan said as he started the Jeep again.

"Do you mind telling me where we're headed?"

"East." His plan was to avoid main roads until they neared the small town of Hogback where he would abandon the vehicle, trying as best he could to hide it. "To Hogback."

"Why?"

"If the deputies locate the Jeep, they might concentrate on a house-to-house search in Hogback. Meanwhile, we're on our way to Cascadia which is only five miles away."

"More hiking?"

"I might hot-wire a car."

"It's not a good plan," she said. "I just told them that I'm a hostage. Don't you think they'll have a couple of people posted in Cascadia?"

"Maybe." It was a risk he had to take. "I want that laptop computer from your Search and Rescue headquarters."

"The computer," she said disgustedly. "That's why you want me with you. That's why you came back."

He negotiated a controlled swerve to the left. "Let's get something straight, Emily. I wanted the boots and the jacket. And the computer is going to be an invaluable tool. But those things aren't why I came back.''

''Then why?'' she challenged.

''You,'' he said. He'd hung around in the trees, waiting to see if she was okay. As he watched her caring for the deputy, Jordan realized how much he'd come to rely on her presence—not only her mountaineering skill but her spirit, her encouragement. Going on alone seemed too damned hard. ''I need you, Emily.''

''Oh, Jordan.'' He heard the smile in her voice. ''That's exactly what I wanted you to say.''

She reached toward him and lightly squeezed his right arm. He glanced away from the road and saw the warmth in her eyes. Apparently, their argument was over.

He would never understand women.

Chapter Six

The scarlet and gold of sunset flamed above Cascadia as a prelude to dusk when night predator birds would take to the skies. From a mountainside perch, with Emily and Pookie beside him, Jordan watched a hawk soar on air currents in a deadly silent quest. His sympathies were with the prey.

Over the police radio, he heard the helicopter search being curtailed while the manhunt continued with trackers and vehicles. State police and a unit of the National Guard had joined the sheriff's department. Jordan was referred to as "possibly armed and dangerous." The dispatcher urged caution due to the "hostage situation." There was no mention of a bounty.

He turned off the radio. A mountain stillness covered the wide valley where the scattered houses of Cascadia seemed as tiny as faraway matchboxes. Way up here, halfway to the clouds, he should've felt safe, but he couldn't shake a nagging tension. There was danger approaching, and he didn't want Emily to be caught in harm's way.

After abandoning the deputy's Jeep and hot-wiring two other cars which they also ditched, she'd led him to this flat rock, far off the beaten path. Here, they would wait for dark when they would climb down to S.A.R. head-quarters and borrow the laptop computer. Technically, they weren't really breaking any laws. Emily had a key to the headquarters, and Jordan intended to return the computer—fully loaded with upgrades—after he proved his innocence.

"It's a beautiful evening," Emily said. She sat beside him, hugging her knees. A relaxed smile curved her lips, and the sunset burnished her gold-blond hair. She reached over to stroke Pookie who was sleeping beside her.

Ever since he said that he needed her, she'd been sweet as honeysuckle. He didn't understand why her mood had changed. Maybe it was the nurse thing; she needed to be needed. In any case, he didn't question her attitude.

Jordan lay flat on his belly on the rock, stretching the knotted muscles in his lower back. Though tired, he felt stronger today than yesterday. The hiking boots and warm leather jacket made a positive difference.

"Isn't it pretty?" Emily asked.

"Hmmm," he agreed.

"Even you have to admit it. The mountains aren't so bad."

"Ever been to the ocean? Florida?"

"I've been to Oregon and to San Diego on vacation. It's warm in southern California, so I guess it's almost the same as Florida."

"Not even close," he said.

Compared to the lush, sultry Florida climate, San Diego was a desert by the sea. Jordan closed his eyes and allowed the vivid Gulf coast colors to flood his mind. As always, his memories refreshed him. He envisioned so many shades of green, none of them muted like the mountain conifers. "Where I live, it's semitropical. The flowers are scarlet, orange, purple. Green leaves, ferns, palms. Yellow and teal birds.''

''Sounds kind of paisley,'' she said disparagingly. ''I prefer my Colorado sunsets.''

''You'd like being out on the ocean. It's vast. Like the mountains.''

''It's flat,'' she pointed out.

He opened his eyes and turned toward her, propped on one elbow. How could he explain the rolling of the waves, the constantly changing landscape of liquid swells and troughs? How could he tell her about the mesmerizing translucence on the underbelly of a whitecap? ''I'd like to take you home with me, Emily.''

For a moment, she held his gaze, not saying yes or no. She could've put him in his place, reminded him that he was an accused murderer on the run without a penny to his name. She could've laughed at him, told him that his suggestion was insanely optimistic, considering the obstacles to leaving this mountainside, much less hopping a plane to Florida. But Emily was generous. ''I'd like to see the Atlantic,'' she said. ''And the beaches.''

In his sleep, Pookie mumbled agreement. ''Moof.''

''What kind of bathing suit do you wear?''

''A one-piece tank suit like the Olympic swimmers.''

He'd expected as much from this practical woman. ''Is it cut high on the thigh?''

''High enough.'' She arched an eyebrow. ''And you? Speedo briefs or trunks?''

''Both,'' he said. Given his druthers, he'd never wear anything but swimsuits so he could always feel the sun on his bare chest and the sand between his toes.

Overhead, the rosy tint faded, and the stars began to flicker against the graying palette of sky. Lying on a rock in the cooling Colorado dusk, Jordan imagined Emily on a beach in her one-piece tank suit, sprinting through the lapping waves, graceful as a sea sprite.

"Tell me about your business in Florida," she said.

Since she knew nothing about computers, she wouldn't appreciate the complexity of developing and manufacturing a superthin, flexible, heat-resistant chip base which was constantly being redesigned for greater miniaturization. "We make computer parts," he said.

"How did you get started?"

"I've been a computer nerd since the first Apple units came on the market. My family didn't have a whole lot of money, so when the machines broke down, I took them apart and fixed them myself. I started up a little repair shop and made enough money to pay for college."

"What was your major?"

"Business. But my true love was computers. The business just sort of grew."

"Who runs things while you're away?"

"You mean when I'm in jail?" He forced the bitterness from his voice. Though cognizant of the ever-present danger, he needed to think positive. "My sister takes care of the accounting and paychecks. Ramon Delgado oversees the manufacturing process. He's a good man."

"A friend?"

Jordan didn't have many friends; he wasn't a social animal. But Ramon came close. He was ten years older than Jordan, had six children and big appetites for food, wine and laughter. "Ramon and I hooked up about seven years ago when I needed to expand and couldn't find skilled help. Ramon sought me out in Florida after closing his own computer business in Mexico. We got along, had the same vision. So we hired a lot of his former workers and got them work visas. When they moved to

Florida with their families, we hired a tutor on staff to teach English to the kids.''

When he looked at Emily, she was beaming.

"What?" Jordan asked.

"You're usually so quiet. But when you talk about Florida, you have a lot to say."

"I'm proud of my business." He rolled to his back and looked up at the stars. "If I went to jail, my sister would sell the company. It'd be a shame to put all those people out of work."

"If they're skilled, they can find something else."

"Not really. The whole green card thing is pretty specific, *comprende?*"

"You speak Spanish?"

"Si."

"So do I," Emily said. "A little bit."

She'd learned the rudiments of Spanish while working in the Denver emergency room so she could better communicate with Spanish-speaking victims and their families. More than once, her language skills had helped save lives.

Staring into the sky, counting each star as it twinkled to life, Emily felt pleasantly warm inside. Speaking Spanish was something she had in common with Jordan.

Otherwise, they were nearly opposite. They came from very different worlds with different flowers, birds and trees. Their chosen fields of expertise couldn't have been more disparate. In emergency medicine, Emily worked with people. Jordan focused his attention on machines.

Perhaps the most disturbing difference lay in the grayish area of morality, the personal codes by which they lived. Even if Jordan's escape from custody had been a setup, he had seized the opportunity and gone on the run from the law. Emily was so completely law-abiding that she used her turn signal on deserted mountain roads.

However, her stringent rules of right and wrong—the legacy of trying to please an MIA father—had somewhat loosened since she'd been in Jordan's company. She had aided his escape by misleading the searchers. She had stood by while he hot-wired cars. And now, she was planning to steal one of the S.A.R. computers. Who'd have guessed she had these latent criminal tendencies?

Her gaze lowered from the stars to the scattered lights of the town. Cascadia didn't have much of a nightlife outside the burger shop, the diner and the tavern. Most people came home from work, had dinner and kicked back. Still, she thought they should wait until after nine o'clock before approaching the S.A.R. headquarters.

"In about an hour," she said, "we should start the climb down and go into town."

"What are we going to do with Pookie?" he asked.

At the sound of his name, the puppy looked up and made a noise. "Moof?"

"Yeah, you," Jordan said. "You're a good dog, but you're about as stealthful as a rock band."

It hadn't occurred to Emily that Pookie would be a problem, probably because she wasn't naturally someone who undertook nefarious activities. "I wish I could leave Pookie with Yvonne."

"Who?"

"Yvonne Hanson. She's the Brownie troop leader and she raises rescue dogs."

"It could work," Jordan said. "We could tie up Pookie in her yard."

"But then Yvonne would know I'd been here." By now, Emily was sure the information about her status as a hostage had spread through every twig of the local grapevine, and she already knew how Yvonne felt about Jordan. "She'd call the sheriff."

"If you give me your key, I could enter the S.A.R. headquarters and find the computer by myself."

Lying on his back with his fingers laced across his lean belly, Jordan appeared to be totally relaxed, staring up at the night sky. But she sensed his tension. How strange! Though they were different, she immediately understood every nuance of his moods. Right now, he was hiding something from her. "What is it, Jordan? What are you trying to say?"

"You're off the hook, Emily. You promised to stay with me until nightfall, and you've been true to your word."

"And?"

"You and Pookie stay here. I'll go into Cascadia alone. It's time for us to go our separate ways."

But she didn't want to leave him. More than ever, she was convinced of his innocence and wanted to make sure his escape attempt was successful. "I can't abandon you now. It wouldn't be right."

"But it might be smart. Ever since Collins told you about the bounty, something has been bothering me. I've finally got it figured out," he said. "If they shoot me in cold blood without a warning, they won't leave you behind as a witness."

"What do you mean?"

"They'd have to kill you. It's logical."

She hadn't considered the possibility of danger toward herself. "Jordan, these are deputies, policemen and national guard. They wouldn't shoot a hostage. I haven't done anything wrong."

"Neither have I."

He was still looking up at the stars. Their soft glow

outlined the strong line of his jaw and cast a stark shadow below the high cheekbone on the unbandaged right side of his face. A sudden twitch tightened at the corners of his eyes and mouth. For the first time, she saw something resembling fear in his expression. "Em, honey, if anything bad happened to you, I couldn't—"

"I'll be all right," she assured him. "I've spent most of my life taking care of other people, nursing them back to health. Really, you don't need to worry about protecting me."

"Can't help it." His gaze descended from faraway contemplation and focused intently upon her face. His low, deep voice carried gently on the wind. "I care about you, Em."

His words unlocked a sensitive place deep inside her. His caring flowed like sunlight into the secret garden of her heart. The poignant glow startled her. Too much light! It glared. Emily had always been able to give of herself, but she wasn't comfortable when affection came the other way. Though his caring might nurture the delicate buds into full bloom, her garden choked with weeds—former hurts, disappointments and tragedy. There had been too much death in her life, starting with the loss of her father. Could she allow herself to be vulnerable?

She'd be crazy to open herself to Jordan. He was a fugitive with a bounty on his head. And yet, when he reached up and touched her cheek, she felt a connection that went far deeper than a caress. She would help him, not the other way around. "I won't leave you, Jordan. You need me."

"In ways that you'll never know," he said.

She leaned down and kissed him. In contrast to the cool night air, his mouth was hot and demanding. When she started to pull away, he held her and kissed back with fierce desperation. His rough stubble chafed her skin. His strength overwhelmed her as he dragged her down on top of him. She felt like the last woman on earth, and he was the only man.

When he finally released her, she collapsed in his arms, cradled against his chest and breathing hard. The logistics of making love on a chill September night on a hard rock surface seemed almost possible.

"Right now," Jordan said in a ragged drawl, "your survival is all I care about. I need for you to be safe."

She couldn't think. His kiss had sent her swirling into a different universe.

"Do you understand, Em? For once, would you do what I say? Leave me."

She was powerless to object. In a small voice, she said, "Okay."

"That's good." He kissed her forehead. "We're going to say goodbye but not forever. When this is over, I'll see you again."

She stretched her arm across his chest, holding on, not wanting to be apart. "I can still help you."

"Explain."

"For one thing, I won't tell the searchers which way you're headed." A plan fell into place. She felt more capable, more in control. "I'll follow up on this whole bounty thing. It's against the law, you know. I'll tell the sheriff and maybe get an investiga—"

"No!" He abruptly sat up, dislodging her from the sweet comfort of his embrace. "I don't want you stirring up any trouble."

"Why not?"

"The person who framed me is a murderer. Don't you

forget that. Not for one second. If you start poking around, you'll be a target."

"I can take care of myself."

"You don't even lock your front door, Emily."

"I can learn to be suspicious," she said.

"You keep your gun stashed in a closet and your bullets in your panty drawer."

"An obvious safety precaution." Her passion was rapidly turning to anger. "I'm perfectly capable of asking a few questions and pointing the investigation in the right direction."

"You're not," he said.

"Why not? Do you think I'm an idiot?"

"Hell, no. You've got a fine brain. But you've also got the strongest sense of right and wrong that I've ever seen."

"Is that a bad thing?"

"Only when you're dealing with bad people," he said. "You expect everybody to do the right thing. You heard what Deputy Collins said. He was trying to shoot me for the bounty. But you still can't believe a lawman might be dishonest."

"Damn your logic," she said, acknowledging the truth of his statement. "But you're only partially right about me. I can adjust my beliefs based on circumstance. After all, I started out thinking that you were a criminal, and I changed my mind."

"I do thank you for that, Em."

As they stared at each other through the dark, she realized she couldn't leave him yet. Once he had his stupid computer, Jordan wouldn't be obsessed with this particular goal. He'd concentrate on hiding. He might make it.

A thought occurred to her, and she scrambled to her feet.

Startled into wakefulness, Pookie went from sleeping dog to wide awake. Tail wagging, he peered into the darkness as if he'd been vigilant for hours. "Moof."

Emily said, "I should've thought of this before. Sandra Lomax is going to have a baby."

Stiffly, Jordan rose. "I'm real happy for your friend. But I don't see how this affects—"

"Sandra's had a difficult pregnancy. I've been checking in on her at least once a week. Anyway, she and her husband went into Denver three days ago so she'd be near a hospital. Their cabin is vacant."

"You're sure about that?"

"Positive," she said triumphantly. "We can leave Pookie there while I help you get the S.A.R. computer."

"You should stay there with the dog," Jordan said. "Too many people are looking for me. It's dangerous."

"Not for me," she said. "Not in Cascadia. I know everybody in town. They won't hurt me."

Before she could set off through the forest, he caught hold of her arm. "You've got to stop trusting people. Until the murderer is caught, *everybody* is a suspect. *Anybody* could hurt you."

Emily didn't want to peer at the world through a veil of fear. She was accustomed to sharp definition and twenty-twenty vision. To appease Jordan, she said, "I'll be careful."

"Promise," he demanded. "I want your word, Emily. You won't take any risks."

She hesitated. "How about this? Once we're in town we'll stay a half block apart. I'll go first and signal if the coast is clear. If there's any shooting, I can run inside a house where I know somebody."

Before he could extract another promise, she took off across the familiar cliffs and ravines outside Cascadia.

Though they were miles from her cabin, she knew these hillsides well. Even in the dark, her sense of direction was perfect.

After about thirty-five minutes, she descended by the back route to the Lomax cabin. Every window was dark, and the porchlight remained unlit. For a moment, she wondered if Sandra had given birth and offered up a little prayer that the labor had gone well.

Though the front door was locked, Emily knew where the spare key was hidden, and they entered.

"Don't turn on the lights," Jordan warned. "They might have somebody checking the cabin for them."

The moonlight streaming through the windows was sufficient illumination. In the kitchen, Emily found a sack of dry dog food for Pookie. After setting out a bowl of food and water for the puppy, she stroked the golden fur. "You're going to have to stay here, Pook. I want you to be a good boy and not make a mess in Sandra's house."

"Moof." He slapped her face with his tongue.

"No barking," Jordan added as he patted the dog's head.

"Moof. Ruff. Ruff."

"Yeah, don't do that."

The dog glanced between them, then plopped onto the linoleum floor with his front paws possessively surrounding the bowl of food.

"He'll be okay," Jordan said. "Let's go."

Shedding their backpacks, they left the cabin. For a while, they followed the graded road that led past other turnoffs. Cabin lights blinked through the trees, but there was no one outside and not a single car or truck. It was after nine o'clock. Most people had settled in for the night.

At a bend in the road, she signalled a halt. "Up ahead

is an intersection with a couple of main arteries. That's a good place for a lookout to be posted."

"After your warning about Mammoth Rock, I trust your judgment," he said. "Which way from here?"

She pointed left toward a trickling stream beside the road. "We should go through the forests."

He followed her. "Too bad. Walking on the road was nice compared to tripping over rocks."

"You're not complaining, are you?"

"Not a bit." He stretched his arms wide, touching tree trunks on either side. "I'm not carrying a fifty-pound pack. I've got good boots and a warm jacket."

"You almost sound like you're enjoying yourself."

"Oh, yeah," he said sarcastically. "I'm as happy as a lobster in a pot of boiling water."

"We should be quiet from here on."

They'd only walked a little further, when she signalled a halt. Through the trees, Emily saw a vehicle parked at the side of the road about thirty yards away. Two men leaned against the hood. One of them was smoking. They were so close that she heard snatches of their rumbling conversation and deep male laughter. From the shape of their hats, she knew they were deputies.

Nervously, she glanced toward Jordan. They had to move with absolute silence through the still September night. Any sound—the snap of a twig underfoot or the rustle of a tree branch—would alert these armed searchers. Deputies, like Collins. They'd shoot first and ask questions later.

The danger Jordan foretold was upon them. Too easily, she imagined herself being fired upon, shot, bleeding, injured, dead. Apprehension tightened her muscles. Her pulse raced. In a whisper, she cautioned, "Slowly."

He nodded. As she moved forward on silent feet, Jordan stuck close behind her, walking in her footsteps, making little more noise than a shadow.

Just ahead was a sharp bend in the road where they could cross, hidden by a wall of conifers. From there, it was less than a mile to the outskirts of Cascadia.

Coming out of the thick forest at the shoulder of the two-lane road, Emily confronted a bull elk with a four-foot rack of antlers. He was grazing on the remnants of high grass near the side of the road.

Startled, she gasped. Her swift intake of breath sounded as loud as a tornado.

The elk looked up. His square black nose pointed directly at them. Emily made shooing motions with her hands.

"Hey," she heard one of the deputies say, "did you hear something?"

The elk continued to stand and stare, too acclimated to the presence of humans to be frightened.

The other deputy responded. "It came from down there. At the bend in the road."

"Let's check it out."

Nervously, Emily glanced back at the forest. They could make it back to the trees.

Jordan rose up behind her and waved both arms at the elk. The animal bolted, rounded the curve in the road and went toward the deputies.

"Look at him! Man, I wish it was hunting season."

Would they come this way to investigate? She grabbed Jordan's hand and pulled him across the road. On the opposite side, they ducked down in the high grass and waited.

Her heart hammered against her rib cage. Open-mouthed, she tried not to breathe too loudly. Her gaze aimed at the bend in the road, watching for the men with rifles and orders to shoot.

Her consciousness went fuzzy at the edges. She didn't deal well with sudden stress. Something clicked inside her head. It felt like she left her body. Then she woke with a start to the echo of a scream. A panic attack. When she worked in the E.R., they came too often. When she told one of the resident psychiatrists, he suggested therapy and told her that her symptoms might be flashbacks. To what? Emily hadn't experienced any severe trauma— at least, nothing she could remember. Her life was calm and average. She had no reason for post-traumatic stress disorder.

Jordan tapped her shoulder and motioned downhill. Cautiously, they entered a stand of trees, a relatively safe distance from the sentinels.

"Good job," he whispered.

"Except for that elk."

"What about it?" he asked.

"Didn't you hear me gasp? It sounded loud as an explosion."

"Quiet as a gust of wind." He wrapped an arm around her shoulder for a quick hug. "You saved my butt again, Em. I wouldn't have known where to look for those guys."

Not wanting him to notice the fear that trembled through her, she quickly stepped out of his embrace and set a course toward town.

"If Pookie was with us," Jordan said, "we wouldn't have encountered any wildlife. That dog's loud enough to scare off a whole herd."

If Pookie were with them, they'd be caught. Emily tried not to think about the consequences of their actions. Instead, she reminded herself that her cause had merit.

She was helping an innocent man find the justice he deserved.

She maintained silence until they were in sight of Main Street where streetlights banished all shadows. There would be no place to hide from a cruising police car. Almost anyone on the street would know her. She had to be invisible.

Hiding beside a garage, she explained breathlessly, "It's a two-story house. On a corner at the south end of town. White picket fence in front. And a sign."

"Are you okay?" His voice was low and quiet.

"Fine." She inhaled and exhaled slowly, hoping to slow her heart rate. If she didn't calm down, she'd hyperventilate. More firmly, she said, "I'm fine."

"What's the sign outside the house say?"

"Dr. Spence Cannon, General Practitioner." She touched the pulse at her throat. Though strong, it was fast, too fast. "He lives in an upstairs apartment and has his offices downstairs. The S.A.R. headquarters is an add-on behind the house. A little larger than a double-wide garage."

"Sounds like an all-purpose residence," Jordan said. "Tell me about Spence. Is he likely to be awake?"

"How should I know?"

"Is he a friend?" Jordan asked.

"Yes, but I don't spend the night with him."

"I'm glad."

She looked into Jordan's dark eyes and saw an absolute absence of fear. In spite of the danger, his self-control held strong. He took her hand. "You don't have to do this, Emily. Give me the key, and I'll take it from here."

"I can manage."

"There's no need," he said. "I'll find the house."

She wasn't a coward. Her father died a hero, and his blood flowed through her veins. If she succumbed to panic, she didn't deserve to be his daughter. "Let's go. I'll stay a half block ahead. You follow."

The only activity in town centered on the tavern on the north end of Main Street, two blocks away from Spence's house. Even there, it was fairly quiet.

She circled around the Cascadia Elementary School, avoiding the well-lit playground and the asphalt marked with basketball hoops. Though she knew every inch of this town, the streets seemed to narrow and the shapes of buildings distorted as if she were seeing them through the back end of a telescope.

A square of light shone from the doorway behind the local grocery. They were closed at seven o'clock. Was someone still there? Emily darted to the opposite side of the street and ducked behind a parked car. Staring at the plain, flat-roofed structure, the outline wavered. Her peripheral vision blurred.

Her eyelids squeezed shut, blocking out the panic. She forced herself to look across the street toward Spence's house. From his upstairs apartment came the bluish flicker of a television set. They'd have to be quiet. They couldn't dare disturb him.

Using extreme caution, she crossed the street. Light-headed, she barely felt her legs moving. Almost there. She floated like a wraith, physically insubstantial, without form.

She took her keys from her pocket and clutched them in her fist. Her hands trembled too much to keep them from jingling. She'd never be able to fit the key into the lock.

At the door to the S.A.R. headquarters, Jordan came

up beside her. Silently, he took the keys and opened the door.

"No lights," he whispered.

Dim illumination came through two high windows. The outlines of jacket and emergency equipment looked like an army of deputies, watching and waiting with their guns drawn.

Jordan crept through the dark toward one of the desks.

"Not there," she said quietly. Her voice seemed to resonate back at her on visible waves of sound. She couldn't speak again if her life depended upon it.

There was a noise. A door opened. The overhead light came on.

Emily froze. Inside her head, she saw tall black trees. The sky lit up with strange fireworks. Shooting stars. Tracer bullets.

Fire exploded in symmetrical rows across a flat rice field. Moans of pain became shrill. Endless screaming pierced her eardrums as the harsh orange flames consumed the forest.

Napalm bombs burst once, then again, raining fragments of molten metal. A burning man staggered toward her. His flesh charred and melted. He fell.

She sank into the sand below her feet.

Chapter Seven

Jordan stared down the long, dull metal bore of a double-gauge rifle. A man in jeans and a sweatshirt aimed directly at his chest. The chase was over. Jordan had failed. He'd lost his freedom. Would he also lose his life? And what about Emily?

He glanced toward her. She stood frozen, staring across an incomprehensible and terrifying distance. Something was wrong! Was she hurt? A grimace twisted her mouth in a silent scream. Her body went limp, and she collapsed to the floor.

Forgetting everything else, Jordan ran to her side and knelt beside her. He turned her onto her back, grasped her hand. Her skin felt cold. Dread tightened inside his chest as he remembered holding Lynette in almost the same position. "Emily, wake up. Dammit, you've got to wake up."

He felt a hand on his shoulder. A firm voice ordered, "Step aside. I'm a doctor."

Her eyes opened. Her breath came in ragged, tortured gasps. Convulsively, she flung her arms around Jordan and buried her face against his chest.

He held her trembling body, grateful she was all right and sorry for putting her through this life-and-death chase. The stress had been too much for her. "Are you okay, Em? Talk to me."

"I remember..." She spoke in the tiny frightened voice of a child. "It's impossible. But I remember."

The doctor squatted down beside them, still holding the rifle but not aiming. In a calm voice, he said, "It's me, Emily. It's Spence. Can you look at me?"

"Don't hurt Jordan." She clung to him. "Please, Spence. Take care of him. He's innocent."

Still holding her, Jordan confronted Spence's probing blue eyes. Though he seemed too young to be a doctor, his grave expression weighted his presence. He frankly assessed Jordan before making a decision.

Slowly and deliberately, Spence set his rifle on the floor. "I believe you, Emily. I've never known you to lie."

This quiet display of loyalty was impressive. As far as the doctor knew, Jordan could have been the cold-blooded wife-killer described in the local newspapers. Spence had no reason to think otherwise, except for Emily's opinion, and he chose to believe her. Spence Cannon would be a good man to have for a friend.

He stood, walked over to a Formica table and pulled out one of the metal folding chairs. He set another chair opposite him. "Bring her over here. I'd like to take a look at her."

"Come on, Emily." Jordan urged her to stand. "Let's make sure you're all right."

Relinquishing her grasp, she allowed him to help her up. No longer trembling, she stood without wavering. Her head bowed, avoiding his gaze.

He stroked her cheek and gently tilted her chin. The corners of her eyes tightened. When she finally looked at

Jordan, her green eyes flashed wide. The lashes fluttered then steadied as she brought herself under control.

"What happened?" he asked.

"It's all right." A nervous smile twitched her lips. "I'm fine."

"I'll be the judge of that," Spence said. "Get your butt over here, Emily Foster. Sit in that chair. Now."

With a sigh, she did as instructed. Jordan watched as Spence checked her reflexes and asked a series of questions. Though his attitude was professional, his obvious concern showed a firm friendship.

Jordan couldn't help wondering why these two hadn't gotten together. Both in the medical profession, they had much in common, including a love for the mountains. Even their coloring was similar. Jordan drew the obvious conclusion: Spence must be involved with someone else.

With the examination over, Jordan asked, "Is there a Mrs. Spence?"

"There should have been, but it didn't work out."

His comment spoke volumes. During the course of a man's life, Jordan believed there might be dozens of sweethearts, women who were special, each in their own way. But there would only be one true love, a soul mate. She would mesh perfectly into a man's life, fulfill his dreams and answer his needs.

Jordan had known from the start of his marriage that Lynette wasn't his soul mate, but he'd grown cynical, tired of waiting for the perfect match. Logically, he believed his heart could learn to love his wife. He'd been wrong. If he survived this ordeal, he would not make that mistake again.

Emily leaned back in the chair, her elbows tight at her sides and her neck stiff. Though she seemed okay, a weird, residual tension caused her to move in a disjointed fashion—almost as if she didn't truly inhabit her own body. She'd been scared out of her skin.

Again, Jordan regretted his decision to drag her into his personal nightmare. He'd been selfish, but their sojourn was over now. As soon as he was sure she'd be safe, he would leave her in Spence's care.

"I'm just fine." She glanced between the two men. "How many times do I have to tell you guys?"

Spence folded his arms across his chest. "People who are 'just fine' don't collapse on the floor."

"Like I told you. I haven't eaten much today. Or had enough water. I'm a little weak. When you turned on the light, I was startled."

"Nonetheless," Spence said, "I'd like to take some blood samples and send them in to the lab."

"Doctors!" Teasing, she rolled her eyes. "You're never happy unless you're sticking somebody. All I really need is a sandwich and a chance to wash off some of this trail dust."

"I can handle that prescription," he said. "Let's go upstairs."

Though Jordan felt the urgent need to escape from Cascadia as quickly as possible, he couldn't grab the computer and run until he was certain Emily would be all right. For that, he needed Spence's help.

While she was in the bathroom taking a shower and washing her hair, Jordan sat at the kitchen table in Spence's upstairs apartment. Pleasant furnishings with no knickknacks, this was definitely a bachelor pad with a couple of dishes in the sink, sneakers by the door, newspapers and professional journals lying around on the counter.

Spence opened the refrigerator door. "So, Jordan, what's it going to be? A sandwich, right?"

"Right."

"Bologna, tuna fish or the truth about what's going on?"

"Truth," Jordan said. "With a side of bologna."

He needed to talk fast. There was a lot to explain before Emily got out of the shower. "I was framed for my wife's murder. My escape was a setup, but I didn't recognize it at the time."

"Why do you think you were setup?"

"I was at Aspen airport, ready to be transported to Denver for a change-of-venue trial. The deputy left me and another prisoner alone in a room at the hangar. He removed the cuffs and shackles."

"That's not standard procedure?"

Jordan shook his head.

Spence asked, "Who was the deputy?"

"Frank Kreiger."

"Frank's a good man. I've worked with him on S.A.R." Without ceremony, Spence threw together a sandwich. "What happened next?"

"The other prisoner opened a window and went out. I followed him. I wasn't twenty yards away when the other guy hit the dirt, and the bullets started flying."

"You think Kreiger wanted you to run so he could shoot you as an escaped prisoner." Spence frowned. "I'm not sure I'd buy that."

"Neither did I. Until I heard about the bounty."

Glancing over his shoulder to make sure Emily wasn't listening, Jordan explained what had happened with Deputy Ed Collins. He concluded, "Here's the important part. After tonight, I'm going on alone, without Emily. She's talking about starting up an investigation into the bounty."

"Sounds reasonable." Spence tossed the sandwich

onto a plate and set it on the table. "Finding out who offered the bounty might lead to the killer."

"Exactly," Jordan said. "If Emily causes trouble for this cold-blooded bastard, he'll come after her. She'd be in danger."

Spence frowned as he absorbed the logic of Jordan's thinking. Though every word made sense, the overall concept must be difficult to swallow. Spence first had to accept that Jordan was innocent. If not guilty, why had he taken Emily hostage? Why should Spence believe the local police were corrupt enough to arrange a fake escape?

Jordan continued, "I won't be here to protect her. You've got to do it, Spence. Don't let her poke her nose where it doesn't belong. Keep her safe."

He gave a quick nod. "You can count on me."

Jordan rose and held out his hand. "You're a good man, Doc."

When they shook hands, the bond between them was sealed. Jordan knew he could trust Spence to do the right thing.

"The problem," Spence said, "is how to control Emily. Short of locking her in a closet, I don't know how I can keep track of her."

She was a problem, all right. Emily might live like a hermit, but she was no shrinking violet. Seeking justice, she would charge forward.

"There are certain people to watch out for," Jordan said. "Even if he seems like a good guy, be careful of Frank Kreiger. And Ed Collins admitted he was after the bounty. If either of them come sniffing around, it's bad news."

"What about the state police?" Spence asked. "There must be somebody in law enforcement we can trust."

"Ninety-nine percent of the cops are okay. But we don't know who's clean and who's dirty. If you talk to the wrong person, Emily is in danger."

"It's safer to say nothing," Spence agreed. "Who do you suspect for the murder?"

Mentally, Jordan ran through the short list of suspects: The three cousins who inherited, Lynette's brother, Brian Afton and the pro skier who rented the guest house, Sean Madigan. Without investigation, Jordan felt a reluctance to point fingers. There were so many other possibilities. Former lovers, business associates, lawyers. "If anybody from Aspen shows up in Cascadia looking for Emily, consider them a suspect."

"You don't know how right you are," Spence said without rancor. "The beautiful people don't often visit our little hamlet, unless they're looking for a chauffeur or a housemaid."

"If I figure out anything definite, I'll let you know."

"How?"

Good question. Jordan would be on the run, hiding in the mountains. He wouldn't have a fixed address. Though he could pick up a cell phone, that kind of signal would be too easily traced. It was too risky for Jordan to be skipping in and out of Cascadia every day. How could they communicate?

The answer dawned with the clarity of a high resolution monitor. "Have you got a computer, Spence?"

AFTER HER SHOWER, Emily wiped a circle in the steamed-up bathroom mirror and stared at her reflection, searching for traces of madness. Her eyes seemed normal. The pupils neither dilated nor constricted. The fine wrinkles at the corners seemed more pronounced, and the twin frownlines between her eyebrows had deepened, but she didn't look "wild-eyed." Nothing wrong with her nose, apart from a sunburn and a few light freckles. Her mouth set in a calm, no-nonsense line.

She moved her lips. "I'm not crazy."

Downstairs in S.A.R. headquarters, when Spence turned on the lights and startled her, Emily had her usual reaction to sudden stress. She'd frozen, but there was nothing insane about that. When confronted by danger, the natural human instinct was fight or flight. Freeze might be considered a version of flight, retreating into oneself.

Twice in the past couple of days, she'd had the same reaction. Once when she saw the snake. Again when Collins fired upon them. The pattern was not unusual for her. Several times in the emergency room, she had seized up tight. Usually when confronted with the aftermath of violence.

In the back of her mind, she remembered the blood, the gunshot wounds, the torn limbs from a car accident or burn victims. When the gurneys came rolling in, she heard the shouts from paramedics, saw the victim and froze, solid as ice, while chaos reigned around her. Fortunately, her paralysis lasted less than a minute, and she went back to work—shaken but able to do her job.

Before she quit and moved to the mountains, her panic reactions had occurred more frequently, but she chalked it up to stress. Until now, she recalled nothing of her panic other than a blank awareness of being immobile.

Now she remembered.

Vietnam. How could she have a flashback to a place she'd never been? Why? Why did she vividly remember a war she'd never experienced?

Her reflection in the mirror winced, and Emily forced her expression to return to an impassive calm. She was fine. She'd be all right. She'd survive this little bump in the road—a minor psychiatric problem. There were any number of specialists, trauma nurses and psychiatrists she might call for an opinion.

But she felt reluctant to reveal this part of herself. She'd never told anyone the details about her father's death, about his time as a medic and a prisoner of war. No one had heard even part of her story, except for Jordan.

"Why?" She mouthed the word in the mirror. Why had she confided in a man she barely knew? Certainly, there were parallels between his situation and the perils of combat. Jordan was unjustly accused and persecuted by men with guns. Spending time with him was like being in a war zone.

The answer to her panic, her impossible flashback, existed in her relationship with Jordan. She had to find out why.

Instead of wrapping herself in Spence's terrycloth robe, Emily climbed back into her filthy clothes. She found a blow-dryer in a cabinet under the bathroom sink and attacked her curly hair. She would be ready to accompany Jordan when he went on the run again.

When she rejoined the two men, they had their heads together over a computer screen in Spence's second bedroom. He'd inherited this house—with the downstairs clinic and the upstairs apartment—from another doctor who lived here with his wife before they had children and could afford a separate residence. The wife's feminine touch was obvious in the rose-patterned wallpaper and chiffon curtains. Otherwise, the decor was pure male clutter with overflowing bookshelves and sports equipment ranging from basketballs to cross-country skis. The furniture included mismatched chairs draped with discarded T-shirts, a heavy wooden desk and a dark blue comforter on the bed. The room looked like it was half-way through a sex-change operation.

Sardonically, she murmured, "Love what you've done with the place."

"Glad you like this room," Jordan said as he swiveled in the squeaky desk chair to face her. "Spence said you could stay here for a couple of days. Until things quiet down."

"Here?" She regarded the mishmash of interior decorating with disgust. "I don't think so."

He rose and came toward her. "Your cabin is too isolated, Emily. It's dangerous for you to be alone."

She resented the implication that she wasn't able to take care of herself. Ever since she had left her mother's house, she'd lived by herself, and she liked it that way.

"Besides," Jordan said, "I can communicate with Spence. And with you. Through e-mail."

Spence had moved to occupy the chair Jordan vacated. Consumed with the graphics on the monitor, he tapped at the keyboard. "Take a look at this stuff, Emily. Jordan showed me some incredible Web sites."

"Computer stuff." She frowned. When she worked in E.R., she'd had to learn several computerized tasks, and she hadn't enjoyed any of them. Rows of numbers on a screen were not to be trusted, and she hated the jumping green scribble of a heart monitor that would drone suddenly, horribly into a flat line.

The hands-on techniques of emergency medicine used by Search and Rescue suited her far better. She could see what needed to be done. She could sense a patient's distress.

"You wouldn't have to stay here for long," Jordan promised. "Only until we can be sure you're safe."

"I'll think about it," she said to avoid further discussion. "Right now, I'm going to get some food."

Turning on her heel, she left the boys with their toy and went to Spence's kitchen. From the slim pickings inside his refrigerator, she managed to put together a sandwich. Anything was better than trail food and granola bars.

She discarded a greenish slab of bacon that had been hiding in the back of the meat drawer. Live here with Spence? Not a chance! Though not overly fastidious, she preferred having things arranged in her own way. Besides, she intended to accompany Jordan. He wasn't going to palm her off on Spence with a pat on the head and a warning not to make waves.

When Jordan came into the kitchen, she spoke in her strictly no-nonsense tone. "You should take your shower now."

"That sounds like an order."

"You'll be safer," she said, "when we're out of Cascadia."

Her subtle use of the word "we" had not escaped his attention. "I'm going on alone from here, Emily. Spence is going to give me a lift down the road. Then, I'm gone."

We'll see about that. "Take your shower."

"Did you leave me any hot water?"

She grinned. "You sound just like my brothers."

"I hope you don't think of me as a brother."

"What if I did?"

"You can call me your friend," he drawled as he sauntered toward her. "Or your boyfriend. Or even your lover. But you can be damn sure I'm nothing like a brother to you."

Proving his point, he slung his right arm around her

waist and snugged her close against him. He kissed her forehead. "Your hair smells good."

"Thank you," she said primly. It felt strange to be smooching in Spence's well-lit kitchen.

In a low voice, audible only to her ear, he said, "I could lose myself in the perfume of hair, the satin of your skin, the sweet fullness of your breasts. I could spend a lifetime admiring the line of your chin and the green of your eyes. I might be leaving, but I'll come back to you, Emily. You know I will."

Abruptly, he released her and went down the hall, leaving her breathless and confused. She took a bite of her sandwich and sighed. When Jordan decided to talk in full sentences instead of cryptic, two-word conclusions, he had a lot to say.

But she wasn't going to let him vanish into the night with an embrace and a comment about the sweet fullness of her breasts. She was going with him. She had to rescue him. And she had to find out why he touched this dissonant chord within her soul.

She went down the hall to find Spence who was intently reading the text on the computer screen. He spun around in the squeaky chair. "Do you know the one thing I miss about living in Denver?"

"What's that?" she asked.

"Access. In the city, I have access to other medical professionals. I can read the latest journals and discuss them. There are conferences." He gazed longingly at the monitor. "It never occurred to me to use the computer like this. I can access the author of an article. When I think of all the time I've wasted playing games on this machine, I—"

"Spence, we need to talk."

"In just a few minutes. Jordan showed me how to really use the Internet. He's amazing."

"He's a fugitive," she reminded. "The searchers are out to kill him."

Spence nodded. "He told me about the bounty. Hard to believe."

"I heard it from Ed Collins's own mouth." She hoped to recruit Spence to her side. "I need to stay with Jordan, to help him survive in the mountains."

"No way."

"You're on *his* side," she accused. "After knowing me for two years and working with me, how could you take *his* side?"

"Because it's—"

"Don't you dare say it's logical." Jordan had infected Spence—who was supposed to be *her* friend—with his rational, male-pattern thinking.

"I was going to say that it's dangerous for you to be with him. The search is more intense. The sheriff wants to rescue you, the hostage."

"But Jordan doesn't even know how to put up a tent," she argued. "He'll stumble into capture. Spence, he might be killed."

"You'd be more help if you went to the police, turned yourself in and misdirected them. Tell them that Jordan is headed toward Denver." He frowned. "But you can't mention anything else, Emily. Not about the bounty. Not about your belief that Jordan is innocent."

"I can't believe you're advising me to lie to the police."

"Jordan's right. There's a killer on the loose, and you don't know who you can trust. And you're definitely staying here with me. You need protection."

The two men were united against her. If she objected,

they'd only be more firm in their decision. A quick plan formed in the back of her mind. Pretending to acquiesce, she said, "I guess you guys are right. But I'd like a chance to say goodbye to Jordan. Will you help me?"

He grinned. "What kind of goodbye are you talking about?"

"One that's none of your business."

"Well, well, well." Spence regarded her with a bemused expression. "Finally, our little Emily falls in love. I can't say I'm surprised that he's an unjustly accused fugitive with an army of searchers after him. You've never been one to take the easy route."

"Fallen in love?" she squeaked. "Jordan and I are just friends. Like you and me."

"Oh, sure."

His teasing smirk was positively infuriating. "Are you going to help me or not?"

"What do you want me to do?"

"I left Pookie at the Lomax cabin. I knew it would be vacant because Sandra is in Denver having her baby. Drop us off there, both me and Jordan. I'll say my goodbye, then spend the night at the cabin while Jordan takes off in his own direction. Tomorrow morning, I'll talk to the sheriff."

"Sounds okay to me," Spence said. "But you'll have to convince Jordan."

She could bring him around to her way of thinking. She had to. Otherwise, he'd be on his way, walking alone into danger and taking the answers to her questions with him.

HIDING UNDER a grungy tarp that smelled like the residue of a thousand campfires, Emily hid in the back of

Spence's minivan, pleased that she'd brought the two men around to her way of thinking.

"This is a bad idea," Jordan muttered. Though he was under the tarp beside her, he did not embrace her. In fact, he avoided touching her as much as possible. "The searchers will be able to follow my trail from this cabin."

"I already told you. In the morning, after you have an all-night headstart, I'll hike back to my own cabin. That's when I'll call the sheriff and tell him I'm okay."

"Don't get the idea you're coming with me," he said. "After I leave, you promised to stay with Spence for a while."

She shuddered at the thought of sleeping in that cluttered room. If she couldn't change Jordan's mind, that was the price she'd pay. "I promised."

They jostled along in silence. Nearly midnight, she figured there would be almost no other traffic on the road. Still, they were taking a back route to avoid an encounter with the deputies posted at the turnoff. Though Doctor Spence was a well-respected man in Cascadia, they might insist upon a search.

In the quiet, her mind considered the possibilities. Change Jordan's mind. Or stay in that dreary little room in Spence's upstairs apartment. She hated the idea of sharing her living space. Even as a girl, when she was home with her mother and two brothers, she'd been uncomfortable.

Her mom, Linda Foster, had been a successful real estate agent in Twin Bluffs, Nebraska. She'd made a lot of money. Yet, Linda Foster refused to move from the small house she had purchased with Emily's father. Every time she was forced to part with a worn-out piece of furniture or even a broken appliance they'd bought together, she wept as if losing him all over again.

The Twin Bluffs house was a shrine to his memory, and that was one of the reasons Emily loved escaping to Colorado, to the cabin outside Cascadia which had originally belonged to her grandparents. Her father had never been here. His ghost was not in residence.

When they were at her family's cabin in Cascadia, her mother seemed calmer at first. She laughed more often, and they went for endless hikes, talking about everything, except her father. After a week, her mother would occasionally mention that their father would've loved this view or that flower or a sunset behind the mountains. By the time they left Colorado, she'd miss him so desperately that Emily half-expected him to be waiting for them in Twin Bluffs. In a way, he was.

The minivan jolted to a halt. They had reached the Lomax cabin without incident.

"We're here," Spence said unnecessarily. Pookie was already making the announcement to the world at large.

Emily threw off the tarp and leapt from the van. She raced inside to quiet the dog, bracing herself for the lavish puppy greeting that might have been appropriate if she'd been gone for years instead of hours.

"It's okay, Pookie. I'm here."

As she went down on one knee and ruffled the golden fur, Pookie's barking settled into tail-wagging and a quieter, happy-sounding, "Muff, muff, ruff."

She glanced around the cabin. Nothing seemed amiss. "Were you too tired to get into trouble?"

His tongue lapped her face. "Woofle."

Jordan entered and closed the door. He had a backpack of supplies provided by Spence and the all-important laptop computer from S.A.R. He'd also exchanged his prison clothing for a pair of Spence's Levi's and a forest green Pendleton shirt. Jordan had shaved. The stitches on his cheek were covered by a flesh-colored bandage. He seemed angry.

Chapter Eight

In the uncertain illumination of moonlight through the windows of the Lomax cabin, Emily couldn't see Jordan's expression clearly, but she felt the palpable hostility emanating from him in waves. Big waves. Tidal waves.

She wanted to talk with him, but the atmosphere she needed was one of warmth and safety. Emily definitely wasn't looking for a fight.

"All right," he said in a cold, controlled voice. "Why was it so damn important for me to come here with you?"

"Would you please calm down?"

"I could've been miles down the road, Emily. Answer my question."

"I wish I could. If I had a simple—"

"Moof?" Pookie interrupted. The dog approached Jordan, slinking across the carpet and whapping his long tail on the carpet like a metronome with a cockeyed beat. At Jordan's feet, Pookie flipped to his back and presented his belly to the acknowledged Alpha male in a canine gesture of subservience. Apparently, Jordan was the leader of their little wolf pack.

He squatted down, gave the puppy his pats, then stood

again, not in the least distracted by Pookie's display of slavish loyalty. "Come on, Emily. What's going on?"

"Not like this," she said. He was too hostile. What happened to his desire to live forever in the glow of her eyes and the sweet fullness of her breasts? "I can't talk to you when you're acting like you want to rip my face off. This is the wrong atmosphere."

"Well, that's a shame," he drawled, "because I'm fresh out of champagne and roses."

"Candlelight," she said, moving toward the backpack she'd left in the kitchen earlier. "We could have candlelight."

He followed, caught her arm and whirled her around to face him. "This isn't a game. If I'm caught, I'll lose my freedom. Maybe my life."

"But at Spence's house, you were—"

"We had a few minutes to relax. But that time is gone. I need to make tracks before first light. Why did you want me here?"

"Maybe I made a mistake." In the pale night glow through the kitchen windows, she stared at his cool, handsome face. With a fresh set of clothes and a shave, he looked like he belonged with the jet-setters in Aspen. Not here with her. "I've never talked about my father, and for some reason I don't understand, I confided in you. I thought you might be some kind of key to my memories."

"Me?"

"Obviously, I was wrong. You have just about as much sensitivity as a backhoe."

He held out his hand, palm up. "Give me the candle. We're going to talk."

"Forget it. I wouldn't want to trouble you."

"I don't have time for sarcasm," he said. "We need

to find a place in this house where we can light a candle and not have the light show through to the outside.''

Unlike the downstairs rooms, the upstairs bedrooms in the Lomax cabin had shades and curtains. She directed him to the guest bedroom where she'd spent the night on one occasion when Sandra needed her.

Jordan secured the window coverings, making sure the flicker of their candle would not be visible to anyone outside. After lighting the plain white votive, he placed it on a saucer from the kitchen.

She glanced toward the old-fashioned brass bed in the guest room. If she lay on that bed beside him, she feared what might happen. Even when he was angry, Jordan exerted a powerful attraction. If she succumbed right now to her desires, she would surely regret it.

"Put the candle down," she said. "We'll sit on the floor."

"Fine."

When Pookie snuffled toward the light, Jordan banished the dog from the room. "Sorry, Pook. You're going to have to wait outside."

"Moofle murf," the dog said with an inflection that sounded awfully resentful.

Emily knelt on the pastel blue area rug that matched the colors in the handmade quilt. Opposite the candle, Jordan stretched out on his side and leaned on his right elbow.

"Is this better?" he asked.

"Yes." With candlelight dancing against warm pine-panelling, the room felt snug and cosy, as if they were set off from the rest of the world. But she was no longer in the mood to bare her soul. Too many harsh emotions lurked in the shadows, waiting to pounce.

"Reminds me of a seance," he said. "Have you ever been to one of those?"

She shuddered. "I'd rather let the spirits of the dead rest in peace."

A silence spread between them. She listened to the beating of her heart, concentrated on taking deep calming breaths. She hoped to recapture a mood of sensitivity and solace, to gradually build toward talking about her disturbing vision.

"I know where to start," he said. "Let's talk about when you keeled over in the S.A.R. headquarters."

"You like to cut to the chase."

"I've seen you do the frozen panic thing before," he said. "But this was different. Way different. Why?"

If she knew that answer, Emily wouldn't need to talk to anyone. She could happily continue in her solitary life, untouched and secure. "Jordan, do you think I'm crazy?"

He smiled, and his dark eyes warmed encouragingly. "You're the sanest, smartest woman I've ever known."

"I saw…things." Unaccustomed to sharing her personal feelings, Emily stumbled incoherently over her own words. "A vision, you know. There was fire and explosions. Oh damn, I can't explain. It was crazy. Impossible."

"Like a bad dream." He reached around the candleflame to touch her hand. "Em, honey, this nightmare is my fault. I had no right to drag you into my hell."

"Don't apologize. You brought something into focus."

"You've had these panic attacks before?"

"Oh, yes. When I was working in the emergency room, I'd freeze up. I thought it was stress, burnout. The other nurses and doctors always said I got too personally involved with the patients.''

"Sounds like a positive trait for a nurse," he said.

"But it's not entirely true. I'm too deeply caught up in my own history, memories of a father who I don't consciously remember."

Staring at the candle, she recalled her vision of the burning man staggering away from the trees. Emily looked toward a dark corner, holding her eyes open, afraid to blink. She couldn't bear to revisit that internal horror.

"Emily." Jordan spoke softly. "What are you thinking?"

"I don't know." She closed off her imagination.

"Maybe," he suggested, "when you saw other people who had been hurt, you were reminded of your father."

"It's possible." But she didn't believe that rationale. "I'd like to think I'm sane enough to tell the difference between an emergency room patient and a man who died over thirty years ago."

Across the candlelight, she gazed at him. The anger had passed, and the bittersweet complexity of their relationship had returned. She didn't want to lose him.

With a sigh, she continued, "Your situation also reminds me of my father. The danger. Being pursued by enemies. But, believe me, I don't have any trouble distinguishing between you and my father."

"That's good," he said. "I never wanted to be a father figure, except to my own children when they come along."

"When do you think that might be?"

"Soon, I hope."

She'd known he was ready for kids. Like her, Jordan

was in his thirties. The old biological clock was ticking. "Me, too."

"How are you feeling now, Emily?"

"A little better."

"Tell me something, Em. You said you've never spoken to anybody else about your father."

"That's right."

"Why not? It's not logical to avoid talking about him. You've got nothing to be ashamed of."

Not logical. "It's emotional, Jordan. When I was growing up in Twin Bluffs, everybody knew about my father. He died a hero. I didn't have to explain."

"But now?"

"My family legacy isn't a topic that generally comes up in casual conversation."

And Emily steered away from deep, heart-to-heart talks. With her friends, she usually listened to their problems instead of the other way around. These few days with Jordan had been her most intense relationship in years. How strange! She had to be taken hostage to let herself get close to a man.

"Have you talked to Spence about your father?"

"It wouldn't be appropriate. Spence and I are professional associates as well as friends. I don't want him to think I'm going to have some kind of weird panic attack when he's working with me."

Jordan rolled onto his back and stared up at the ceiling. He seemed to prefer the prone position when he was thinking. "The first time the sheriff slapped the cuffs on my wrists, I wanted to crawl in a hole and die. I'd never felt humiliation so dark and deep. By the time I escaped, the cuffs were a habit, like putting on a necktie. I hated being a prisoner, but it didn't hurt me anymore. I accepted my shackles. I think, Emily, it's something similar for you.''

''If I talk about my past and accept my father's death, it won't hurt me as much.''

Predictably, Jordan's solution was simple and rational. Probably too easy, she thought, but his idea offered a thread. If she started pulling, other issues might unravel.

''Try it,'' he said. ''In one sentence.''

Slowly, she said, ''My father was a medic who was captured in Vietnam and died there.''

The heavens didn't rain thunderbolts and the earth did not quake beneath her feet. Her statement didn't even sound like a secret.

''You're going to be okay, Emily.'' He pushed himself off the floor and stood. ''It's time now. I've got to be moving on.''

As she stepped in front of him, the truth jumped up and splashed her in the face like a bucket of cold water. Talking to Jordan about her father was only part of her goal. She wanted to be with him, to explore this strange attraction. ''Stay with me tonight.''

''I'd like nothing more.'' He lightly stroked her cheek. His gaze melted over her. ''You're making it damn hard to be a gentleman.''

''What do you mean?''

His hand lingered at her jawline, lightly tracing the bone beneath the flesh. ''I won't take advantage of you, Emily.''

''Excuse me? I'm the one who asked you to spend the night. Not the other way around.''

''I'm a man with no future. I can't let you do something you might regret. Emily, you've got to remember who I am.''

"A fugitive." She caught hold of his hand and kissed the palm. "You're *my* fugitive."

A spark flared in his eyes.

Without another word, Jordan dragged her into the circle of his arms. His fierce, ravenous kiss took her breath away. Her fears and memories banished, there was only passion, an overwhelming thirst.

Anxious to be rid of her filthy clothing, she shucked off her shirt and turtleneck. So many layers! She sat on the bed and fought with the laces of her boots. Her socks came off. She wriggled out of her jeans.

Immediately, Jordan was on top of her. He tore off her bra, yanked down her panties. His legs tangled with hers. His hard flesh pressed against her.

A frantic desire consumed her. Her body temperature soared. Her pulse throbbed at a ferocious pace as if her heart would explode inside her rib cage.

His legs straddled her hips, and he rose above her. In the shimmering candlelight, she beheld his broad shoulders and muscular chest. He was perfect, a dominant male presence. And she was ready to succumb, eager to drown in the sheer power of his need.

He caressed her breasts, tweaked the sensitive nipples. Exquisite shivers went through her. She'd never made love like this. Not with such naked hunger.

When she grasped him and stroked, he shuddered.

Now she was the aggressor. In an instant, she changed positions. She was on top, sliding over his body, licking his warm flesh, fondling him.

He gasped. "Emily."

"Mmmm." She couldn't speak. Not now.

"I don't have a condom."

"Don't care."

"I do." He held her. Carefully, tilted her off his body.

They lay side by side, on the blue-patterned quilt, breathing hard. "We could look around. Maybe your friends have—"

"Sandra is nine months' pregnant. Before that they were trying to have a kid. They don't have condoms." Oh God, she didn't want to stop! "Are you trying to tell me you have an STD?"

"What?"

"Sexually transmitted disease."

"Hell, no."

In her head, she tried to calculate the number of days since her last period, but she didn't keep track anymore. And the rhythm method couldn't be considered reliable. What if she got pregnant? "I'll take my chances, Jordan."

He leaned over and thoroughly kissed her lips. "Em, honey, there are other ways I can make you happy."

"And vice versa." Languidly, she smiled up at him. "I'm very familiar with the human body. After all, I am a nurse."

He started with her throat, then her breasts, then he went lower with his tongue and pressured strokes. The rhythm of their lovemaking had changed from frenzied animal passion to an erotic, sophisticated tango. A responsive partner, she savored each touch, each subtle manipulation as he urged her toward shuddering, climactic release.

Swollen with passion, she cried out as she reached the peak and collapsed into a swirling eddy of sensation. Oh, this felt so right, being here with Jordan, sharing the night. He fulfilled her in so many ways.

She closed her eyes. Instead of burning forests, she saw wide vistas of restful green. In the distance, a serene ocean beckoned. Sunlight sparkled on the waters. Emily knew she'd sleep peacefully tonight. But not yet.

She opened her eyes and gazed into his handsome face. Now it was her turn to pleasure him.

DOWNSTAIRS in the Lomax cabin, Jordan shouldered his backpack. Thanks to Spence, he was well-supplied for a stay in the wilderness. More important than the camping gear, he had a G.P.S. instrument to guide him with global mapping technology, and he had the S.A.R. laptop computer, complete with powerful battery and wireless Internet connection. With these tools, Jordan felt confident. If he managed to evade the searchers and establish a safe base for operations, he could find the murderer and clear his name.

At this moment, his only regret was being separated from Emily. She'd been beyond amazing last night. Though Jordan had known she was resourceful and skilled, he never suspected that her talents extended to the bedroom. Though they hadn't technically consummated their relationship, he'd been fully satisfied. Twice.

He glanced toward the stairway leading to the bedroom where she was still asleep. He couldn't wake her to say goodbye because she'd insist on accompanying him. Nor could he leave a note telling her how deeply he cared. A written scribble would be evidence that might fall into the wrong hands. The worst thing that could happen was if the murderer discovered a link between them and went after Emily.

Jordan prayed she'd be sensible, that she wouldn't take off on her own investigation that might bring danger down upon her. Emily was too damn courageous for her own good.

He reached down to scratch Pookie who stood beside

him, looking up and ready for action. Quietly, he said, "Take care of her, Pook. Keep her safe."

"Moof." The puppy wagged his tail.

As a first line of defense, the goofy golden retriever was not reassuring. Jordan wished he could stay and protect Emily. But he had to go. On the run, again.

He opened the cabin door and slipped into the starlit night.

WITH POOKIE snuggled on the bed beside her, Emily woke slowly from an unremembered but pleasant dream. Her fingers slipped through the dog's soft fur.

She didn't want to open her eyes and face the dawn because she knew the other side of the bed would be empty. Jordan would be gone. Last night, she'd felt his absence as surely as if someone had amputated a piece of her heart. A painful sorrow spread through her veins. She didn't want to face his absence. Even worse was the abiding apprehension. She knew, firsthand, of the peril he would face. Too easily, he could be hurt. Killed. Caught and locked away from her forever.

Her solace was to retreat into the minefield of remembrance, the stories of her father, her mother's shrine, the emergency room. She avoided all those and replayed the fresh memory of lovemaking from last night, lightly touching her bee-stung lips, still pleasantly swollen from his demanding kisses. Her body trembled at the thought of his caresses. Behind her eyelids, she saw his magnificent body and his passionately intense dark brown eyes. Often she would visit this place in her mind. She would nurture these delicate buds and bring them to bloom.

She was grateful to Jordan for being wise enough to avoid the possibility of pregnancy. Though Emily was, in many ways, ready to have a child, she certainly wouldn't choose to have a baby with a man whose very survival was in question. The pattern was too similar to her own history.

A doggy paw pushed into her shoulder, forcing her onto a corner of the bed while Pookie sprawled in the center, taking up far more than his fair share of the mattress.

"That's enough, Pookie."

Instantly awake, the dog rubbed his cold wet nose against her chin. "Murfle."

"Jordan's gone, isn't he?"

"Moof."

She wanted to reassure the dog and herself that everything would be all right, but Emily was painfully aware of the many obstacles that faced Jordan's escape. A bounty on his head. A murderer still at large. And there were the unestimable hazards inherent in mountain survival. Though the weather had been relatively mild, the first snow could come at any time.

She had to help him. But she'd given her word that she would stay with Spence and keep a low profile. She couldn't betray her solemn promise. Even if it was ridiculously over-cautious.

A spark of anger ignited within her. Though Jordan believed in her intelligence, he didn't give her much credit. Why did she need Spence looking over her shoulder? She could be smart and safe at the same time she helped him in his investigation.

She threw off the quilt. Her first task was to obliterate any clue that she and Jordan had spent the night in this cabin. No problem. There was a washer and dryer downstairs to handle the bedsheets.

Then she'd hike back to her own cabin. She'd take a shower and call the police. After that came the hard part.

Emily would have to lie to the sheriff. She had to pretend she'd been an unwilling hostage.

HOME. THE CABIN had never looked so beautiful to Emily as she trudged the last few yards. She'd taken her time on this hike, circling around and backtracking. She'd even set up a fake campsite where she could claim she and Jordan had spent the night in case the trackers decided to pick up his trail from where he supposedly left her.

Though she'd hoped for a few moments of quiet relaxation by herself, a police vehicle was already parked outside her door. It was almost noon when she climbed the steps onto her front porch.

"Emily, you're here." Deputy Frank Kreiger greeted her at the front door. A stocky man in his mid-thirties, Kreiger was an extreme skier, well-known for his heroism in S.A.R. avalanche rescues. He was not smiling at her.

At the sight of him, Pookie went wild, barking furiously. "Arroo, arroo."

"It's okay, Pookie." She tried to calm the dog. "Kreiger is a friend."

Her first lie. Jordan had warned her to be especially careful around Frank Kreiger. He was the deputy who'd removed Jordan's cuffs and shackles at the Aspen Airport. More than likely, Kreiger was involved in setting up the arranged escape attempt that was supposed to end with Jordan being shot dead.

"Are you all right?" the deputy asked.

She added a heaviness to her step that wasn't altogether fake. "Would you please notify the sheriff that I'm okay? And contact Doc Spence."

"Are you hurt? Did that bastard hurt you?"

That bastard was the man of her dreams. "Jordan Shane was a perfect gentleman. But I'm exhausted, maybe a little dehydrated. I want the doc to check me out."

When the deputy grasped her elbow to help her into the house, Emily forced herself not to recoil. She couldn't allow herself to show the revulsion she felt toward him, a dirty cop. "If you don't mind," she said, "I'd like to take a shower and get out of these filthy clothes."

"Sorry," he said. "I need to debrief you right away. In a search like this, every minute counts. And you're our best lead."

"You'll have to wait," she said. "I'm not going to face the sheriff and everybody else looking like this."

Beneath his sun-streaked blond hair, Kreiger's forehead pinched in a scowl. "I never thought you were the girly type."

"I'm not planning to get dressed in pink ruffles." She yanked away from him and stalked toward her bedroom. "By the time you call the sheriff and Spence, I'll be out of the shower."

She grabbed a change of clothes, went into the bathroom and locked the door. Taking a shower was part of her strategy. She needed to erase the scent of Jordan on her body, and she couldn't allow the sheriff to think she'd paused last night and cleaned herself.

True to her word, Emily hurried. Not even taking the time to dry her hair, she dressed in clean clothes and emerged from the bathroom, carrying the truly disgusting clothing she'd worn for the past three days toward the small washing machine in the kitchen.

"I'll take those," Kreiger said. No one else had yet arrived.

"My clothes? You want my dirty clothes?"

"You'd be surprised what kind of forensic evidence we can turn up with DNA, fibers and—"

"The only thing you'll find on my clothes is a very bad case of body odor," she said.

"Nevertheless," he said, "you want to cooperate, don't you?"

"Fine." She tossed the bundle at him. "Burn them when you're done."

Belatedly, Emily remembered that she was supposed to be so exhausted that she needed to stay with Spence so he could keep an eye on her. She had to pretend weakness. Sinking into an armchair, she said, "I'm so tired."

"Can I get you anything?"

"A bottled water from the fridge."

He returned quickly and sat opposite her. His tense posture showed an uncomfortable edginess. "Emily, how well did you know Jordan Shane before he took you hostage?"

"We'd met." She'd expected this line of questioning. Why her? Why had Jordan come for her? Fortunately, she didn't need to lie about his rationale, his very logical rationale. "About a year ago, he came here to my cabin and dropped off a donation for the Cascadia S.A.R. After his escape, he remembered that I was a nurse and came here for medical attention."

"And you patched him up?"

"He had my gun," she said coldly. "I didn't have a choice."

Kreiger's expression showed clear disdain. "Are you saying he forced you? Without any encouragement or compliance on your part?"

"Exactly." His implication appalled her. "Are you saying I should have struggled? That I should have risked being shot? That kind of thinking went out when cops finally dropped their assumption that every woman who was raped was asking for it. I'm the victim here.''

"According to your friend, Yvonne Hanson, you thought Jordan Shane might be innocent.''

Who could have guessed that her casual conversation with Yvonne when they were watching the Brownies would come back to haunt her? "Until proven guilty," Emily said.

"What do you think now?''

She bit her lip. Lying was the hard part. While she was walking this morning, she'd practiced dozens of possible responses to this question. The answer she settled upon was a variation on the truth. "Jordan was wrong to escape police custody. He broke the law. It was a terrible mistake. But I don't believe he murdered his wife.''

"You're wrong, Emily. He's guilty." The deputy's eyes were hard, piercing. "You never knew Lynette Afton-Shane. She was the most beautiful woman I've ever seen, but she could drive a sane man crazy with her teasing.''

Had Jordan's late wife driven Deputy Kreiger crazy? Emily sensed that his connection with Lynette went deeper than friendship. He was a skier, and she owned the lodges. How close were they? How deep was his need for revenge?

"Make no mistake, Emily. Jordan Shane will be caught, and he will pay for his crime.''

"Is this personal?''

"I'm a law officer," he said. "I'll do whatever it takes to bring a criminal to justice. I need as much information as you can give me. Where was Shane headed when he left you?''

Again, she sidestepped a blatant lie. "He wanted to go back to where he lives in Florida. To get there, he'd have to make it to Denver International Airport and catch a plane. Do you have people watching at the airports?''

"Damn right, we do. But how could he get there? We've got roadblocks and surveillance on the highways.''

"While I was with him, Jordan hot-wired two vehicles, not counting the one he stole to come here. He's real good with mechanical stuff.''

Kreiger leaned back in his chair, regarding her steadily. From the front of the house, she heard another vehicle arriving, and Emily was glad she'd be facing a different interrogator. Deputy Kreiger carried a heavy grudge. It was even possible that he was the person who offered the bounty for Jordan's capture, dead or alive.

"You have to help us, Emily.''

"Of course.''

"And we need the information fast, real fast.''

She understood the need to move quickly. But why was he emphasizing speed? "I'm not sure I understand what you're saying.''

"I'm surprised at you." The frown lines on his forehead deepened. "An S.A.R. person like yourself ought to be more aware of the weather. There's a cold front coming in. There's snow predicted for tonight.''

As soon as he spoke, she felt the drop in temperature. Snowfall would be a boon to Jordan's escape, making it near impossible for the trackers to follow his trail. And the helicopters would be grounded. But how could Jordan survive the biting cold of the high Rockies? She should have gone with him. Here in the cabin, she was unable to help. *Be safe, my love.*

Chapter Nine

Though he'd taken every precaution not to leave a trail, Jordan didn't glide gracefully through the mountain terrain. Hauling his well-stocked backpack, his bulk loomed large as a Mack truck, crashing through the forest. Twigs snapped with every step he took. He ploughed through low-hanging branches and shrubs, sending the native wildlife scattering.

He didn't belong in this environment. If he'd been stranded on a tropical island, he could've survived easily. But here? He was a beached whale, a fish out of water.

At midafternoon, he entered an aspen grove, hoping to recapture his appreciation for this country. He gazed up into the quaking bower of golden leaves but found no enchantment. Without Emily, the aspens were nothing more exciting than a bunch of yellow trees. Without her, nothing seemed as important.

Jordan hunkered down beside a creek to catch his breath and listen to the police band radio. He was nearer to the town of Aspen—another place where he'd discovered a dearth of magic—and the dispatcher's signal came through clear. "...looking for one man, possibly armed and presumed dangerous. Repeat—the hostage is free. Her physical condition is A-OK."

A measure of relief loosened the knots of tension in his shoulders and lower back. Emily was safe. At least, for the moment.

Jordan celebrated with a swig of water and a protein bar that tasted like chocolate cardboard. God, he was exhausted, tired of running, tired of hiding under the trees so the searchers wouldn't see him. After dark, he could move faster, cutting across meadows and open spaces, following the directions indicated on the G.P.S. instrument.

"...a weather alert," the monotone voice on the police radio reported. "Three to five inches of snowfall predicted for tonight."

Overhead, the dark-bellied clouds had begun to blanket the sky. No wonder the golden aspen leaves had lost their shimmer. The sunlight was almost gone. "Not snow."

He hated the cold. Stretching out on the ground, he rested his head against the backpack. So tired. He needed warmth, needed sleep. Maybe if he rested his eyelids for a few quick minutes...

He woke to the infernal whir of a chopper, coming closer. Hidden beneath the aspen leaves, he'd be invisible, especially since the shadows had lengthened into dusk. It was almost dark. Let them fly overhead. They'd never see him in this thick grove.

Then he heard another noise that pumped adrenaline through his veins. The baying of hounds.

While he was "resting his eyelids," the searchers had come closer. They were onto him.

As soon as the noise of the chopper faded, Jordan leapt to his feet and donned his pack. How close were they? In these vast open spaces, a shout could echo and carry for miles.

He hiked straight up, clawing at the rocks until he

reached a high ledge. From this vantage point, he hoped to see them coming before they spotted him.

Through his binoculars, he scanned the darkening hillsides. The September nip in the air had turned to bitter cold. Jordan turned up the collar on Deputy Collins's leather jacket and pulled the black knit cap down over his ears.

There they were! He saw their flashlights, snaking through the dark. Four of them. The bloodhounds wailed again.

He tried to estimate their distance. Probably only a mile and a half. An open field stretched in the opposite direction. Should he take his chances and go that way, putting distance between himself and the search team? Or should he stay on the rocks where it would be harder to follow his tracks?

He wished Emily were with him. She'd know what to do.

Tentatively, he moved along the ridge, unsure whether he was headed in the optimal direction. There was no time to consult his instruments. Another few steps. His foot slipped on the loose gravel. He fell. Before he could register what was happening in his logical mind, Jordan careened down the hillside, sliding on his backpack and his butt.

Nature had made his decision for him. At the bottom of the hill, he bounced to his feet. No injuries. Instinct told him what to do: *Run, you idiot!*

He took off across the field like a sprinter running for an Olympic gold medal. He went straight across, trampling grass, laying out a trail. His only hope was speed. He had a headstart and an unplanned nap. Jordan needed to cover ground. If only he could catch a break!

He darted through a line of conifers, up a hill, down

into a wider forest. Gasping for breath, he stopped in a clearing, a circle of trees. His lungs ached. Over the past few days, he'd become acclimated, but he wasn't a native. He gulped down oxygen, turned his face skyward.

The first wet snowflake splattered on his chin. He hated the Colorado cold. He despised the icy weather. But now, it might save him. A good snowfall would obliterate his tracks. "Come on," he murmured. "Let it snow, let it snow."

He got his wish. Within minutes, the blizzard engulfed him. Falling as hard and steady as rain, the snow covered the ground with a thick, white icing. His Levi's were drenched, clinging to his legs, but his boots stayed dry. Apparently, Deputy Collins had the foresight to waterproof his footwear.

Aware that his footprints in the snow were at least as obvious as the other trails he'd left, Jordan consulted his G.P.S. instrument and headed for a road where his progress would be less obvious.

He found asphalt. The solid paved road felt good beneath his feet. From this point, he was less than fifteen miles from Aspen. Though he ran the risk of encountering a minivan full of deputies, Jordan decided to take his chances. He could see headlights coming toward him as an early warning and could dive into the ditches at the shoulder of the narrow two-lane road. *Run, you fool.*

Burning body heat would keep him warm. Staggering, jogging, he kept going. He entered the zone where his body kept moving without thinking, without cognizance. One foot ahead of the other. *Keep going.*

The falling snow surrounded him with incredible silence, like a vacuum. Only once did he see a car, and he fell back into the woods. It passed him without slowing.

He left the road at a turnoff. He was going uphill. He

had to find a place to stop. He had to wrap himself in thermal blankets and sleeping bags.

He'd make it. He had to survive. For Emily. She'd be mad as hell if he froze to death.

EMILY COULDN'T SLEEP. In the cluttered guest bedroom in Spence's upstairs apartment, she sat at the window and stared into the night, worrying about Jordan. Had he found shelter? Would he stay warm?

The storm was already sputtering, about to die. Though the downfall had been sudden and heavy, it lasted only a few hours, a positive prelude to a winter everyone hoped would provide enough sparking powder to transform the mountains into a winter wonderland for tourists with platinum credit cards tucked inside their ski boots. In the Aspen area, snow meant commerce, and the local residents welcomed the downy, drifting, icy flakes.

But not now! Jordan wouldn't know how to cope. She should've talked to him about treatment for hypothermia and frostbite.

"Damn." She paced across the floor in the small bedroom, stepping over a catcher's mitt and a snowshoe.

Roused by her activity, Pookie sprang off the bed and paced in her tracks.

"I have to find a way to help him."

"Moof," Pookie said.

Emily's part had gone extremely well. After facing the vengeful hostility of Deputy Frank Kreiger, her other interviews with the Pitkin County Sheriff, state police and national guardsmen were a piece of cake. To a man, they were solicitous of her health, deeply concerned that she'd been forced to endure such an awful ordeal. She permitted herself a slight smile. If only they knew the secrets of her "ordeal," they would've offered congratulations rather than apologies.

Apart from Kreiger, the lawmen were pleased that she escaped without injury. And they seemed to believe her when she hinted that it was Jordan's fondest wish to return to his home in Florida. Why shouldn't they believe? It was the truth.

He hated the mountains, and the snowfall would only reinforce his opinion that the entire state of Colorado was out to get him.

When she halted in front of the computer, the puppy ran into her calves.

"Go back to bed, Pookie."

"Ruffle muff." He didn't need to be told twice.

Emily glared at the machine and pressed a few keys. Spence had shown her how to check for Jordan's e-mail. She waited for the electronic reassurance, but nothing came. Her mailbox was empty.

"Please," she whispered, "Jordan, let me know you're all right. You've got to survive."

For the rest of the night, she alternated between the window and the computer—watching and waiting until she was overcome by exhaustion.

SEATED IN A CHAIR by the window with her arms resting on the sill, Emily felt a hand on her shoulder. She wakened with a start. Her dreams had been so full of Jordan that she half expected to see him standing behind her.

It was only Spence.

"Mmmmrrr," she groaned like a squeaky hinge.

"Nice noise," he said. "You've been spending too much time with Pookie."

Squinting, she looked out at Cascadia's Main Street where the sun was shining from a clear blue sky. Snow piled up at curbside, but the slush had begun to melt. How many hours had passed? She checked her wristwatch. Almost noon.

Anxiety clenched ominously inside her. The searchers would be out. And the helicopters. She should've been keeping track on the police radio. "What's going on, Spence?"

He grinned. "You've got mail."

She stumbled toward the computer. With trembling fingers, she clicked open the message from Jordan.

"I'm okay," it said. "Emily: Don't get into trouble."

She read it once, twice. Then she rubbed her eyes and read again. "That's all?"

"He's got to conserve his batteries," Spence said. "He really can't go into details."

She didn't believe that excuse. Jordan enjoyed dropping these pithy little comments that he considered logical. "How do I respond?"

Spence pushed a few keys and quietly left her alone. She began to type.

Dear Jordan,
Have you found a warm, dry place to stay? You need to be careful about exposure in the snow. Here are the symptoms of hypothermia…

She typed energetically, detailing the causes and treatments for various exposure-related conditions, including snow blindness which meant he should wear his sunglasses. Also, the warm cap and mittens. Geez, she sounded like his mother! Changing gears, Emily gave instructions on frequent cleaning of his gunshot wound to avoid infection.

As for your suggestion that I might have behaved in an inappropriate manner, i.e., getting into trouble, in spite of my promise that I would be excessively cautious, I have one word for you—Hah!

She proceeded to type in another hundred words telling him about her discussions with the law. She ended with,

Deputy Kreiger is very, very, very suspicious. Was he in love with your wife?

She pressed the button to send her message and nodded emphatically at the machine. "I dare you to come up with a one-sentence response to that message."

She left the depressing little bedroom and went to the kitchen where Spence sat at the table, reading a journal. Without lifting his eyes from the page, he said, "You're looking a lot more perky."

"I'm glad Jordan's all right. Even that brief message was better than nothing."

"Emily, I think we should avoid mentioning you-know-who by name."

"You're right." She needed to be vigilant or else her so-called "perky" mood would lead to a slip of the tongue.

"You've got a ton of phone messages on the answering machine," he said, "from friends, a couple of reporters and the sheriff. I suggest you call back the sheriff and leave the others on hold."

"Why?"

"Because you're supposed to be recovering from exhaustion, remember? That's why you're staying here."

She peered into his refrigerator. The minimal contents—beer and bologna—had not been replenished. "There's nothing to eat. I should go to the store and get us something for dinner."

"No store."

"The market is just across the street."

Spence marked his page in the journal and set it down on the kitchen table. "You're supposed to be sick."

"Yes, but—"

"No trips to the store. No visits with friends. Talk to as few people as possible. The less said, the better." He rose from the table and reached for his white lab jacket that hung from a peg near the door. "I promised you-know-who that I'd take care of you, even if it meant locking you in a closet for your own good."

She glowered at him. Just like her big brothers, Spence seemed to enjoy telling her what to do. In this case, however, he was right. She needed to regard everyone as a suspect, keeping a very low profile. "I'll act like a sick person," she promised. "I've been around enough of them to know what that looks like."

"I need to get back to work," he said.

"Have you been listening to the police radio?"

He nodded. "The searchers and helicopters are back out this morning, but they have no leads."

"Good."

"By the way, Sandra Lomax had her baby. A girl. Six pounds, five ounces. They're both doing well, but Sandra had a C-section, and they're going to stay in Denver for another week."

A glimmer of joy lightened Emily's mood. In the midst of worry and crazy visions, life went on. A baby! A blessing! "What's her name?"

"Diana Marie." Spence headed for the door that lead

downstairs to his practice. "Remember, you're supposed to be sick."

Diana Marie Lomax. Emily inadvertently touched her own flat, barren belly. She was thirty-two with plenty of childbearing years left, but she was ready for a baby. Both of her brothers had children, so their mother didn't feel the need to exert any extra pressure on Emily to reproduce. The family legacy was already being carried on by her nieces and nephews.

The yearning came from deep inside Emily. A baby. A sweet cuddly newborn with perfect little fingers and toes. Oh God, she wanted to have a child, to be wakened in the night by soft fussy noises, to be fulfilled, to nurse an infant at her breast...

"Might be wise to find a father first," she muttered under her breath. Typical of her messed-up life, the first man she'd been interested in for years was a fugitive.

With a bottle of water in her hand, she meandered back to the computer. No mail.

In Spence's front room, she punched the button to replay phone messages. Yvonne hoped she was getting better and offered to take care of Pookie. There were three calls from reporters which Emily summarily erased. The sheriff wanted to talk to her. Two other friends from S.A.R. offered to bring over casseroles.

"Yes!" Emily said. "Decent food. Bring on the casseroles."

The last message was an unfamiliar voice: "Hello, Ms. Foster. My name is Brian Afton. My sister, Lynette, was the victim of Jordan Shane. I wish to extend my condolences for your inconvenience in this terrible situation. If there's anything I can do to help, please call."

She pressed the repeat button and listened again. Brian Afton was the brother who inherited all of Lynette's holdings. He owned two ski lodges. Why would he bother calling Emily?

Possibly, Brian Afton was a nice guy with an over-developed sense of responsibility about anything surrounding his sister's death. Possibly, this was a clue.

Her first instinct was to call him back and set up a meeting. She might be able to ferret out some information the police had missed. But she ought to ask Jordan.

Returning to the computer, she followed the directions to input another e-mail message. She typed, "Brian Afton called. Should I talk to him?"

She pressed Send and went to return the phone call from the sheriff, call Yvonne and arrange for casseroles.

When she returned to the computer, she had mail. Jordan wrote:

No Talking To Brian Afton. Deputy Kreiger in love with Lynette? Why do you think so? I'll be out of contact until later tonight. Gotta run.

Gotta run? Was that Jordan's idea of fugitive humor?

She responded with a detailed recounting of her conversation with Deputy Kreiger, including his vengeful attitude and his praise of Lynette who he called "the most beautiful woman he'd ever seen."

Emily paused, staring at the words on the computer screen. She typed:

If I had known your wife when she was alive, I might have resented her wealth and her beauty. But I can't be jealous of a dead woman. She's gone, murdered.

But Lynette had not truly departed. Her restless spirit reached out from the grave, touching so many other lives with memories of what had been and unfulfilled wishes for what could have been. What did she want? Was she searching for justice, demanding revenge? Or did she just want to be left alone to rest? No one would ever know.

Thinking of her father as much as Lynette, Emily typed:

It's strange how the dead stay with us. We live our lives, trying to make them proud. And they never answer. I've looked to the sky for angels, but I've never seen their wings. Not even a single pearly feather. I still keep looking up, hoping to see into heaven, waiting for the last goodbye.

She pressed the Send button, and leaned back in the squeaky swivel chair, imagining her words flying through space and time. Maybe she could write to her father this way. Send him a message. Tell him what was going on in her life. Ask him what she should do about Jordan.

She was fairly sure her father would tell her to help Jordan, to be active instead of laying low. But she'd promised not to stir up trouble.

And so, Emily spent the rest of the day in her bathrobe, trying to act sick while a couple of S.A.R. friends dropped by with casseroles. Since she couldn't stand to meet visitors in the cluttered little bedroom, she arranged herself in the front room in a comfy chair with a crocheted afghan over her legs. She kept all but one of the shades pulled and turned off the ringer on the phone so she wouldn't be tempted to answer.

Yvonne was the only one who pushed for details about Jordan, but Emily stuck to her standard response. ''I think he's innocent of his wife's murder, but he was wrong to escape from police custody.''

She sent Pookie home with Yvonne where her puppy could be free to roam instead of being fenced in the small yard behind Spence's house.

Halfway through the afternoon, the sheriff arrived. She really didn't know Sheriff Litvak well enough to trust or distrust him. He'd always been pleasant, as quick to smile as a politician running for office. But he'd botched the investigation into Lynette Afton-Shane's murder.

"How are you doing, Emily?"

She spoke softly, trying to sound weak. "I'm very tired."

"I won't take a minute," he promised. "I had a couple of questions about the incident with Deputy Ed Collins."

Would he mention the bounty? Should she tell him? Emily bit her lip to keep from speaking out. "Yes?"

"Deputy Collins claims he was injured while in pursuit of the fugitive. Is that the way you recall?"

Emily wouldn't exactly call it pursuit. Collins had been standing on a cliff, shooting at an unarmed man. The thought of his cowardice angered her, and she shifted her legs under the afghan. "I'd have to say Collins was doing his job to the best of his ability."

"And the fugitive was on the run. Is that correct?"

"Yes," she said.

"What were you doing?"

"Calling for help," she said. "Sheriff, is there some reason you're asking me these questions?"

"Procedure," he said.

From her work with S.A.R., she knew that "procedure" was an all-purpose response that meant "no comment." Sheriff Litvak had something to hide. If one of the newspaper reporters had gotten wind of the dead-or-alive, ten-thousand-dollar bounty, the sheriff would need to protect the reputation of his department.

"When you were treating the deputy's injuries," the Sheriff said, "did he voluntarily disarm himself?"

"Yes. The equipment on his belt made him uncomfortable."

"In spite of the fact that there was a known fugitive in the vicinity?"

"Ed was in pain. He took some headache medicine and passed out." Emily threw up a stone wall to block further questions. "I can't say what Ed was thinking."

"Then you were taken hostage again."

"Yes," she said.

"Why didn't the fugitive, Jordan Shane, take Collins's guns?"

The answer flashed across her mind: Because he's not a mad dog killer. Because he never wanted to hurt anyone. Because you were wrong, Sheriff Litvak. Jordan didn't murder his wife.

All that Emily said was, "I don't know."

She repeated that phrase a few more times before the sheriff departed. He wasn't smiling when he left the room, and Emily decided to add him to her list of suspects which now included Deputy Kreiger, Brian Afton and the skier, Sean Madigan, who she really didn't know much about.

After dinner, she planted herself in front of the computer, waiting for Jordan's e-mail. It was eleven o'clock at night when he finally wrote back to her.

"Doing okay," his message said. "Tomorrow, I start investigating. I miss you."

Rapidly, she typed back, "Miss you, too. Sheriff Litvak. Could he be a suspect?"

Though the turnaround time was less than fifteen minutes, it felt like hours.

She opened his e-mail which said, "Don't Investigate. You promised. Will check in tomorrow."

But how could he expect her not to help? She hated the inactivity, the passivity. She couldn't just sit here like lint on carpet.

She endured four more days of supposed recuperation with cryptic messages from Jordan, indicating that he was fine. She wasn't. Emily had a serious case of cabin fever. It had been five long days since she'd been outside. Her pent-up energy felt strong enough to power a small city. Emily couldn't pretend to be sick anymore. And why should she?

The search efforts had been cut back to almost nothing. State police and national guard had left the area. According to local gossip, Jordan had fled from Colorado and was on his way to some mysterious island off the coast of Florida.

When the telephone rang, she grabbed it. "Hello?"

"Emily? This is Ed Collins."

It was a measure of her high level of boredom that she was actually happy to hear from this rude, obnoxious man. "How are you doing, Ed?"

"They did the operation on my knee. It's feeling better, but I can't walk yet. I'm still in the hospital."

She didn't envy the physical therapists who had to work with this uncooperative patient. "I'm glad you're going to be all right."

"Hey, listen," he said gruffly. "I wanted to thank you. For the first aid and...for the other."

"What other?"

"You know, when the sheriff came by. You could've got me in trouble."

Interesting. Was Collins referring to the bounty? His trigger-happy approach? Or was it something else altogether. It might be useful to ask a few questions. "Why don't I stop by for a visit? Later this afternoon?"

"Yeah, sure. Why not?"

After she hung up the phone, Emily felt a grin stretch the corners of her mouth. *Freedom!* She wasn't actually breaking her promise to Jordan. A visit to a sick friend in the hospital could hardly be called an investigation. She scribbled a note to Spence, telling him she'd be visiting someone in the Aspen Hospital, grabbed her jacket and whipped down the stairs and out the door.

Her ancient Land Rover sputtered a few times before the engine caught, but when they hit the open road, the old girl hummed. The one-hour drive from Cascadia to Aspen went through some lovely mountain scenery. Today, the view seemed even more spectacular than usual. The snow had knocked the leaves off the trees, revealing bare branches and rugged stands of rock above the dark forests. The surrounding peaks, freshly iced with pure white snow, hinted at the beginning of ski season in little more than a month. Emily felt good to be alive, to be moving around. After being cooped up for five long days, colors were more vivid. Every sound was like a melody. She cranked the radio to high volume and sang along with Billy Joel.

About eight miles outside Aspen, she pulled up at a stop sign and turned down the radio. From behind the Land Rover, she heard the revving of a motorcycle.

Emily looked in the rearview mirror. The cyclist behind her was dressed all in black leather. He wore a black helmet with tinted visor that made him look like a faceless alien.

When she merged into traffic, he stuck on her tail. The hairs on the back of her neck prickled as she remembered

Jordan's warnings. There was a murderer at large. She could be in danger.

Though the motorcycle rider was probably only following her because he, too, was going into town, she decided to try a slight evasive action. At the next corner, she turned right.

The motorcycle followed. A coincidence?

Emily went left, then right again. The faceless rider stayed with her.

She looked for another turn, a way to get back to traffic, but she was stuck on a winding road that hairpinned higher and higher past multimillion-dollar homes with impressive gates and huge acreage.

She stared in her rearview mirror. The cyclist had flipped up his visor. His face was visible.

"Oh my God!" It was Jordan.

Chapter Ten

Jordan guided the Harley around her parked Land Rover to the driver's side window where Emily stared up at him. Her green eyes bulged round as cue balls. "It's you," she said. "It's really you."

"Follow me," he directed. "It's not safe here."

He revved the bike and pulled in front of her Rover. Though he should've been angry about the way she ignored his warnings and drove carelessly into danger, a fountain of sheer joy gushed up inside him. He'd missed being with her, hearing her laughter, holding her and feeling her heart beating against his. He missed seeing her. The more he learned about Emily, the more he appreciated her beauty. His pretty Colorado gal in her jean jacket, white turtleneck, broad belt and hiking boots glowed with sweet vitality. One tendril of her curly blond hair was more magnificent to him than a mountain range at sunset.

On the Harley, he led her away from the private property where surveillance might include video cameras at the gate. As they entered National Forest land, he took odd twists and turns until he could be certain no one was following them.

During the past five days, the search had been downgraded to mere vigilance. Jordan was presumed to have left the area. Using his computer, he'd managed to set up a few phony credit card transactions in busy stores in Texas where check-out clerks couldn't pick his face from the crowd. The law enforcement people, now including the FBI, were following those false leads in a nationwide manhunt.

Jordan swerved the Harley into a designated rest area with a picnic table. There were no other cars in sight. Before he dismounted, Emily was running toward him. She stopped short a few feet away from him, beaming.

"Look at you!" she said. "Black leather and a Harley."

"That's right." He swung his leg off the bike. What was she trying to say? Had he missed something?

She reached toward his face and touched the tender place where the stitches had been. "Almost healed," she said. "I did a good job. You look great. Jordan, you look like…a stud!"

"I feel like a man who's been too long without his woman."

He caught hold of her hand, pulled her into his arms and kissed her mouth. She tasted sweeter than strawberries fresh off the vine. Her lithe body fit tightly against him, awakening memories of their night of passion. He was already hard when he separated from her and held her at arm's length.

Dreamily, she murmured, "I always knew you were a handsome guy, but there was this whole computer nerd part to your personality. Very sweet and intelligent…"

"Emily, we need to talk about what you're doing here."

"…I mean, you look like a bad boy, an updated Elvis, every mother's worst nightmare." A teasing smile tugged the corners of her mouth. "I don't know that I like the idea of you driving around like that, all sexy in black leather."

"It's practical. Leather is the best protection against the Colorado cold."

"It's logical." Laughing, she tossed her head and the sunlight danced in her hair. "That sounds more like the Jordan I know. Tell me how you got the Harley."

"I bought it online, walked into the dealer and drove away."

"I thought if you used a credit card the police could trace the transaction," she said.

He didn't bother to explain the complex computer hacking system that bounced offshore and back again half a dozen times, allowing him to circumvent discovery. "Let's just say, I'm using my own money. By the end of the month, my sister who does the accounting for my company will figure out what I'm up to. Until then, there's not a clue."

"Why a Harley?"

Only a woman would question the choice of this fine riding machine that held the road and was capable of off-road driving. At least once in his life, every man should drive a Harley.

He tapped the black helmet. "Let's just say I bought it for accessories. This helmet is the best disguise in the world. I can see out and nobody can see me."

"Well, the crotch rocket suits you, stud."

"Thank you, ma'am." Jordan forced himself not to grin back at her. He didn't want her to get the idea it was okay to leave Spence's apartment and strike out on her own. "Why'd you come to Aspen?"

"Back up," she said. "How did you know I'd be here?"

He pulled a beeper from his pocket and showed it to her. "Spence notified me."

"Wait a minute! Aren't phone calls traceable?"

"He contacted me via e-mail. His computer talked to my computer, bouncing the signal off a digital receiver and—" Her eyes were beginning to glaze over, so Jordan summarized, "He didn't use the phone. Now, it's your turn. What's this about visiting a sick friend in the hospital?"

"Do you mind if we walk while we talk? It seems odd to be with you and not be running for our lives."

"The danger isn't gone," he reminded. The worst mistake he could make was to become complacent. "I'm still a fugitive."

Some of the sparkle left her eyes. "I didn't mean to be thoughtless, but I'm so glad to see you. Did you get all my e-mails?"

"Yes." Page after page about her heritage and the tragic death of her father took him back in time. He'd been able to see her as a sober little girl in Twin Bluffs, trapped in her mother's shrine to a dead man. He read about her decision to become a nurse, like her father was a medic in Vietnam. She shared her pain, her fears and also her dreams.

"Thank you," he said. "Your words reminded me why I want to go on living free. You've given me a gift."

"What's that?"

"The key to your mind."

She slipped into his arms again. "And to my heart."

Jordan didn't know what he'd done to deserve her affection, but he would gladly accept her precious offering. Emily was one in a million. He'd had to climb to the top of the world to find her, and he meant to keep her safe.

He leaned down and whispered in her ear. "Tell me why you're going to Aspen."

"Because I'm bored out of my mind at Spence's apartment." With a sigh, she separated from him. Avoiding his gaze, she sauntered toward the picnic table beneath a stand of evergreens. "I hate being sick, and pretending to be sick is even worse. I want to help, Jordan. I want to do something."

"Who's the sick friend in the hospital?"

She climbed onto the bench and sat on the top of the picnic table. "Deputy Ed Collins called me. He thanked me for not getting him into trouble when I talked to the sheriff, and I thought he might be referring to the bounty. I thought if I went to see him, I might get some information about who offered the ten thousand dollars for your capture, dead or alive."

Jordan considered. An important guideline in investigating was Follow The Money. If he found out who had put up the bounty money, it might lead to the person who'd arranged for Jordan's easy escape from the Aspen Airport. The frame-up for the escape had to be connected to the frame-up for the murder.

The logical sequence pleased him, but he still didn't want to get Emily involved. "Why would Collins tell you anything?"

"Maybe he came to his senses and realized that I saved his miserable life." Her pretty green eyes earnestly searched his face. "I need to do this, Jordan. I want to help."

He was sorely tempted to accept her offer. After five days investigating and setting up his base of operations, he wasn't much closer to finding the murderer. There were too many questions that needed to be asked in person. But he didn't want that person to be Emily. "I can't put you in danger."

"Nobody suspects we're connected," she said. "I haven't been menaced or threatened in any way."

"Because I had you safely tucked away with Spence," he said.

"I'll try this one thing. Talking to Collins. And that will be all."

He joined her at the picnic table. When he studied her expression, he saw intelligence and cool sensibility. Emily ought to be able to handle a conversation with an idiot like Ed Collins without getting into trouble.

Though it went against his better judgment, Jordan said, "Just this once."

FOLLOWING Jordan's instructions, Emily found a parking place on the street outside the hospital. She checked her wristwatch. At exactly fifteen minutes past two o'clock, half an hour from now, she would meet Jordan in the enclosed parking area on the top level. If he wasn't there, waiting for her, she had other instructions.

Feeling like an espionage agent, she went toward the front entrance to the hospital. A cheerful bounce lightened her step. Finally, she was able to do something useful. After her talk with Collins, she felt certain that Jordan would realize how necessary she was to his investigation. Instead of being relegated to the cluttered guest bedroom in Spence's apartment, she'd ride off with the stud muffin on his brand-new Harley.

Emily sucked in her cheeks and put on a friendly, hospital visitor expression. Not too happy. It would definitely not be appropriate for her to skip through the sterile hallways, giggling and singing.

Though she'd never met the desk nurse before, Emily

decided to introduce herself and dig for a little inside information. "I'm Emily Foster, emergency nurse for S.A.R. in Cascadia."

"I've heard about you." The young woman stood up straight behind her counter. She was near six feet tall and athletic-looking, a typical Colorado blonde. "You're the one who was a hostage."

"That's right. I'm here to see Deputy Collins. Has he had many visitors?"

The other nurse confided, "Hardly at all. It's kinda weird. Usually, when we have a cop injured in the line of duty, there's a crowd."

"Collins is a little difficult," Emily said.

The blonde rolled her eyes. "You can say that again. We ended up putting him in a private room because he irritated everybody who had to stay with him."

"I think he's friends with that deputy who's an extreme skier. What's his name? Kreiger?"

"Kreiger, that's right. He's been by a couple of times. Good-looking dude but a little short." The desk nurse leaned toward her. "So, tell me about Jordan Shane. From his photos in the newspaper, he's a total babe."

"Actually," Emily said, "he's kind of a computer nerd."

She waved goodbye and went down the hall to the private room where Collins sat in his bed, scowling at the closed drapes. His injured leg was encased in a bulky removable cast. "Hello, Ed."

"You got here damn quick." His thin lips twisted in an unpleasant sneer. "Not much going on in your life, is there?"

"I manage." Her nurse personality took over as she went to the drapes and yanked them open, flooding the square room with sunlight. Then she tidied up the tissues he'd thrown on the floor. On the dresser sat one small bouquet of wilting carnations with a get-well note from the sheriff's department. The card wasn't personally signed. Apparently, Collins wasn't the most popular guy on the force. "I assume your operation went well," she said. "Are you making progress in physical therapy?"

"You must feel real guilty, rushing over here so fast."

"Guilty?"

"This injury is your fault," he said. "You distracted me while I was pursuing the fugitive."

Emily bustled to the door and closed it. She stood at the foot of his bed. "We both know it didn't happen that way, Ed. You fired without warning. You did nothing to protect me, a hostage. You left your walkie-talkie in the car. And you fell off the mountain all by yourself."

"Maybe," he said grudgingly.

"Nothing you did was even close to correct procedure." She made a guess, based on his attitude and the fact that he wasn't being treated like a hero. "It's not the first time you've goofed. Is it?"

"Nobody's perfect. You don't understand how hard it is to be a cop."

"Even harder to be a good cop." She checked her wristwatch. Only sixteen minutes before she had to meet Jordan. If she wanted to come back to him with solid information, she didn't have time to be subtle with Collins. "You probably think you're overworked and underpaid."

He stiffened his neck. The tendons stood out in angry cords. However, in his patterned hospital gown, the deputy wasn't at all intimidating. "What are you getting at?"

"You mentioned a bounty. Ten thousand dollars. I want to know who's paying the money."

"Why should I tell you, nursey?"

"If you don't, I might feel obliged to call up the sheriff and explain what really happened on Mammoth Rock."

She laid down her trump card and waited, fully expecting Collins to provide her with information. The deputy was too cantankerous to form an alliance with anyone, even the slimeball who offered the bounty.

"I heard about the bounty though Kreiger," he said. "But it's not his money. Frank Kreiger ain't rich."

"Then why did you believe him?"

"Kreiger's got friends, you know. He's a skier." Collins clamped his thin lips together. "That's all I'm going to say."

"Thanks, Ed. I was curious." It wasn't much of a revelation but better than nothing. With six minutes left to spare, she backed away from his bed. "Don't worry about me shooting off my mouth. I won't be the one who gets you in trouble with the sheriff."

She didn't feel obliged to report him. Collins's abilities were such that he'd probably hang himself without any help from her. She waved a fluttery goodbye. "Be seeing you."

"Hey, wait!" He glanced toward the clock on the dresser. "You're not taking off already, are you?"

Her eyes narrowed. What was going on here? He obviously didn't like her, and the feeling was mutual. "Was there something else you wanted to say?"

He swallowed, and his Adam's apple yo-yoed up and down. "I thought we could be friendly-like."

"We're not friends, Ed." Four minutes left. "What do you really want?"

Resentfully, he gave up the pretense. "There's somebody who wants to meet you. I told him you'd be here."

"His name?"

There was a tap on the door to Collins's room. She

opened it. The man who stood framed in the doorway had coal black hair, combed straight back from his forehead. His eyes were a startling ice blue. Though he was probably only in his late twenties, he seemed older. His carefully assembled appearance showed very expensive taste. In a modulated baritone, he said, "I'm Brian Afton. Lynette Afton-Shane was my older sister."

"I'm Emily Foster." She shook his hand. His grip felt soft with carefully moisturized skin and a buffed manicure. His cuticles were more perfect than hers had ever been. Was this the hand of a murderer?

Suddenly edgy, her gaze lifted to his face. Had he killed his sister? "I was just leaving."

"You never returned my phone call, Emily."

"I've been ill," she said hastily. Her allotted time was nearly spent, and she didn't want to leave Jordan waiting. But she had to ask, "Why did you call me?"

"I was concerned about your ordeal. This incident does, after all, involve my family." He must have read the skepticism on her face because he added, "I also wondered what else you could tell me about Jordan Shane."

"Everything I know, I told the sheriff."

"I'm more interested in your impressions than in the facts," he said. "You spent nearly two days with the man. You must have drawn some conclusions about his character, his likes and dislikes."

"If there's one thing he dislikes more than anything else, it's the mountains. He has no appreciation for the sunsets or the wide open vistas." She hadn't meant to say that much. Brian had a seductively sinister quality, like the mesmerizing glare of a predator. "You'll have to excuse me."

He leaned his shoulder against the edge of the door,

effectively blocking her escape. "Tell me more, Emily. I want to know every detail about the man who killed my sister."

She stifled the urge to protest Jordan's innocence. "I have to run. Maybe another time."

"Perfect. I'm having a little get-together at the house tomorrow night." He reached into his jacket pocket and pulled out an engraved business card with his address. "Eight o'clock. I'll expect you to be there. Feel free to bring a guest."

She accepted the card. "I'll think about it."

"It would be a comfort to me," he said. "It's always difficult to accept the death of a loved one."

His blue eyes flashed, and she seemed to recognize a deep, sincere grief. Either he was truly affected by his sister's murder or Brian Afton was the most accomplished liar she'd ever met.

Emily dodged around him and marched stiffly down the hospital corridor, forcing herself not to sprint though she was five minutes late to meet Jordan. *Act natural.* She didn't want to attract attention to herself.

To all outward appearances, she was calm, even nonchalant. But her heartbeat accelerated. Under her denim jacket, she was sweating. An invitation to the Afton home was not to be ignored. By reputation, the château was magnificent, even by Aspen standards. More importantly, a get-together would probably include most of the suspects on Jordan's list. She wanted to be there, to interrogate every last one of them.

On the top floor of the parking garage, she stood for a moment, took a breath and looked around. No one here. Had Jordan given up on her? Had he disappeared again?

"Come on," she muttered, "I'm only five minutes late."

She heard the Harley before she saw him. He parked in front of her, flipped open the storage pannier and grabbed a helmet that was exactly like his. "Put it on. Let's go."

Though she might have guessed he'd pick her up on the bike, Emily hesitated. Never before had she ridden on a motorcycle. She was a sensible woman who believed in safety first. In the E.R., she'd seen the horrifying aftermath of motorcycle accidents.

"It's okay," he said. "I'll be careful."

Why should she trust this hot, sexy, dangerous man in black leather? Visions of Hell's Angels, beer brawls and evil tattoos flashed in her head. But she put on the helmet. This was Jordan, she reminded herself. He would never do anything to hurt her. Emily straddled the leather seat behind him and wrapped her arms around his torso.

The Harley between her legs felt huge and powerful, and when Jordan pulled away from the curb, she screamed. It wasn't a huge, panic-stricken shriek, only a tiny eek. But he stopped. "Emily, honey."

"Yes?"

"The idea here is to be subtle. Not to attract attention to ourselves. Try not to make a lot of noise back there."

"Ever since I met you, I've been doing things I never considered, even in my wildest dreams."

"And I do appreciate that," he said patiently. "If you're scared, you might want to close your eyes."

"I'm not scared." But when he moved forward again, she had the same gasping reaction. Circling through the parking garage, she jolted stiffly with each turn. She squeezed her eyes closed. That was worse. *Don't scream.* But she had to let the excitement out. Under her breath, she whispered a mantra, "Oh dear, oh dear, oh dear, oh dear."

On the street, he accelerated, and she hung on for dear life. They weren't going much faster than a bicycle, but it felt faster. The parked cars seemed too close. Her knees gripped tightly.

Jordan avoided the center of town. In minutes, they were careening along the open road. The roar of the engine deafened her. They picked up speed. The trees flashed by like a VCR tape on fast-forward. "Oh dear, oh dear, ooooooh..."

She felt airborne as if she were flying, soaring beyond the bonds of gravity. The sensation reminded her of downhill skiing on a straightaway slope, hanging onto control by the merest thread. Then, suddenly and unexpectedly, you'd hit a mogul and lift off in spontaneous flight. The speed was seductive, exhilarating.

She abandoned her death grip on Jordan's waist and welcomed the wind that tore around her, sliding down her collar and up her sleeves. She closed her eyes and became one with the whistling currents of air.

This time, the sound that escaped her lips was laughter, high and delighted. She loved the Harley! Why hadn't she ever done this before? So much of her life had been dedicated to doing the right thing that she'd missed out on all kinds of naughty fun. She'd needed a change, needed Jordan to tear into her life and shred her conventional thinking.

Miles to the north of Aspen, they crossed the shimmering rapids of the Roaring Fork River. On a gravel road, she jostled and bounced against him. "Where are we going?" she yelled.

He stopped. "Hang on tight. It's off-road from here."

On hard-packed dirt, they made a haphazard ascent. In the midst of thick brush, he parked and turned off the engine.

She pulled off her helmet. Though the Harley was silent, her head still echoed with the engine's roar. Her teeth still chattered from the bumpy ride. "F-f-fantastic," she stammered.

"We're home," he said.

Unsteadily, she dismounted and watched as he removed a large portion of shrubbery. He wheeled the bike through the opened space. A few paces beyond, she saw the boarded-up entrance to a mine shaft, not an unusual sight in the formerly gold-rich Rockies. Using an almost invisible hinge, Jordan opened a door to the cave. He took the bike inside and she followed.

He handed her a flashlight. The entrance area, braced by ancient timbers, was just large enough for a square-sided, eight-foot tall, black tent. Was he living here?

"Is this safe?" she asked. "Aren't these mine shafts prone to cave-in?"

"It's safer than setting up a tent anywhere else," he said. "The searchers have given up, but they're still checking at campgrounds and watching for anybody new to the area."

He went through the front flap to the tent and lit a Coleman lantern. "Make yourself at home while I close up the bushes and the door."

Emily entered his small domain. On the floor of the tent was an inflatable mattress and sleeping bag. On a narrow bench, he had a battery-operated hotplate, water purifier and cooking implements. The rest of the space was an office of low collapsible tables covered with electronic equipment. She recognized her walkie-talkie with the police band radio and the S.A.R. computer, but the rest of these doohickeys were new.

Jordan slipped inside and closed the flap. "What do you think?"

"I'm glad to know you're not freezing to death. Are you getting enough to eat?"

"Just enough," he said. "But I'd give my IRA for a thick, juicy, medium-rare, T-bone steak."

"Did you buy all this stuff online?"

"Mostly. And I also put my hands on some cash money that went through a dozen wire transfers."

"I'm impressed. Are you sure this stuff can't be traced?"

"It can," he said, "but I made it so complicated that it'll take several days, assuming they know where to look."

He peeled off his leather jacket. Underneath, he wore a black knit sweater, and he still looked studly and completely in control. An amazing transformation. She remembered the first day they'd spent together when he stumbled across the hillsides, virtually helpless, not knowing which way to turn. Now, he seemed to be surviving very nicely without her help.

"Sit on the bed," he said, "and tell me what you learned from Collins."

"Number one," she said as she curled her legs under her and sat on top of the sleeping bag, "he's not only a jerk. He's an incompetent jerk. Ed Collins doesn't have many friends in the sheriff's department."

"No surprise there." Jordan sat beside her. "What about the bounty?"

"Collins didn't know who was paying the cash, but he heard about it from Deputy Frank Kreiger who's apparently a lot more popular than Collins."

Jordan nodded. "So, that's number one. What's number two?"

"The real reason Collins called me was to lure me to

his hospital room. There was somebody he arranged for me to meet. Brian Afton.''

"Damn," Jordan said. "You met Brian?"

"He invited me to a party at his house tomorrow night."

"His house," he repeated bitterly. "It belonged to Lynette. The château wasn't built with Afton money."

"It wasn't? I had the impression that Brian came from a wealthy family."

"Not the kind of money that comes from the well-managed ski lodges that belonged to Lynette's first husband. After he was killed in a small plane crash, she inherited everything. And she was a top-notch business-woman. Within seven years, she doubled the net worth of her holdings and became a true diva of Aspen society. The château was her pride and joy. And she worked damned hard for her success." He frowned. "Now, baby brother Brian sashays in, with no effort, and inherits everything."

"Do you think he's the murderer?"

"I don't know." He gestured toward the electronic equipment. "I've checked all his financial records. About three months ago, a few weeks before Lynette was killed, Brian was strapped for cash."

She nodded. "Sounds like a motive."

"But Lynette bailed him out. She made him a loan that was really a gift, requiring a payback of less than ten cents on the dollar. She was always generous with her family."

"What about the cousins who inherited?"

"I've pretty much eliminated them as suspects. None of them were desperate to commit murder. And there's no way they had a key to the house or knew the security codes."

"Who does that leave?"

"Brian. And Sean Madigan, the professional skier who lived in the guest cabin on the château grounds."

"The skier." A logical connection clicked inside her head. "When Collins mentioned Deputy Kreiger, he referred to him as the skier."

"That description applies to half the people in Aspen," Jordan said.

"Not really." There was a hierarchy of skiing expertise that ranged from snow bunnies who couldn't manage a snowplow to free-stylers to Olympic-caliber experts. "Kreiger is an extreme skier. He and his buddies hitch a ride on a chopper and are dropped off on remote peaks. Among the reckless, it's considered the coolest form of skiing. I'll bet Kreiger is tight with Sean Madigan."

"But the real question," Jordan said, "is whether Madigan could afford a ten-thousand-dollar bounty."

Chapter Eleven

Using problem-solving logic and a spectacular amount of computer data, Jordan had narrowed his focus to two main suspects: Sean Madigan or Brian Afton. In less than an hour, Emily had drawn the same conclusion from a cursory knowledge of the case and a few conversations.

Though only factual evidence was admissible in a court of law, there was no substitute for physical investigation—talking to people, observing them. And Jordan was denied this opportunity. He was a fugitive. He couldn't show his face.

"I'm keeping an open mind," he said, "but I think our murderer is either Brian or Sean."

"Or Kreiger," Emily said.

"Also possible," he conceded.

She stretched out across his sleeping bag. Every night, he had imagined her being here, lying beside him on the uncomfortable air mattress. Her frequent, rambling e-mails had given him a glimpse inside her mind. Now he wanted her body.

"Tell me," she said, "about your logic."

"The two basic issues are motive and access to the house. Remember that Lynette had tight security requiring a key and an access code to get inside and to get back out again. Whoever killed her knew the code so they could escape.''

''I don't suppose anybody confessed to having the code,'' she said.

''I did. And I also had a key.'' Those facts were a damning but largely irrelevant piece of evidence against him. ''Not that I needed one. I was already in the house.''

An adorable frown tugged at her lips. Though not a striking beauty like Lynette, Emily was a hundred times more attractive. Her loveliness radiated from within, surrounding her with a virtual spectrum of charm. Her every gesture fascinated him. ''What about motive?'' she asked.

Jordan dragged his mind back to the case. ''Brian's motive is obvious. Money. He was set to inherit the lion's share of Lynette's assets. But he wasn't desperate for cash. His sister generally gave him whatever he needed.''

''Taking handouts isn't the same as ownership. Maybe Brian had big ambitions and wanted it all.''

''Far as I can tell, Brian's only goals in life are to dress well and have a good time. He's not a businessman.''

''What about Sean?'' she asked. ''I thought he was just renting the cabin on the grounds. What are his motives?''

''For one thing, he inherits the cabin and the acreage it sits on,'' Jordan said. ''That might not sound like much, but we're talking about prime Aspen real estate. That cabin—which isn't much bigger than yours—is worth over half a million dollars.''

''Wow!'' Her green eyes popped wide. ''I guess it's true when Realtors say the value of a home is based on three things—location, location, location.''

''It's still not an unimpeachable motive. Like Brian, Sean benefited by having Lynette alive. She used to take him on trips and buy him things. She gave him a brand-new Jeep Cherokee. And there's something else.''

Jordan glanced toward his computer. From his skilled hacking, he had obtained access to virtually all the facts in the case, including the coroner's report and data gathered by the Pitkin County sheriff's department. ''Madigan's fingerprints were found in Lynette's bedroom.''

''Aha! Doesn't that make him the number one suspect?''

''It made him her lover.''

''Even better,'' Emily said. ''He killed her because of a lover's quarrel.''

''That's not the way the police interpreted the facts.'' He shook his head. ''Their reasoning was completely without logic. On one hand, they claimed I killed my wife because she wouldn't agree to a divorce. On the other, they assumed my motive was jealous rage when I discovered that she'd taken a lover.''

''Did you know about the affair?''

''I might have guessed. We'd been estranged for over a year, and Lynette wasn't the type of woman to go very long without a man to admire her.''

''What about you?'' Emily asked. ''Are you the type of man who can go for—''

''I respected my marriage vows, even though it was damn obvious that the relationship was doomed.''

''I should've guessed,'' she teased. ''Always the gentleman.''

''Maybe I wasn't tempted. I hadn't met you.''

''But you did. You came to my cabin with that donation for S.A.R.''

At the time, his visit to Emily hadn't seemed very important. He'd been bored, needing some task to occupy his day, and a trip to Cascadia filled the time. He'd looked forward to seeing Emily again. She was bright and pretty.

At the time, Jordan dismissed his trip as a mere diversion. He hadn't known that he had stumbled across his destiny. "If I hadn't been married, that little visit might have turned into something more."

"You mean dating?"

"Maybe."

"But that would've been so dull. Going out to dinner, seeing a movie, doing all the standard courtship rituals." She laughed. "It was much more effective to hold a gun on me and take me hostage."

"Is that the only way a man can tie you down? To literally knot a rope around your waist?"

"It helped," she said with absolute honesty.

Emily knew she'd been so tied up in her own stress that she could barely see beyond the tip of her own nose. She'd been busily helping others and hiding herself. When Jordan grabbed her, she had been shaken to her core, torn away from the safety of solitude. Now, she was changed forever. She no longer wanted to be alone.

Her enforced seclusion at Spence's cluttered apartment had been difficult instead of refreshing. Still, she'd used the time. She'd purged herself in a volume of e-mails to Jordan and had faced the fact that she might just have a few unresolved father issues. "I wouldn't prescribe kidnapping for every single woman who has lost interest in dating," she said. "But it worked for me. Especially when the kidnapper is someone like you."

A grin lightened his features. "Someone *like* me?"

"A man who's infuriatingly logical and too smart for his own good. A nerd. A gentleman. A sexy black leather stud."

"I like that sexy part," he said.

When he reached toward her, she caught hold of his hand. Though Emily was anxious to revisit the physical part of their relationship, she wanted to hear everything, every single word, about his investigation.

Jordan might not need her help when it came to surviving in the wilderness, but he couldn't possibly complete his investigation without asking some face-to-face questions. And that was where she came in. Emily could be his eyes and ears. She could attend the party at Brian's house and come up with some answers.

"Tell me more about your investigation," she demanded. "Are there other motives for Sean Madigan?"

"There's one more piece of evidence," he admitted. With obvious reluctance, he withdrew his touch. "We ought to take our boots off, Emily. This air mattress is kind of delicate."

"What else about Madigan?"

"I'm not sure if this applies to Madigan or Brian or even to Rita Ramirez, the housekeeper," he said, leaning down to unlace his boots. "Do you remember when I told you Lynette asked for a month to straighten her affairs before we went ahead with divorce proceedings?"

She nodded, vaguely recalling this conversation. "Did it have something to do with rewriting her will?"

"Not according to her attorney. He would've come forward with information like that in a murder investigation."

"Then why?" she asked.

"It took me a while to figure this out," he said, kicking off his boots. "I hacked through documents from her attorney, from business managers, from the ski lodges and Lynette's personal papers. I found the clue with her accountant."

Jordan wasn't one to brag, but his smug expression

showed a certain pride in his deductions. "And?" she prompted.

"Lynette had an outstanding art collection, including paintings, sculpture and even a Fabergé egg. Only about half her stuff is on display in the house. The rest is in storage in the basement."

"Shouldn't it be in a museum?"

"Possibly. Anyway, about a month before she was murdered, she had an expert come in to catalog and evaluate her artwork. I compared his evaluation with another one, filed with her accountant, taken about three years ago. Several objects were missing."

"She might have sold them," Emily said.

"There was no paperwork for sales. These objects weren't masterpieces. Probably only worth a couple thousand bucks apiece. But they would've been documented."

"So, you're assuming these artworks were stolen. By Brian?"

"I don't think Brian would bother with stealing. That's a little too much effort for him."

"What about the housekeeper?"

"I have to consider her, but I can't believe it. Rita Ramirez was the closest thing I had to a friend in Aspen. I used to spend more time in her apartment behind the kitchen than I did in my wife's bedroom. I think the thief was Madigan."

Undoubtedly, Jordan was leading toward a logical conclusion, but Emily wasn't sure exactly what it was. She was further distracted when he stretched out her leg and started unfastening her hiking boots. "How does the theft connect to murder?"

"Lynette's ego would never allow her to admit that her lover was stealing from her, so she never turned the new evaluation over to the accountant. She'd want to clean up her own mess before we got started with the divorce paperwork. And that meant getting those things back from Madigan.''

"So she confronted him," Emily said.

"That's what I figure," he drawled. "Madigan probably put her off with one explanation after another. When I showed up at the house, asking for time alone with Lynette, Madigan saw an opportunity to get rid of her and frame me.''

"Why don't you take this to the sheriff?"

"It's only a theory." He eased the boot off her right foot. "There's no hard evidence. No receipts. No sudden bumps in his bank balance.''

"But the artwork itself." Her focus on his logic was severely eroded by his gentle strokes on her ankle and foot. "Couldn't the new owners be found? Couldn't it be traced back to Madigan?''

"I'm sure he went through a broker. Maybe even a fence." He removed the left boot. "Even if we could prove he sold the artwork, he could claim that Lynette generously gave him the artwork as presents.''

"It gives him a motive for murder. If she discovered his theft, she might have been getting ready to dump him. Jordan, I think we should…'' Emily's words trailed off as he massaged her foot, flexing the ankle and bending her toes. His caress on her instep shivered up through her body, relaxing and arousing her at the same time. "…oh, that feels good.''

"I know something that might feel even better.''

In contrast to their frantic animal passion on the night when they stayed in the Lomax cabin, Jordan took his time undressing her, gliding her turtleneck higher on her torso, one slow inch at a time, as he nuzzled against her stomach, her rib cage, her breasts.

As he unbuckled her belt and unzipped her Levi's, Emily's sense of anticipation soared to an almost unbearable level. When he touched her most private core, she gasped, trembling at the edge of sweet release. More, she was greedy for more.

"Jordan, did you happen to buy—"

"A twelve pack," he said.

"You're going to need them."

She helped him off with his sweater, noticing that the wound on his arm was healing nicely. She touched the scar. "I did a good job of nursing you."

"You saved my life," he said simply.

And he had done the same for her. Though her wounds were not visible, she'd been in pain. Hiding. Alone. In so many ways, Jordan had healed her.

LATE AFTERNOON, cruising back toward Aspen on the Harley, Jordan felt invincible. Against all odds, he'd found a reason for hope. And her name was Emily.

Behind him on the motorcycle, her slender arms wrapped around him. As he swung into a sharp turn on the road above the Roaring Fork River, she hugged him tight, and her breasts pressed into his back. Then she leaned back, and he heard her laughter as the chill September breeze swept around them.

Apparently, Emily enjoyed riding the bike. Matter of fact, she seemed open to almost any adventure he had to offer. This thing they shared—this relationship—was so good and true that he couldn't believe the universe would take it away from him. He had to find proof of the murder and clear his name.

Tomorrow night was the party at the Afton Château

which meant the usual security would be relaxed while guests came in and out. Though there'd be a lot of witnesses, Jordan figured tomorrow night was a good time for him to move inside the grounds. He wanted to plant a couple of listening devices. Plus, he'd like to get inside Sean Madigan's cabin and take a look around.

Entering Aspen, he kept to the residential streets where he'd be unlikely to encounter deputies or state cops. In this quaint, well-maintained town with Victorian-style houses, it was hard to believe anything as sordid as murder might exist.

He pulled into a gas station, parked and turned off the engine. Though he would've preferred taking off his helmet and kissing Emily goodbye, he didn't dare to show his face. "I can't take you directly to your car," he said. "Someone might be keeping it under surveillance."

She pulled off the helmet and shook her head. Her curly hair tumbled around her shoulders. Less than an hour ago, his fingers had tangled in that blond mane. He'd lost himself in the emerald green of her eyes as they'd climaxed together.

"I'm going to Brian's party," she said.

He'd been expecting this declaration, almost waiting for it. She must have told him a hundred times that she wanted to help, that he needed her in his investigation. Though he preferred for her to stay safely tucked away, she was determined, unstoppable as the winter snow in the mountains. "I can't order you not to go," he said, "so I'll agree."

Her eyebrows raised. "You're not going to object? What about telling me it's too risky and I'll be in terrible danger, yadda yadda."

"Would it do any good?"

"No," she said.

"Then, I have two requests," he said. "You have to wear a wire, a listening device, so I can hear who you're talking to and what they're saying."

"Sure." Emily couldn't believe he was conceding so easily. "What else?"

"Take Spence with you."

"No problem."

He touched her shoulder, glided his hand down her arm and squeezed her hand. "I guess I need your help again."

"Jordan, you know I'll do anything for you."

"Stay safe," he said.

When he kick-started the Harley and drove away, she watched until he had disappeared into traffic. *Stay safe.* That went double for him.

She should've felt pleased that she'd gotten her way. Now she was part of Jordan's investigation, helping him no matter what the danger. Her heart knew she was doing the right thing. How could she stand idly by while he struggled alone? Jordan had been unjustly accused and imprisoned. She simply had to help him.

Yet, she feared that she was terrifically ill-suited for the role of undercover detective. She was a nurse, an average citizen, law-abiding and naturally honest. What did she know about wearing a wire and being under surveillance? Would she be able to anticipate danger before it popped up and smacked her in the face? Her life had been dedicated to treating the aftermath of violence, not anticipating an assault.

Wishing she'd read more spy novels, Emily made her way through downtown Aspen where quaint storefronts and boutiques offered all manner of overpriced merchandise. The charm of her surroundings passed in a blur. Second thoughts dogged her footsteps.

When she finally reached her car, parked on the street

outside the hospital, she easily recognized the first sign that the police had taken notice of her ancient Land Rover. A parking ticket. With any luck, this citation would be the worst thing that happened to her.

On the drive back to Cascadia, Emily tried to think positively. She could help Jordan solve this crime. Then, he'd be free. They could explore the possibility of a real relationship. Selfishly, she wanted that chance. When the danger has subsided, would they have anything in common? To be sure, they were sexually compatible. She desired him with every fiber of her body, and he fulfilled her completely. But he was from Florida, for goodness sake. He'd already tried marriage to a mountain dweller and failed. Could she adapt to palm trees and ocean beaches? Would he give the mountains another chance?

Don't put the cart before the horse. Her main focus needed to be gathering evidence and solving the murder.

Emily tried to imagine what might happen during tomorrow's get-together at the lavish, glamorous home of Brian Afton. She'd heard there were twenty bedrooms and sixteen bathrooms. Marble floors. Crystal chandeliers. Genuine Chippendale antiques. But Emily wouldn't have time to gawk. She had to find the murderer. She needed a strategy.

Her conversation with Deputy Collins had been easy because she had a threat to dangle over his miserable head. There'd been no need for subtlety which, frankly, was not her forte.

The party tomorrow night required a different approach, less forthright. Somehow, she needed to direct the conversation toward incriminating topics. The bounty. The codes and keys needed for the security system. In Sean's case, she could focus on the artwork in the house.

But how? She'd never been good at small talk, much less at ferreting out information.

If only she had a threat, something to convince them to cooperate, she might make headway. Aha! She could *pretend* to have evidence linking them to the murder. After all, they didn't know she was coming to the party empty-handed.

With evening approaching, she flicked on the headlights. At the side of the road, she saw two deer. They watched her Land Rover with startled eyes as she slowed to drive past them. With a flash of their white tails, they bounded toward the surrounding forest, and Emily wished she could go with them. Mountain survival was second nature to her. She belonged here. Not at a trendy party in Aspen.

She imagined a glittering ballroom filled with beautiful people whose hair was never mussed and whose makeup was always perfect. Would there be celebrities? Movie stars? What kind of food would be served? "Oh my God, what am I going to wear?"

She needed help. Instead of returning to Spence's upstairs apartment, she drove to the home of Yvonne Hanson where she could get some advice on wardrobe.

As she parked in the driveway, Emily was greeted by a chorus of barking from the spacious kennel area at the rear of the house.

Emily opened the chain-link fence and stepped into the yard. She heard a familiar sound that lightened her worries.

"Murfle moof!"

"Pookie!" She bent down and held her arms wide as the golden retriever puppy charged toward her, greeting her with such enthusiasm that she was almost knocked flat on her butt. "How's my boy? How's my baby?"

"Not real bright," Yvonne said. She stood in the doorway, silhouetted against the lights from inside. "I guess you're feeling better?"

"What?" Belatedly, Emily remembered she was supposed to be recovering from exhaustion. "I'm fine. Great, in fact."

Life had been so blessedly simple when her only problem was taking care of Pookie and getting through each day. It was easy, but empty. She didn't regret knowing Jordan.

"Are you going back to your cabin?" Yvonne asked.

"Yes." She needed a return to normalcy to replenish her spirits. "But I have to talk to you about something."

"Come on inside. John had to work late, so the kids picked dinner. Mac and cheese. I'm having a salad."

"Can I bring Pookie?"

Yvonne scowled and spoke directly to the dog. "Don't bark. Don't cause trouble with the other two dogs who are already in the house. Understand?"

"Moof," Pookie quietly replied.

The interior of the Hanson household was warm and pleasantly chaotic with four children and two dogs. Libby the Brownie was the oldest. She bounced up to Emily and grinned. "I like your dog. He's goofy."

Pookie's tongue flopped out of his mouth and he bobbed his head in agreement. His entire body wagged as he approached Libby for a pat on the head.

"Undisciplined," Yvonne pronounced. "If you want Pookie to be a rescue dog, you need to start training him now."

She dished up a bowl of salad for Emily and ordered the children back to the table where they fidgeted, chattered, nudged and giggled, occasionally taking a bite of the glaringly orange macaroni and cheese.

"So?" Yvonne questioned, "what do you need to talk about?"

"I've been invited to a party in Aspen tomorrow night, and I don't know what to wear."

"Well, la-di-da! A party in Aspen! Who invited you?"

"Brian Afton."

Yvonne scowled. With a glance at the kids, she asked, "Is this the house where the *M-U-R-D-E-R* took place?"

"Murder," Libby said, translating her mother's spelling for her younger siblings. "Mom's talking about murder."

"I'm going to murder you," Yvonne said, "if you don't eat that dinner."

Turning toward Libby, Emily changed the subject. "What do you think I should wear to a fancy party?"

"Pink," she said as if it were the most obvious answer in the world.

Yvonne reclaimed the conversation. "Is this a sit-down dinner or cocktail party?"

"He called it a get-together, so I assume it's fairly casual. But it is Aspen."

"Right. Most people who live there spend more for their boots than I put out for my mortgage payment." Yvonne chewed thoughtfully. "Stick with the Western look. Wear your dress-up cowboy boots with black Levi's and a silk blouse. I've got a Western-cut blazer you can borrow."

Emily speared a cherry tomato, realizing that she hadn't eaten since lunchtime and was hungry for more than a salad. "What about jewelry?"

"I have some costume jewelry, but these are people who can spot a cubic zirconia at a hundred yards. Have you got anything real?"

The only genuine gemstone Emily possessed was a

yellow diamond on an old-fashioned platinum locket with matching chain. A family heirloom, it was given to her on her twenty-first birthday by her mother. Inside the locket was a picture of Emily's father. She never wore the necklace; it always felt too heavy around her throat. "I have a diamond."

"Then, you're all set," Yvonne said. "I've actually been to that house. It's fabulous."

Vaguely, Emily recalled Yvonne mentioning a visit to the Afton Château. "You said it was a kid thing?"

"It was after I did a demonstration in Aspen with the rescue dogs. This adorable little Latino girl couldn't stop petting and hugging the dogs. Her name was Isabel, just as sweet as she could be. She couldn't speak much English and seemed lonely."

Emily smiled. It was so typical for Yvonne the Earth Mother to take a special interest in a sad child who loved animals. "What happened next?"

"After everybody else had left, it was obvious that Isabel and her mother didn't have a ride home. The mom looked a little bit pregnant and a little bit queasy, so I gave them a ride."

"When was this?"

"The beginning of the summer. Probably a month before the you-know-what," Yvonne said with a glance at Libby. "Anyway, they were visiting the housekeeper, Rita Ramirez, and she gave me a quick tour. Unbelievable house. It's huge."

Emily turned this new piece of information over in her mind. Jordan hadn't mentioned anyone else living in the house, and it seemed important in light of the art thefts. But maybe Isabel and her mother had only stayed for a few days.

After the children had finished eating and dispersed to

their various evening tasks, Yvonne served her a cup of strong, black coffee and a thick slab of homemade apple pie. In a quiet voice, she said, "I'm worried about you, Emily."

"Don't you have enough to keep you busy?" Emily attacked the pie. "This is delicious."

"You know what I mean," Yvonne said. "I've never known you to be sick, and you've been holed up at Spence's apartment for nearly a week."

"Five days," Emily said. Five long days. "But I'm better now."

"How did you get yourself invited to the Afton house? Excuse me for noticing, but you're not exactly one of the jet-setting crowd."

"I bumped into Brian Afton," Emily explained, "and he asked me."

"Why?"

A good question. What did Brian Afton want from her? She took another huge bite of the pie. "Maybe he thinks I'd be good for conversation, having just been a hostage and all."

Yvonne shook her head. "Your opinion that Jordan is innocent won't be real popular. What's really going on? What have you gotten yourself into?"

Emily hesitated with her mouth full of sweet, flaky pie crust. Her life had gotten so complicated. She couldn't reveal the truth, but she couldn't lie. She swallowed. "I'm doing the right thing, Yvonne. You'll just have to trust me."

All four kids and Pookie dashed into the kitchen. The children chattered all at once and pointed. Pookie made moofing noises and chased his tail.

"Stop it!" Yvonne silenced them. "Libby, what is it?"

"A police car! In front of the house! The lights are going round and round and round and—"

"That's enough," Yvonne cut her off. She reached over and patted Emily's arm. "No matter what happens, kiddo, I'm behind you a hundred percent."

Emily rose to her feet. "I'll go see what they want."

Standing on Yvonne's doorstep, Emily recognized the square shoulders of Deputy Frank Kreiger, striding toward her. She ought to be glad for another opportunity to talk to a suspect, but a dark, ominous wave of foreboding swept over her. In a falsely friendly voice, she called out, "Can I help you?"

"I thought I recognized your Land Rover," he said. "I'd like to ask you a few questions, Emily."

Yvonne stepped onto the porch, shoulder-to-shoulder beside her. "Are you going to arrest my friend?"

"Arrest me?" Shocked, Emily stared at Yvonne. "Why would you think I was going to be—"

"Don't worry." Yvonne winked. "If they put you in jail, I'll have the Brownies bake you a cake with a file inside."

"Is there a badge for that?"

"You bet." Yvonne turned a baleful glare at Deputy Kreiger. "It's called loyalty. When you work together, when you save lives together, you learn all about loyalty. Do you know what I mean, Kreiger?"

He nodded. Though he didn't back down, Emily thought he looked uncomfortable as he removed his cap and raked his hand through his short blond hair.

She said, "I'm not going to get arrested, Yvonne, because I haven't done anything wrong." Except for aiding and abetting an escaped convict. She turned to Kreiger. "You weren't planning to take me into custody, were you?"

"Just a couple of questions. Come with me."

As Emily accompanied him down the sidewalk to the gate, Yvonne called after them. "Turn off those cop lights, Kreiger. You're getting the kids all excited."

"Right away," he shouted back to her. To Emily, he said, "Yvonne seems worried about you."

"Does she need to be?"

"Not when you're with me." He avoided looking at her. "You're safe with me, Emily. I'm a deputy."

As they approached his vehicle, she noticed someone else sitting in the front seat. Kreiger reached inside and turned off the red and blue flashing lights. The other man stepped out and walked toward her.

"Emily," Kreiger said, "I'd like you to meet Sean Madigan."

Chapter Twelve

Though the porchlight from Yvonne's house was too far away to clearly illuminate the face of Sean Madigan, Emily didn't like what she saw. He was large and muscular, but his face was thin. His sharp features cast hard-edged shadows below his cheekbones and jawline, giving him a skull-like appearance. His most remarkable characteristic was the dark, russet color of his thick hair, pulled back in a ponytail. When he shook her hand, his grip pinched.

"You're the Olympic skier," she said, wishing that small talk would suffice.

"I made the team eight years ago, but I was injured before the competition."

Deputy Kreiger cleared his throat. Again, she had the impression that he was uncomfortable. "It's too bad you never got your chance, Sean. Bad luck."

"Bad coaching," Madigan corrected sharply. "I never should've been out skiing in those conditions."

His comment confirmed Emily's negative impression. She didn't believe in blaming other people for your misfortunes. To be sure, Sean Madigan was an unpleasant person. But was he a murderer? Had he turned a gun against the woman he once had loved?

Such betrayal would require a coldness, an almost inhuman disregard for emotion. But Madigan's deep-set blue eyes glowed like hot embers as he stared. There wasn't much going on behind those eyes. He was dangerously stupid.

Instinctively, she recoiled from him, wrapping her arms around her body as if to protect her delicate inner organs from sudden, vicious attack.

Turning toward Kreiger, who was a paragon of sanity in comparison to his friend, she asked, "What did you want to ask me about?"

"You went to Aspen today," he said, "to visit Ed Collins in the hospital. I wasn't aware that you and Collins were close."

"I always feel a connection to someone after I've saved their life." Emily infused a chiding tone into her voice, hoping to hide the fact that she felt intimidated by these two men. "I wanted to see how he was recuperating."

"And how's he doing?" Kreiger asked. "In your professional opinion."

"As well as can be expected. Knee injuries are always unpredictable."

"What did you talk about?"

"This and that." *You. We talked about how you offered a bounty.* Emily bit her lip, grateful for the dim light that hopefully masked her deception. "Nothing important."

"Collins isn't a great example of law enforcement in Pitkin County." Kreiger fidgeted, adjusted the brim on his hat. It appeared that—like her—he was trying to hide his expression. "I probably shouldn't say this, but he's been known to invent stories to save his own—"

"Don't," she interrupted abruptly. Though her own statements verged on falsehood, she was quick to recognize a lie from Kreiger. He was about to deny the bounty, to say it was a fantasy of Ed Collins's devious mind. "Don't say it."

"What?"

She knew he'd been involved with offering the bounty. Also, Kreiger had been the one who'd removed Jordan's handcuffs at the airport so he must have been part of setting up the escape attempt. He wasn't a man to be trusted.

Yet, she believed he was, at his core, a decent, hard-working cop. She'd seen him on the job. On Search and Rescue operations, Kreiger was fearless, ready to risk his own life to rescue someone else. Possibly she could touch that part of him. "You might have made some mistakes, but it's never too late to change your mind."

"Mistakes?" Madigan inserted himself into the conversation. "What mistakes are you talking about?"

His hostile tone startled her, and she almost blurted out the words on the tip of her tongue. *The bounty.*

Nervously, she lowered her gaze, not even wanting to look at Madigan. He was so intense, predatory, ready to leap down her throat. She had no idea how to handle him.

"Emily?" Kreiger said encouragingly. "What are you talking about?"

Her eyes pleaded with him. Offering a dead-or-alive reward was wrong. Kreiger knew it. He knew he'd stepped outside the boundaries of law enforcement protocol. If she'd been alone with him, she would've mentioned the bounty. But the presence of Madigan changed everything.

Hiding her tension with a shrug, Emily said, "I just don't think you'd want to bad-mouth another deputy."

"Collins is an ass," Madigan said. "He had a clear shot at Mammoth Rock, and he blew it."

"How do you know that?" she asked.

"I went there. Checked it out." He sighted down an invisible rifle, followed his prey and pulled the trigger. "I wouldn't have missed."

His demonstration chilled her. Madigan would've gunned down Jordan in cold blood.

"That's what Jordan Shane deserves," he said. "He's a murderer."

Emily could have argued, but she was afraid. If she crossed swords with Sean Madigan, she might come away dead. Again, she turned to Kreiger. "Any more questions?"

"After you left Collins's room, you didn't return to your Land Rover. In fact, you were gone so long that you got a parking ticket. Where were you?"

"Shopping," Emily blurted. It wasn't totally false. She'd walked past the boutiques and looked in the windows. "I was shopping."

"Where?"

"Downtown Aspen. I walked. Parking is always such a hassle."

A fake chuckle caught in her throat. She didn't dare think about where she'd been for those hours. In Jordan's mine shaft hideaway. Making love. She couldn't allow any glimmer of the truth to show.

"You're lying," Madigan said.

Panic surged inside her, racing her heartbeat. Her

words tumbled out in a rush. "I'd just been invited to a get-together by Brian Afton, and I thought maybe I should buy something new. So, I looked at lots of stuff, but I didn't find anything."

"Liar," Madigan accused. He reminded her of a schoolyard bully, big and stupid and mean.

"I looked at things." Her voice grew louder, more defensive. "I can't afford Aspen prices."

"Liar, where were you?"

"Knock it off, Sean." Kreiger stepped forward. "I'm asking the questions here."

"Then ask her. Quit tippy-toeing."

"Don't tell me how to do my job."

Though Madigan took a step back and raised his palms in an elaborately sarcastic hands-off gesture, his attitude was clearly challenging. "Then do it, Kreiger. Do your damned job."

"It's okay, Emily," Kreiger said.

His tone was gentle—maybe *too* gentle. Were they working a good-cop-bad-cop routine? If so, their ruse was working. She felt off-balance, teetering on the brink of confusion and fear.

"Emily, I need to ask you these questions because I'm following every lead. I don't mean to insult your integrity. Do you understand?"

"I think so." She cringed inside, fearing what he might ask next. She felt incapable of another lie.

"Do you have any information," Kreiger asked, "that might lead to the whereabouts of Jordan Shane?"

"No." The word slipped past her lips. In other interrogations, she'd been careful to phrase every answer to contain a germ of truth. She'd been misleading. Now she was an outright liar. Her complicity with Jordan was now a fact and a felony.

Kreiger nodded and smiled. "That's all I needed to know. Sorry for disturbing your evening."

The deputy started back toward his vehicle, but Madigan didn't follow. Menacing, he leaned toward her, so close that she could feel the fetid heat of his body. Fear wrapped around her like a shroud.

In a low, dangerous voice, he said, "I'll be keeping an eye on you, Emily."

AND I'M KEEPING an eye on you. Through night-vision goggles, Jordan watched the A-frame guest house where Sean Madigan lived. Last night, Madigan had threatened Emily. Tonight, while Brian hosted his get-together, Jordan needed to make sure that red-haired bastard wouldn't come near her again.

Earlier this morning, when he'd read Emily's e-mail recounting her conversation outside Yvonne's house, Jordan's blood boiled. Impotent rage clenched his muscles so tight they hurt. He couldn't abide the thought of Emily being harassed or accused. She was purely innocent, doing the right thing.

Madigan had no cause to come after her. His approach was sleazy, hiding behind his friend, the deputy. And he scared Emily. Though she downplayed her fear, Jordan read between the lines. He imagined her facing two dangerous men in the night. Revenge, he wanted revenge. He wanted to throw back his head and roar, to hunt Madigan down and make him pay. But Jordan had to stay hidden.

The inability to fight back tore at the fabric of his character, and there was no amount of logic that could heal his helpless fury. What kind of man was he? How could he send Emily into danger?

He wrote back to her, "Forget the party. Don't go."

She responded, "I already have an outfit to wear. I'm there."

He didn't argue. There was no point. She'd made up her mind and wouldn't be swayed. But he couldn't allow her to proceed without his protection.

With the security systems relaxed for guests to arrive, he'd entered the grounds outside the well-lit granite-walled château. Two square miles of landscaped terrain surrounded the house itself. Beyond the property line was natural forest, protected by city covenant.

Jordan had left the Harley in the forest, camouflaged behind shrubs, and approached through the forest, moving as silently as the whisper of cold September wind through the evergreens. Was it only a week ago that he'd stumbled on the forest paths, clumsy as a heifer in snowshoes? He'd adapted to his surroundings. He still hated these cold mountains, but he'd learned how to survive.

From his current vantage point, he could see the vehicles pull up and park on the circular drive. It appeared that this little "get-together" included over thirty people and a caterer. His night-vision goggles focused on the guest cabin that Madigan hoped to inherit, outlining every detail in infrared.

Jordan moved closer, took off the goggles. With his naked eye, he stared through an unshaded window. Inside, he saw Madigan, shirtless with his dark red hair hanging loose past his shoulders. He walked with an athletic strut. His chest puffed out. He must've been working out because his pecs were taut. His flat belly looked hard as a ridged washboard. Even when nobody was looking, Madigan posed and postured.

Through the receiver in his ear, Jordan heard Emily's voice.

"Okay, I've activated the wire. Jordan, can you hear me? I wish there were some way to make sure."

They'd tested the transmitter earlier today, and it worked perfectly. Though he'd considered giving her a receiver so he could communicate with her, the device would be clearly visible in her ear. She could talk to him, but he couldn't respond.

"I'm driving to the house," she said. "Bad news. Spence couldn't come with me. There was a bad car accident outside Cascadia, and he had to respond with medical aid."

Damn. Jordan had been counting on Spence's physical presence at the party to keep Emily safe. Now she was alone, vulnerable.

"Don't worry," she said. "I know where I'm supposed to meet you. At ten forty-five."

He checked his wristwatch. Almost nine o'clock. In an hour and forty-five minutes, they'd planned for her and Spence to leave together. He was supposed to stop at a particular gas station for a fill up while Emily subtly disappeared with Jordan. Now, she'd have to leave her car. Their escape would be obvious.

"Jordan." She spoke his name as gently as a caress. "Be careful."

You, too. From the edge of the dark forest, he watched as Emily parked her Land Rover on the paved circle drive with the other cars—gleaming SUV's manufactured by Cadillac and BMW. She was only fifty yards away from him but separated by a chasm as wide as the Grand

Canyon. He couldn't go to her, couldn't step onto the well-lighted flagstones leading to the house. Jordan was trapped in fugitive darkness.

When she climbed out of the Rover, he thought she looked good in black jeans and a burgundy blazer. Her long, curly hair was tied at her nape with a thick black ribbon.

Jordan's thigh muscles flexed. He ached to sprint toward her, scoop her off her feet and carry her to safety. *Don't go inside.* She was walking into a nest of rattlesnakes.

"Geez," she whispered into the wire. "This is some amazing joint. I can't believe you lived here."

Fists clenched, he watched as she disappeared into the front door. Never before had he been eager to attend one of these get-togethers. He'd give anything to be standing at her side, protecting her from harm.

Crouched beside a tall, thick pine, he listened to Emily's conversations as she mingled with the other guests. Half a dozen times, she was asked the predictable question, "What was it like to be a hostage?"

Her standard response came quickly, "I'd rather not talk about it."

She directed the conversations toward S.A.R. rescues and her EMT work. But mostly, she listened to other people who were only too happy to rattle on about themselves. It all seemed pretty much innocuous. Maybe he'd been overreacting by expecting danger.

He focused on Madigan's cabin. As soon as the arrogant bastard left, Jordan planned to sneak inside and look for proof that Madigan had been stealing artwork from Lynette. Finding receipts was too much to hope for. But maybe there'd be an address for an art dealer or the key to a safe-deposit box, some kind of clue.

While he was in the cabin, Jordan would also plant a listening device. He carried three other bugs in his pocket: two for Brian Afton, and one to be placed in Rita Ramirez's apartment behind the kitchen.

Jordan had been surprised when Emily e-mailed him about the little girl, Isabel, and her mother who had been visiting Rita. He doubted Lynette would approve of the housekeeper having overnight guests. One of the reasons she'd hired Rita was because she had no family in Colorado, and she'd be unlikely to have boyfriends since she was a mature woman and married. Her husband lived in Mexico. Every month, Rita sent him half her paycheck to pay for a farm.

When Emily's e-mail suggested that Rita's guests might have stolen the artwork, Jordan again dismissed the idea. Rita was an honorable woman. He'd spent a lot of time talking with her while he was bored in Colorado, and he deeply regretted that she'd been the one who found him holding Lynette's dead body. Rita was convinced he'd killed his wife.

Through the earpiece receiver, he heard Emily's whispering voice, "Jordan, I'm in the bathroom. Unbelievable! It's bigger than my living room. There's a skylight over the tub which happens to be big enough to swim laps. Why am I telling you this? You lived here."

Good, he thought, she was hiding out in the bathroom. *Stay there, Emily.*

"I said hello to Brian," she continued, "and I met some guy who's on television but I didn't recognize him. Should I be impressed? Kreiger is here, but I haven't seen Madigan yet. I'll keep looking. Bye now."

At nine-thirty, Sean Madigan left the guest house. He stood for a moment on the porch, scanning the area, sniffing the air as if he could smell an intruder.

An overpowering temptation urged Jordan to reveal himself, to step forward and challenge this red-haired man who had been his wife's lover and, possibly, her murderer. It took every effort of his self-control to stay back. *Evidence, he needed evidence.*

Twice, Jordan had been drawn into a trap. He'd been framed. It wouldn't happen again.

Swinging his muscular arms, Madigan strolled along the pathway that led to the flagstone sidewalk by the drive. His house was vacant. This time, Jordan would be smart.

Still listening to Emily making small talk at the party, he approached the modified A-frame cabin which had been built several years after the main house. The cabin was typical of Colorado architecture with shake shingles and cedar walls. Jordan recalled some story about how it had been built in the sixties as a hideaway for the château owner's mistress. Apparently, Lynette had seen fit to continue the tradition.

Though he had a selection of skeleton keys and lockpicks, they were unnecessary. Madigan had left the door unlocked—a sign of incredible arrogance or blatant stupidity. Jordan slipped inside and donned his infrared goggles.

The layout of the A-frame was simple. Upstairs was a sleeping loft. Downstairs was a kitchen, living room, bathroom and a closed room that could be used as a second bedroom. He started with the second bedroom. Madigan had turned it into an exercise room, and it smelled like old sweatsocks. The only furniture was expensive equipment designed to isolate and work muscle groups. Jordan opened the sliding closet doors. Inside were shelves stacked tight with heavy ski sweaters and hanging clothes but nothing else.

In the living room, Jordan went to the Scandinavian-style desk. The furniture in the guest cabin had been spared Lynette's penchant for antiques. Mostly, it was plain with clean simple lines. The desk drawers yielded nothing more interesting than bank statements which Jordan had already checked through Internet hacking. Madigan had made no unusual deposits or withdrawals. His credit card receipts might be useful. Quickly scanning, Jordan found only one with a balance over five thousand dollars. The others were lowball, typical of an itinerant professional ski bum.

Jordan's ears pricked up as he heard Emily say, "Hello, Mr. Madigan."

"I want to talk to you," Madigan growled. "Alone."

"Maybe later," Emily put him off. "I'm in the middle of a discussion with Kiki. She's an artist."

In spite of his tension, Jordan grinned. Kiki Felton could talk the arms off a Hindu Siva statue. He recognized the droning voice, greeting Madigan and mentioning how much she'd like to draw him nude as the Creator intended.

Then Emily piped up, "Do you own any art, Mr. Madigan?"

Jordan pleaded silently. *Don't go there, Emily. Don't provoke him.*

"My body is my art," Madigan said.

What a jerk!

Emily wandered off with Kiki explaining some of the finer pieces in the Afton collection.

In Madigan's cabin, Jordan raced up the stairs and glanced around the open loft bedroom. King-size bed. Two dressers. A table and chairs by the window.

Though his search seemed fruitless, Jordan had the sense that he was missing something, something obvious.

Skis! Where did Madigan keep his skis? Jordan went into the small attached garage. Empty. Madigan's car was parked in front. There had to be another storage area, a place he'd overlooked.

Jordan's ears pricked up as he heard the voice of Brian Afton through the receiver in his ear.

"Emily, so glad you could make it to my little get-together. I've been a poor host, haven't paid enough attention to you."

"I'm having a lovely time," she replied politely. "This is a magnificent house."

"Would you like a tour?"

No, don't go with him.

"Sure," she said. "Why not?"

Jordan told himself that nothing would happen. Brian wouldn't pull anything with a houseful of guests. Emily was in no real physical danger.

But he couldn't help remembering her frozen response when frightened, her flashback to a place she'd never been. He didn't want to put her through that agony again.

A glance at his wristwatch showed forty-five minutes until they were scheduled to meet. Too much time.

He needed to finish his search of the guest house quickly, leave and move closer to the house. Then what? He couldn't walk inside and save her. Kreiger was at the party. And Madigan. Men who wanted to take him into custody or shoot him dead.

With the infrared goggles, Jordan scanned the floorboards, looking for a trapdoor. Every joist fitted perfectly.

He was in the kitchen. Cabinets, appliances, countertops. And a door leading to the walk-in pantry. He twisted the knob. It was locked. Jordan fumbled with the skeleton keys. One of them ought to fit.

He heard Brian's voice. "There are original paintings by some local artists upstairs. Come along, Emily."

"Maybe we should take Kiki with us."

Good thinking, Emily. Jordan twisted the key in the lock. The pantry door opened.

"Kiki has been here before," Brian said. "If I didn't know better, Emily, I'd think you were afraid to be alone with me."

"Do I have a reason to be afraid?"

"Of course not."

"I'd love to see the upstairs," she said. "But first, I need to stop at the little girl's room. I'll be right back."

Relief spread through him. She could hide out in the bathroom for a while. She'd be safe.

The pantry was long and narrow. Half a dozen pairs of skis were stacked near the front. At the rear, flat against the wall was a four foot square safe. "Damn it."

Jordan had no safe-cracking equipment with him. He should have thought ahead, should have realized that Madigan hadn't deposited the money from the stolen artwork in his bank account. He'd kept the cash locked away in the safe where it couldn't be tracked by computer.

"Jordan," Emily's voice came over the receiver. "It's me. I'm in the bathroom again. I'm going to have a private talk with Brian. After all, that's why I came to this party. If it doesn't go well, I'm going to leave early. I'll just go to the gas station and wait for you."

Not a good idea, His simple logical plans crumbled around him. He closed and locked the door to the pantry in Madigan's cabin. Moving fast, he left the guest house and went back into the night. If he could plant the bugs, the night wouldn't be a total waste.

Jordan eased through the forests, looking out at the landscaped yard that was mostly brown and frozen though the recent snow had melted.

Through the receiver, he heard Emily talking to Brian again. But their tour was interrupted. Brian had been caught up in hosting duties. The noise level around her increased. *What the hell was going on?*

"Oh my God," Emily said, "Sean Madigan and Frank Kreiger are having a shoving match."

Jordan was sure her remark had been for his benefit. He headed around to the back side of the house where the forest was thick.

"I can't believe it," Emily said, "Kreiger took a swing at Madigan. This isn't a fair matchup. Madigan is a lot taller with a longer reach."

She sounded like a doggoned ringside sports announcer.

The crowd noise made it difficult for him to pick out her voice. Actually, this diversion worked in Jordan's favor. All the partygoers would be preoccupied with watching the fight. He'd have a better chance of approaching the house unseen.

He perched high on a hillside, scanning with his infrared night vision, planning his approach. His gaze travelled upward. On the roof of the three-story stone château were two uniformed snipers.

Again, they'd set up a trap for him. And Emily was the bait.

AFTER THE FIGHT, Emily glanced at her wristwatch. It was ten-fifteen. She might be exactly on time to meet Jordan, after all. But she wanted to leave now.

There was an unmistakeable aura of danger at this party. The beautifully catered food turned her stomach. The chatter seemed threatening and distorted.

Jordan had been right. She never should have come here.

"There you are," said Brian Afton. "Not to worry, Emily. I asked Kreiger to leave, and he went quietly. Just a little altercation. Boys will be boys, you know."

Neither Kreiger nor Madigan had looked the least bit boyish. Whatever had sparked their argument was not a joke. She remembered her earlier impression that Kreiger had been in love with Lynette. And Madigan had been her lover. It was amazing that the two of them were friends at all. "I should be going," she said.

"Nonsense. We'll complete our tour." He lightly touched her elbow to guide her. "Upstairs."

He didn't frighten her the way Madigan did. Brian was carefully affable and not offensive. With his perfectly groomed black hair and expensive cashmere sweater, he didn't look like he would physically harm anyone.

And yet, as she ascended the sweeping marble staircase passing the atrium foyer and a high, twinkling crystal chandelier, she felt like she was climbing the gallows.

At the top of the staircase, Emily was glad she wasn't prone to vertigo. A long cherrywood railing was all that separated the long upstairs hallway from a twenty-foot fall onto the marble-floored atrium below. Brian led her to the other side where a row of paintings hung above wainscoting.

He carefully explained each piece, pointing out the

finer points of brushstrokes and perspective. His continuous monologue had a calming effect on her. "You certainly know your artwork," she said.

"At one time, I considered painting as a career," he said. "I was never an effective businessperson like my sister was. Perhaps, once this affair is settled, I'll try my hand at painting once again."

"After this affair is settled?" she questioned. "You mean, once the murderer is convicted."

"Yes, the murder." His blue eyes, so startling in contrast to his black hair, regarded her coldly as if she were an annoying raccoon overturning a trash can. His lack of emotion while talking about his sister's murder worried her. Emily had dealt with enough bereaved families to know how they usually reacted. Even now, two months later, Brian should be feeling the pain.

She asked, "Do you miss Lynette?"

"Interesting question." He guided her a few steps farther down the hallway toward a pair of closed double doors. "We were never terribly close. Lynette excelled at everything from being prom queen to her straight-A report cards. Perhaps, I resented her success."

Enough to kill her? Brian had stepped into a very glamorous lifestyle by inheriting his sister's estate.

"I know what you're thinking," he said in a teasing sing-song voice. "You're wondering if I murdered her."

Her stomach wrenched. This was the moment she'd been waiting for. Solid proof. A confession. But she feared the answer. If he confessed to her, what would he do next?

"Well, Emily, I'll put you out of your suspense. Did I murder Lynette? The answer is…no."

Could she believe him? "We don't have to talk about this, Brian."

"But I want to. I have a little secret to confide. Due to some complicated legal and accounting issues, I am prohibited from selling any part of Lynette's estate until after Jordan's trial. There's some confusion about his ten percent of the inheritance which is to be held in escrow. To be perfectly honest, I don't care if he's guilty or not. I merely want the issue settled."

"He's innocent," she said quietly.

"And you care about him," Brian said. "There's something going on between the two of you."

"No."

"Don't bother to deny it. Everyone has guessed, even the dim-witted deputies. And that's why you're here, Emily. I'm expecting Jordan to come here and gallantly rescue you."

Apprehension clenched inside her, tying her stomach into a hard, painful knot. "Why should I need rescuing?"

"Because you're going to be arrested." For the first time, she saw emotion in his face. He was amused, almost laughing at her. "You've been aiding and abetting an escaped convict, haven't you?"

The thought of jail didn't scare her. As long as she knew she was doing the right thing, she could endure anything. Hadn't her father been unjustly imprisoned in a POW camp in Vietnam?

Swallowing hard, she clung to the last threads of composure. "Supposing you were right, how would you plan to capture Jordan?"

"I'm well prepared. Among the guests at this party are several trained security guards. Oh yes, and there are snipers on the roof."

"Snipers? I thought you wanted Jordan to go to trial."

"If he's dead, the inheritance issues will be settled just as neatly."

Emily drew the logical conclusion. "You're the one who offered the bounty."

"Indeed I did. Ten thousand dollars is a small price to pay." He flung open the double doors. "Our tour of the house wouldn't be complete without this. Lynette's sitting room and bedroom."

White walls, mirrors and dramatically lit paintings surrounded her. White furniture and white carpet blurred her vision as if she were snow-blind. She wasn't afraid for herself but for Jordan. If he came too close to the house, he'd be shot. The only way he'd escape was if he'd been listening to the wire, knowing about the ambush. She prayed he'd be smart enough to run away.

Brian held her arm, propelling her forward, through another door to the bedroom. More white overwhelmed her. On the carpet at the foot of the bed was a dark rust-colored stain.

Brian said, "According to the coroner, death came in an instant. She didn't suffer. Even in dying, Lynette was admirably efficient."

"I'm going to be sick." Emily clapped her hand over her mouth. Her stomach heaved.

"That way." Brian pointed. "That's the bathroom."

She ran inside, locked the door and barely made it to the toilet before she vomited.

Kneeling on the white carpeted floor, Emily felt weak and helpless. Why had she insisted on coming to this place? Instead of helping Jordan, she'd led him into a trap. She whispered into the wire. "Please be smart. Get away from here before they kill you."

Gathering her strength with a few deep breaths, Emily knew she had to act immediately or else she'd be taken into custody.

"Emily?" Brian called outside the door.

"Give me a moment."

At the sink she quickly rinsed her mouth and face. She then turned on the faucets full blast and went to the glass French doors trimmed in white, endless white. She unfastened the latch and pushed the doors open. Outside was a long terraced balcony with a table and two chairs.

Brian knew the architecture of the house. If she was going to escape, she had not a moment to waste. Emily slipped outside. She slung her leg over the railing, wishing that she'd worn her climbing shoes instead of the slick-soled cowboy boots. Quickly, she lowered herself on the outer side of the balcony. Clinging to the railing, she gritted her teeth and prepared to drop. From her boots to the ground, it was probably ten feet. A dangerous height. She could sprain an ankle.

"Let go," said a voice below her. "I'll catch you."

She released her grip and fell into Jordan's waiting arms.

Chapter Thirteen

Thrilled and terrified at the same time, Emily wrapped her arms around his neck. In Jordan's rich brown eyes, she saw nothing but truth. In his embrace, she felt protected. He wouldn't let them arrest her. But how could he stop the army of hired guns who were after them?

"Nice boots," he said.

She couldn't guess at the logical meaning behind those two words. "Yes."

"How fast do they run?"

"I can keep up."

He squeezed her once and let her go. "Follow me."

Avoiding direct light as much as possible, he stayed close to the walls of the house, running in a crouch, seeking cover behind the landscaping as they put distance between themselves and the balcony. At the edge of a wall, he stopped, glanced around the corner and ducked back beside her.

She stared longingly at the forest that seemed so close. "Let's make a run for the trees. We'll have a better chance in the forest."

"There are snipers on the roof. As soon as we step away from the house, we'll be in their range of fire."

Emily knew these gunmen were sharpshooters, nothing

like Ed Collins. They'd been hired by Brian, and he had the financial resources to buy the best. "We've got to get away from here. Brian hired—"

"I know," he whispered. "I heard everything over the wire. That's why I was ready to catch you when you came onto the balcony."

She hadn't really considered how or why he'd been waiting for her. It was enough that he'd magically appeared when she needed him. "Do you have a plan?"

"Always," he said.

She waited for him to explain, but he said nothing more. "Do you mind telling me what it is?"

"We're near the kitchen," Jordan said quietly. "There's more activity here. Servers coming and going. They won't expect us to be here."

"For good reason," she whispered back.

"If we can make it to one of the catering vans, I'll hot-wire it. Or we can hide in the back."

As plans went, it wasn't much, but she had no better idea. They couldn't risk stepping into the open. Even if they weren't gunned down, the men on the roof would see them. Their pursuers were too close and too well-armed for them to get away.

He peeked around the edge again. "Okay, nobody's out there. Let's go."

She shadowed his movements across the paved service area behind the house. There were no decorative flagstones, only functional asphalt. He turned the rear handle on the van.

Before he could open it, Emily heard footsteps. She turned and faced a stern-looking Hispanic woman who wore a gray-and-white maid's uniform. She looked past Emily to Jordan.

"Rita," he said. *"Buenos noches."*

"Jordan," she said.

Emily braced herself, waiting for the housekeeper to shout for help. Of all the people who believed Jordan had killed his wife, Rita Ramirez had been the most adamant. She'd discovered him standing over the body. She had sworn repeatedly that no one else was in the house.

"I was wrong," she said. "Come with me."

"What?" Emily breathed the question.

"He is innocent." Rita nodded toward the house. "Quickly."

They went through a small windowed door to the left of the main service entrance and down a flight of stone stairs. While they walked through a maze of underground corridors, Jordan and Rita carried on a hushed conversation in Spanish. Though Emily couldn't completely understand their rapid-fire words, she heard the name Isabel. Were they talking about the little girl Yvonne had mentioned?

In the depths of the basement, Rita pulled open a crude wooden door on squeaky hinges. She took a ring of keys from her pocket, removed one and pressed it into Jordan's hand. In English, she said, "I am sorry. I didn't know."

"Take care of Isabel and her mother," he said.

Grasping Emily's hand, he guided her into the wine cellar beneath the house. The light from two naked bulbs illuminated a spacious room with slanted wine racks on either side. Nearly every slot was filled.

Quickly, Jordan took her to the far end where there was an arched entryway. A locked door of fancy metal grillwork separated this smaller room from the rest of the cellar. Jordan used the key, opened the grillwork and guided her inside. Then he signalled to Rita.

She turned off the light, plunging them into total darkness.

"I have a flashlight," Jordan said. The narrow glow from a pocket-size light cut through the blackness. He handed it to her. "If you hear or see anything, turn it off."

He pulled the grillwork closed, locking them into a narrow space with another wine rack and shelves with bottles. "This is the really good stuff," Jordan explained. "Hundred-year-old cognac. Wine that costs upwards of a thousand a bottle."

"It seems wasteful to pay so much for alcohol," she said. "Was your wife a big drinker?"

"She was big on entertaining. The perfect wine to complement the perfect meal." He moved to the side of the stone arch. "There's just enough room here for us to flatten up against the wall if anybody comes down here to search."

"Without the key," she said, "they can't come in here."

"That's the plan."

She slid down the wall and sat on the concrete floor. Though she was anxious to hear what Rita had told him, Emily also felt a sense of foreboding. Their situation was about to get even more treacherous. She cleared her throat. "It's not damp or musty like I expect it to be in a basement."

"The temperature and humidity are controlled." He sat beside her. "It's one of Rita's jobs to check it twice a day."

She held the flashlight so she could see his face. "Can we trust her?"

"Yes." He leaned toward her and lightly kissed her lips. The gesture was meant to be sweet and reassuring, but his kiss deepened. Her hunger for him had not been changed by threat or danger.

She twisted her body to face him in a seated embrace. Her cheek rested against his broad chest.

"It's almost over." He softly stroked her hair. "If we can make it through tonight, we'll be safe."

Though she desperately wanted to believe him, her mind stayed attuned to danger. Her heart still fluttered. If she closed her eyes too tightly, panic would rush in and overwhelm her. "What did Rita tell you?"

"On the night of the murder, Isabel and her pregnant mother were here at the house. The mother is Rita's niece from Mexico."

"Illegal aliens," Emily guessed. "That's why Rita was hiding them."

"She wants them to go back to Mexico. To follow the proper procedures. But the mother, Teresa, refuses to go. It's her dream—right or wrong—for her baby to be born in this country."

"I understand." Immigration laws were not to be thwarted, but she could easily comprehend a mother's fervent desire to give her children the best life possible.

"Isabel and Teresa came back here a couple of weeks ago. That's when Rita discovered the child was having nightmares. She talked about being chased by a monster called Roboso. He had a gun. He killed people."

"She witnessed something."

"Rita finally figured it out. Even though the little girl was forbidden to leave Rita's apartment behind the kitchen, she loved to sneak into the big house after everyone was asleep. She saw the murderer. She followed him up the stairs. She might even have seen him kill Lynette."

Emily's heart ached for this traumatized child. "Ro-boso?"

"Fractured Spanish," he said. "*Roja* meaning red. And *oso* meaning bear. The red bear."

She thought of long russet hair, pulled back in a po-nytail. "Madigan."

"He killed Lynette."

"Why didn't Rita come forward as soon as she figured this out?"

"Teresa refused. She's nine months' pregnant. Any minute now, she could have the baby. After that, she'll let her daughter testify."

Though Emily didn't want to drag mother and child through the ordeal of police questioning and probable deportation, they couldn't wait. "Childbearing is an in-exact procedure," she said. "The mother could be wrong about the timing. This could take weeks. We don't have that much time, Jordan."

"I know," he said.

Jordan felt the danger closing in, tightening around them. He'd heard Brian's threats over the wire. Emily could be arrested.

Leaning forward, he kissed the top of her head. Her hair smelled fresh and clean. He couldn't allow anything bad to happen to her. At the same time, he didn't want to cause further stress for Isabel and her mother. They, too, had been living the fugitive life.

There had to be a way to show Isabel's testimony and still not deliver them to police custody. "Videotape," he said.

She wriggled against his chest and lightly punched his arm. "You have to quit doing that, Jordan."

"Doing what?"

"Blurting out one or two words and expecting me to understand. What about videotape?"

"We can videotape Isabel's testimony and turn it over to the sheriff. It ought to be enough to get me off the hook."

"We couldn't do it," she said. "Not you and me. Nobody would believe evidence from us."

"Right. We need somebody to ask the questions and verify that we're not coercing the child."

"Kreiger," she said.

"No way. Kreiger had to be involved with pushing me into an escape at the airport. He's buddies with Madigan."

"Not after their shoving match tonight," Emily reminded. "I think Kreiger got sucked into cooperating with Madigan because he truly believed you killed Lynette, and he secretly loved her. He wanted to see you dead."

"Which is exactly why I don't want to be friends with the guy."

"I still think he's a decent human being. He made a mistake."

"His little error in judgment almost got me killed." Jordan repeated, "No way. Not Kreiger."

They'd find someone else, someone reputable. At least, they had a plan: Videotape Isabel's testimony about the red bear who crept through the house and killed Lynette.

The sheriff would have to investigate Madigan.

"I don't suppose," Emily murmured, "that you found any other evidence against Madigan."

"I didn't." He sighed. "I searched at the guest cabin, looking for something that could connect him to the theft of artwork, but he outsmarted me."

"I find that hard to believe. You're practically a genius, and Madigan's a dangerous, horrible idiot."

"There's a safe at his house. I'm assuming that inside the safe is cash. Real money is untraceable. It doesn't leave a paper trail that I can follow by computer. I can't prove his cash came from the sale of Lynette's stolen artwork."

He hugged her more tightly against him. "It's ironic. All of my sophisticated computer tools couldn't solve this murder. Dozens of detectives and searchers couldn't find the right answer. It all comes down to a little girl's nightmare."

The outer door to the wine cellar creaked open. Jordan reacted immediately to the sound. He clicked off the flashlight, moved Emily off his lap and against the stone wall beside him.

The bare lightbulbs came on. Carefully, silently, he and Emily stood, flattening themselves against the wall, hiding inside the shadow.

Voices echoed in the cellar. He heard Brian Afton, "Be careful down here. These bottles mustn't be disturbed in any way."

Jordan heard the sound of boot heels against concrete. A rattling noise jangled the air.

"Watch where you're going!" Brian snapped.

"Doesn't look like anybody's here, boss."

One of the searchers stood just outside the grillwork gate. Jordan could feel his presence, could hear his breathing. The searcher said, "Hey, what's back here."

"Get away from there," Brian said harshly. "Any one of those bottles is worth more than your miserable life."

"Got a key?"

"Just look inside. Do you see anyone? No, you don't. Let's move on."

The searcher grabbed the metal grill and shook it against the lock. Jordan tensed. Beside him, he felt Emily freeze.

INSIDE HER HEAD, Emily saw a field of tall grass, swirling in the wind like a whirlpool. The roar of an Apache helicopter assaulted her ears. She felt herself being sucked deeper and deeper, coming too close to the army green chopper.

The grass parted. There were uniformed men on the ground bleeding, screaming for help.

"Medic!"

She saw the flare of gunfire. The clouds overhead exploded in garish orange and black. The trees flamed into giant torches.

She fell to the earth. When she looked up she saw a thatched roof village, burning. People were running everywhere.

"Medic!"

A uniformed man in a helmet stepped out of the trees. He was carrying a white metal box with a red cross.

From faraway, she heard Jordan's voice, calling to her. "Emily, are you all right? Emily, answer me."

She felt her lips move. She heard herself say, "I'm watching a movie. Vietnam. I can see it, Jordan."

"What do you see?" he asked.

There was fire everywhere. The black smoke stung her eyes, but she stared at the man with the red cross. He walked toward her. As he came closer, she saw his face, smeared with grime. He smiled and waved to her.

"It's my father," she said. She recognized him from all the photographs her mother had treasured. He was exactly like the tiny picture she wore in her locket. But he was alive. He was young and strong and alive. "He's coming toward me."

"You can't go with him." It was Jordan's voice again. "You have to stay with me."

"I know."

Her father's face filled her vision, and she felt a gentle serenity, soft as an angel's wing.

"Goodbye, Daddy," she whispered. "I'll always love you."

She blinked. Her eyelids closed for a moment, and she saw only a soothing, velvet darkness. Finally, she was at peace.

When she opened her eyes, she was lying on the concrete floor. Jordan held her. And it wasn't dark anymore.

"It's okay," he said. "They're gone. Nobody's going to hurt you."

"The lights?"

"Brian forgot to turn them off. How are you feeling?"

"I'm all right." She'd had a chance to say goodbye. "I'm fine."

"You don't have to get up. We'll stay here until Rita tells us it's okay to come out."

She snuggled up against him, content to be in his arms as he arranged himself more comfortably against the stone wall in the wine cellar. Her arm stretched across his chest. She knew him so well, so intimately.

Being with him had forced her to touch the deepest part of herself, the unremembered dreams, the nightmares. Yet she knew that soon she would be saying goodbye to Jordan.

"When this is over," she said, "what will you do?"

"I'll go home."

"To Florida."

"That's where my home is." He trailed his fingers along the line of her jaw. "I want you to come with me."

"I can't live there. It's too hot," she said. "Not to mention the snakes."

"Trust me, Em. It's a helluva lot safer in Florida than here."

She sounded the familiar refrain, "You haven't given Colorado a chance."

"I could say the same about you and Florida."

She didn't bother to argue. Jordan was a southern gentleman, and she would never convince him to live with her in the mountains.

After this was over, they might try a long distance relationship. Lots of couples managed to live far apart.

But Emily didn't want to live separate lives. The career path no longer held much interest for her. She wanted marriage, a family, children of her own. It was a lot to ask from him. Maybe...too much.

Jordan stretched out a long arm and picked a bottle off the shelf. "What would you say to a sip of hundred-year-old cognac."

"That would really upset Brian."

"I know," he said.

She flashed Jordan an evil grin. "Go ahead and break the seal."

JORDAN AWOKE to the sudden loud rattling of the metal grillwork. He heard Rita's voice, "Come with me," she demanded. "Quickly. Teresa is having her baby."

"A baby?" He groaned.

Last night, after a few sips of the fine, smooth cognac, he had stretched out on the concrete floor, using his jacket as a pillow and cuddling Emily in his arms.

"Jordan!" Rita shook the grillwork again. "Hurry."

Emily poked his shoulder. "Give me the key."

"What are you going to do?"

"I'm a nurse, Jordan. I can deliver a baby."

He kept the key in his hand. "Hold on, ladies. We still have to be careful. Rita, is Brian in the house?"

"He left early to search."

The search would, once again, be in full gear. "Has the sheriff's department mobilized?"

"*Si,*" she said hastily. "*Madre de dios,* Jordan. We're safe here. The doors are locked. Security is in place. Hurry! Now! Teresa needs help."

Reluctantly, he turned over the key and followed the two women upstairs to Rita's apartment behind the kitchen. Jordan had always liked visiting Rita. The furnishings in her simple one-bedroom apartment with kitchenette contrasted the sterile antiques and art in the rest of the house. In Rita's apartment, there was color, dozens of portraits of family, a guitar, hand-embroidered pillows and postcards from Mexico stuck to the refrigerator with magnets.

While the two women bustled into the bedroom and closed the door, Jordan confronted a big-eyed girl with a long, black braid. She perched on the edge of the sofa, looking very worried. "Are you Isabel?"

"*Si.*"

"*Quantos anos tiene usted?*"

She held up a whole hand of fingers. "*Cinco.*"

She was five years old. Would anybody believe the testimony of a kid? He definitely needed a reputable person to conduct the interview for the videotape. But not Kreiger.

Rita came out of the bedroom, rushed to the refrigerator and pulled out the ice trays. "Talk to her only in English, Jordan. She has to learn."

"Can I help?" he asked. "Should I boil water or something?"

"Sit on the sofa with Isabel and tell her a story."

He approached the girl. "May I sit with you?"

"Yes," she said.

He remembered from Emily's e-mail that Isabel had shown an interest in Yvonne's rescue dogs. "Do you like dogs?" he asked.

"I much like dogs."

"Then I'm going to tell you a story about Pookie the Wonder Dog. He can climb mountains. And he can talk. Have you ever heard of a dog that says 'Moof'?"

She shook her head and giggled.

Rita stood over them. "Jordan, I never should have doubted your innocence. You are a good man."

"It turned out okay," he said. "If this hadn't happened, I never would've gotten to know Emily."

"She is a nurse. Thank God." Rita sketched the sign of the cross on her breast. "I am much relieved."

Responding to a moan from the bedroom, she rushed back to the pregnant mother with a bowl of ice.

Isabel's face pinched in a frown as she looked toward the room where her mother was in labor.

"She'll be okay," Jordan assured her. "Emily will help her. She knows what to do."

"Your wife?"

"No," Jordan said. The thought had occurred to him more than once, but he didn't think Emily would ever leave her beloved mountains. And he sure as hell didn't want to settle in Aspen.

"And now," he said, "the story of Pookie the Wonder Dog."

After an hour of storytelling with Jordan lapsing into Spanish for the more exciting exploits of Pookie putting out forest fires and rescuing children from mine shafts with a single paw, he made lunch for both of them.

In these rooms, with a new life birthing, he had the sense that time stood still. Yet, the danger seemed too close, oozing through the floorboards, creeping around the edges of the windows. The sharp taste of apprehension twitched at the back of his throat. He hated it here.

"Do you like the mountains, Isabel?"

"Yes, but it is cold."

"Have you ever been to Florida?" he asked.

"Does Pookie go there?"

"Sure," he said. "Why not? I remember one time when Pookie the Wonder Dog went swimming with the dolphins…"

Emily had emerged from the bedroom and stood watching them. "Pookie the Wonder Dog?"

"Yes," Isabel said enthusiastically. "He is much, um, much super-duper."

Emily laughed. She'd peeled off her blazer and rolled up the sleeves on her silk blouse. Her hair was pinned on top of her head, and her eyes looked tired.

"Your mother is doing very well," she said. "In just a few minutes, you're going to have a little brother or sister."

"I want a dog," Isabel said. She pointed at Emily's throat. "Pretty necklace."

"It's a locket." Emily leaned down and popped the locket open. "See the picture inside. That's my father. He died a long time ago in Vietnam, and he was a medic. That's kind of like being a nurse. That's what I do."

"He would have been proud of you," Jordan said. She'd come a long way from not being able to mention her father. "I'm proud of you."

Her green-eyed gaze rested gently upon him, and he

knew. He wanted to spend the rest of his life with this woman, basking in the warm glow of her eyes. He wanted her to be the mother of his children...even if it meant living in the freezing shadows of these cold, hard, Colorado mountains.

"I called Spence a while ago," she said. "He's on his way over here so he can officially certify that this baby was born in the USA."

"Did you happen to mention that he might want to bring a video camera with him?"

"Didn't think of it," she said. "I'd better get back in the bedroom. It's almost time."

Just a few minutes later, the groaning from the bedroom got real damn loud. Isabel stared with huge eyes. Her skinny body trembled.

"It's okay." Jordan tried to reassure her. "Your mom's going to be okay."

Her eyes reflected a seriousness beyond her years. She'd witnessed a murder and lived the life of a fugitive. He wished there were some way to console her. "Sometimes, it helps to move around," he said. "To keep your mind busy with something else."

"Show me."

He got up and started pacing. She joined him. Back and forth in the small room, matching steps, skipping steps.

There was silence. Then the loud healthy cry of an infant.

Rita rushed out of the bedroom. "It's a boy. Isabel, you have a baby brother. Are you happy?"

"Yes." But her eyes were still serious.

Rita hugged her. "What do you think we should name this baby?"

She glanced at Jordan. With a giggle, she said, "Pookie."

Isabel went with her aunt into the bedroom, and he was left alone on the sofa, abandoned by the women as if men had no place in the miracle of life. Labour and birthing required a kind of endurance unknown to Jordan. He would rather be pursued by twelve helicopters and a hundred armed marksmen than to pace helplessly and listen to the sounds of pain.

Emily came toward him, holding a tiny bundle wrapped in a soft white blanket. She cooed, "Here's the little guy who was causing all that trouble."

Jordan peeked inside the blanket's folds at a round, pinched face. The arms twitched, and the scrawny neck craned as if the baby was looking around at this strange, new place. "Is he supposed to be so red?"

"It's typical."

Jordan had never seen a newborn before. "Amazing."

"You hold him."

Though he tried to refuse, Emily insisted until the baby was in his arms. He felt it wiggling. The eyes stared right at him. How could this little creature be moving around? What kind of complex circuitry brought a baby to life? "Hello, Pookie."

The infant made a tiny noise. Moof?

A strange warmth spread through Jordan. Though he couldn't explain how or why, he would do anything to protect this infant. He gently returned the little bundle to Emily, and she took Baby Pookie back to his mother.

When she returned, she collapsed onto the sofa. Though she'd washed up, there were smears of blood on her white silk blouse. The hair around her face was damp with sweat. "Having babies is a lot of work."

"But worth it," he said as he sat beside her. "I'd like five or six."

"Spoken like a man."

He laced his fingers with hers. There were other manly words he wanted to share with Emily. He had words pertaining to the exercise of making slow, hot love on a cold Colorado night. There were words describing the fresh beauty of a hardworking, green-eyed woman. He'd say the hard words, too. Commitment. Responsibility. Family. He would tell her how he'd never expected to find his true soul mate, how he'd waited so long and settled for less. He would never let her go. She was the world to him.

He could talk endlessly and never run dry of words. But there were just three that were appropriate at this moment. Three little words. *I love you.*

Her eyes closed. She was nearly exhausted.

Jordan gave her hand a little squeeze and leaned back against the sofa, staring up at the ceiling. *Emily, I love you.*

A buzzer sounded, indicating that someone was at the front door of the big house.

"That must be Spence," she said wearily. "Typical of him to show up after all the work is done."

"Stay here and rest," he said. "I'll get it."

He called to Rita for the security code necessary to open the door and close it without setting off silent alarms.

Jordan left the cosy apartment, which was crammed full with the messiness of new life, and walked through the sterile kitchen, the dining room, the living room. This place was huge, empty, silent. The soles of his hiking boots squeaked on the marble floor in the foyer.

From the corner of his eye, Jordan saw movement. He turned and faced Sean Madigan.

The red-haired skier held a .45 revolver in his hand.

Jordan didn't doubt that Madigan was crazy enough to kill all of them. The red bear. The monster. Somehow, he had to distract Madigan, to get him away from the house. "You don't want to shoot me in here."

"Don't I? It's my right. You're an escaped prisoner."

"Not in the house," Jordan said. "If you kill me here, you'll have to tell the police where you got the key. That brings up other pesky questions about the night Lynette was murdered."

Madigan frowned as he considered.

This guy was no mastermind. Ironically, Madigan's stupidity was what might have saved him. He'd stolen the artwork and kept his payoff in cash. Nothing clever. But his money was untraceable. On the night of the murder, he'd walked into the house, shot Lynette and left the weapon on Jordan's pillow. Straightforward. Simple.

"I have a question," Jordan said. "Why me? Why did you frame me for the murder?"

"Nothing personal." He raised the pistol in one hand and sighted down the barrel. "You were just in the wrong place at the wrong time."

"What about my escape from police custody? Did you plan that with Kreiger?"

"That was Kreiger's idea. He thought you'd get off light because you're rich. And he wanted revenge for Lynette."

"What about Kreiger now?" Jordan remembered that the two men had argued and exchanged blows at Brian's party. "Is he having second thoughts?"

The doorbell rang again, resonating through the atrium foyer.

Madigan gestured with the gun. "Back door. This is going to be fun, Jordan. I'll give you a sporting chance. You can start running before I shoot you."

"Not much of a chance." There was no way in hell they were going to the back door. Jordan refused to lead Madigan closer to Rita's apartment. "I thought you were a competitor."

"Olympic class," Madigan said.

With a big ego to compensate for his tiny brain, Jordan knew which buttons to punch. "Let's settle this like men. Hand to hand."

"You think you can take me?"

Maybe not. But Jordan knew one thing for sure. If he was going to die, he didn't want to be shot in the back. "I'm through running."

Madigan lifted the barrel of the gun, pointing it at the ceiling while he decided what he'd do next.

Jordan charged. One long stride, and he launched himself into Madigan. They crashed onto the marble floor together.

Jordan was on top. He smashed Madigan's gun hand against the marble. He was disarmed.

Sean Madigan, a professional athlete in excellent condition, was stronger. But Jordan had greater motivation. He had a future to look forward to. He had Emily.

Jordan felt a blow to his chin, hard enough to snap his head back and cloud his brain. He was half-stunned. Madigan easily threw him off.

But Jordan couldn't lose. Not now. In the space of a heartbeat, he blanked out the pain. On his feet. He swung hard and missed.

Madigan danced like a professional boxer, flicking out with sharp jabs and dizzying uppercuts.

No way could Jordan compete with this guy and win,

not unless he engaged his brain. Centrifugal force. Triangulation. Momentum.

Jordan dropped his arms, laying himself open to a deathblow. Madigan wound up to deliver.

When the blow came, Jordan dodged. The momentum of Madigan's follow-through propelled him off balance. Jordan connected with his knee to the other man's gut. *Every action has a separate but equal reaction.*

Jordan counterplayed every blow, turning Madigan's strength against himself until the red-haired man toppled to the floor. Beaten.

Through a bloody haze, he was aware of the front door being opened. Deputies, led by Kreiger, came inside.

He felt Emily's arms around him. Looking down, the floor rushed up to greet him. He was going to pass out. All he could manage were three words. "I love you."

Chapter Fourteen

Two days later, Jordan Shane drove through Cascadia and took the turnoff leading to Emily's cabin. He was a free man. The charges against him had been dismissed.

Madigan cooled his heels in the Pitkin County jail. Kreiger was on disciplinary leave of absence for two months. His punishment would've been worse, but he'd belatedly led the final assault to arrest Madigan. Brian Afton had all the papers he needed to control Lynette's estate.

Jordan was also working with immigration officials to arrange for Isabel's mother to come to work for him in Florida. As he explained to Rita, this solution had always been within their grasp if she'd seen fit to confide in him. But it was okay. He didn't hold a grudge. Everything had worked out just fine.

Except for Emily. She hadn't said those three little words back to him.

During the craziness of the past two days, she'd retired to her cabin and had been ominously uncommunicative.

Her silence was about to end. He wouldn't let her close down their relationship without giving him a chance. He wanted to marry her. If he had to tie a rope around her waist and drag her kicking and screaming to the altar, so be it.

They were meant to be together. Soul mates. They could work out the logistics of living in Florida and Colorado. He was willing to compromise on location but not on love. Never on love.

When he parked in front of her cabin and got out of the car, Jordan was greeted by Pookie the Wonder Dog, wagging and moofing. But Emily didn't come out onto the porch. Her front door stayed closed tight. An icy wind swirled around him as he climbed the stairs to the front porch. Snow was in the air.

He tapped at the door. "Emily?"

"Come in."

He opened the door to a riot of tropical color. A potted palm tree. A platter of fresh fruit. A giant map of Florida tacked to the pine-panelled wall. Emily herself wore Bermuda shorts and a Hawaiian shirt. She'd pinned a fake red hibiscus in her hair.

"I thought I'd better get used to this kind of stuff," she said. "Because I'm going with you to Florida, Jordan."

He pulled her into his arms. Unresisting, she fitted her slender body against him. Thigh to thigh, belly to belly. Her arms draped around his shoulders. When he kissed her, he tasted mango-flavored lip gloss. "Why?"

"It's the right thing to do. I never want to say goodbye to you." Her smile was radiant. "I love you."

"Marry me," he said.

"I will," she replied.

And Pookie said, "Moof."

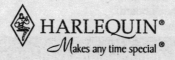

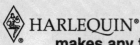

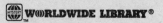